To Yolanda and Joe,
with great affection
Jacobo Sefamí
October 2010

Happy birthday!!

Jacobo Sefamí

Mourning for Papá

A Story of a Syrian-Jewish Family in Mexico

Translated by Kay (Kayla) S. García

Floricanto™

Berkeley Press is an imprint of Inter American Development, Inc.
FloricantoTM Press
650 Castro Street, 120-331
Mountain View, California 94041
(415) 552-1879
www. floricantopress. com
ISBN: 978-1-888205-29-9
"Por nuestra cultura hablarán nuestros libros. Our books shall speak for our culture."
Roberto Cabello-Argandoña,
Editor

Acknowledgements

Kayla García wishes to thank the **Center for the Humanities** and the **Department of Foreign Languages and Literatures** at Oregon State University for their encouragement and financial support during the time she translated this novel.

All the characters portrayed in this book are fictional. Any resemblance to real people, dead or alive, is purely coincidental.

A glossary of words in Hebrew, Arabic and Spanish is included as a book-mark, and at the end of the book.

To Sally
For my children, Carlos, Asher, and Maru

The face does not die, said a wise man. Even absent, it remains a face, moulded on absence as we mould words on emptiness.

Edmond Jabès

Nostalgia in the writing of death is offered as a consolation before the powerlessness of memory; it is the defeat of the word before the inaprehensibility of disappearance.

Raymundo Mier

Characters

Simón Galante, and his wife **Rebeca**.

Narrators: Jaime, Abram, Fule, Saqui, Musa, David, and Beni (all sons of Simón and Rebeca).

Other characters in alphabetical order:

Alicia: Abram's ex-wife.

Azra: León's son-in-law; referred to as the "ratero" (the thief).

Bella: Jaime's wife.

Beto Mochón: someone from the Ḥevra (Jewish orga nization in charge of burials).

Ceci: David's wife.

Concha: housekeeper for the Galantes.

Elena: Fule's wife.

Elías Hanono: narrators' cousin; married to Bella Cohab.

Fortuna: Beni's wife.

Isaac Helfón: paid to pray at funerals and other reli gious events.

Jaime Behar: narrators' cousin.

Jasibe: Rebeca's sister; daughters: **Ruth Mustri, Tere Mustri, and Alegra.**

Lisa: Saqui's wife.

Mago: Simón's niece.

Raquel: narrators' sister who died; also name of Re beca's sister and Tío Leon's daughter.

Rosa: daughter of Rebeca's sister Raquel.

Salomón Behar: narrators' cousin.

Sofía: daughter of Rebeca's sister Raquel.

Teófilo Buzali: Director of the Ḥevra.

Tía Pola: Simón's sister.

Tía Rosa: Simón's sister.

Tía Sara: Simón's sister; sons: **Jacobo, Jaime, and Salomón Behar**.

Tío Leon: Simón's brother; married to **Terri**. Step daughter**: Dorotea.** Children**: Morris, Raquel**.

Zequíe: Rebeca's sister.

1

29 Elul 5756 (Yom Shishi)/
1 Tishrei 5757 (Shabbat) Rosh Hashanah

13 September 1996 (Friday afternoon)

ONEN. THE BEREAVED PERSON IS CALLED ONEN BEFORE THE BURIAL; AFTER THE BURIAL HE IS CALLED AVEL. THE ONEN CAN EAT BEFORE THE BURIAL, BUT HE MUST NOT EAT MEAT NOR DRINK WINE. FURTHERMORE, HE CANNOT SHAVE OR BATHE. IT IS FORBIDDEN TO EAT OR SMOKE IN THE ROOM WHERE THE DEAD PERSON LIES.

Shema Israel, Adonai Eloheinu, Adonai Eḥad! Shema Israel, Adonai Eloheinu, Adonai Eḥad! Mamá was mumbling these words over and over, hoping for a miracle. Deep groans punctuated her prayer, and a painful expression distorted her face. Mamá knew it was the end, for this time nothing more could be done. Papá was stretched out on the hospital bed, gasping for air as usual, but this time his whole body shook so violently that the bedrails rattled. Ceci, Musa, Beni and Tía Rosa had been chatting in the next room, but came running when they heard the commotion. The nurses and doctor on duty blocked their path. *Calm down; they just called Doctor*

Charabati and he's on his way. They hustled in and out of the room, with anxious faces, bringing different carts and muttering an occasional *Damn it, Ortiz, move it!,* along the way. Later in a softer tone, they asked to speak to Jaime. *Please come with us. No, the rest of you wait outside. We have to talk to him alone.* But Mamá was already in the room and the rest of us crowded in beside her. We all looked anxiously at Papá, with his wide-open eyes staring blankly, his head wrapped in bandages and his bruised arms hanging limply by his sides. The machines no longer made any noise, and the flashing red numbers had stopped. Mamá began to slap her own face. *Hold onto her! Don't let her hurt herself!,* said Abram with tears in his eyes. *He's left us!,* Mamá managed to say between sobs. We stood immobilized by disbelief, watching Papá who stared without seeing, his face already reflecting eternal serenity. Mamá's whole body trembled, on the verge of collapse. Fule's wife Elena suddenly reacted: *Grab her, grab her, Ceci, don't just stand there.* But Mamá didn't want to be touched. *Call Charabati or García,* Jaime yelled, *maybe there's something they can do. We've got to keep fighting!* Mamá pulled at her hair, her loud sobs unleashing all the anxiety she had been holding inside for so long.

None of us knew what to do, not even Jaime. Our cousin Elías Hanono called from the factory. *Listen, Jaime. Don't leave him like that. He's got to be covered. Close his eyes, lay him down on the floor and cover him with a sheet. You have to be the one to do it, because you're the oldest. Get two candles and put them next to his head. I'm going to call Teófilo Buzali, from the Ḥevra.* Jaime, shaking himself out of his stupor, responded with a tenuous voice: *The Ḥevra? What's the Ḥevra? No, better call León Hamui, he knows everything we need to know and he'll tell us what to do.* But Elías insisted. *No, Jaime, I know what I'm talking about, don't worry. I'll call you back. Tell your sister-in-law not to use her cell phone.* It was impossible to get through.

13

Mourning for Papá

Jaime turned around to gaze at the figure on the bed, and then gently closed Papá's eyelids. He felt the skin, almost cold now, and looked bitterly at the inert body. *His love is gone,* he thought, *his affection is gone; but, you have to give your father his kiss.* Jaime pulled the sheet over his head, but we hesitated to put him on the floor. David hid his face in his arms, sniffling. And a little while later, what time was it?, the phone rang again: *This is Teófilo Buzali, shafalkon. Look, roḥi, try to console your mother; all of you should calm down. We can't do anything right away. We can't bury him, because everything stops for the holy day. Besides, it's Shabbat. Your cousin Elías was wrong. You can't set candles by him or lay him on the floor; you're going to have to take him down to the basement, roḥi. I'll fix everything with the hospital. You should all go home, but first, tell your brother Beni to go ahead and ask them to fill out the death certificate there. Remember, you can't tell anybody. For some reason he died today, on a sacred date, the eve of Rosh Hashanah and also of Shabbat. It's God's will.*

Mamá sank into an easy chair, her gasping sobs becoming increasingly dry and hoarse. Yet another call came from David Atie, telling us we should go to the knis. Somebody mumbled a curse. We stood in awkward groups, hugging each other as we wept. Beni muttered that they weren't even going to send shomerim to guide us in our grief. *If everybody goes to the knis, who stays with Papá?* We looked at each other in despair, grasping the rails of the hospital bed. None of the hospital personnel had dared to intervene, but suddenly two attendants arrived, *they gave us orders to take him down to the basement...we're really sorry...* A new wave of wailing shook the room. It was already dark by the time they rolled out the bed with Papá's body on it. We didn't all fit in the elevator, so Beni, Musa, David and Abram ran down the stairs, panting as they reached the bottom. The attendants had entered a cold room, with several enormous refrigerators. Jaime tried to placate us, *calm down now, we're going to have to leave him here, there's no other way.* Saqui went running to the bathroom, unable to control a sudden attack of diarrhea. Looking in the mirror, he realized that his eyes were irritated and his nose was stuffed up. Just then Beni rushed in and vomited violently into the urinal; he couldn't even make it to the toilet. Saqui reached for paper so Beni could clean the drool off his mouth and chin.

Papá had been very ill. Three months ago he had begun to talk nonsense. Then Charabati had told us, *it looks like the lack of oxygen has affected his brain. It's very serious; I'm going to have him in intensive care; we'll see how he reacts. I'll call a neurologist to take a look at him; the other problem is that he has an infection in his blood and he hasn't responded to treatment.* We were all very worried, *whatever you say, doctor. What neurologist do you recommend?* Charabati was ready with the answer: *Dr. Constantino is the best.* We felt relieved to find a thread of hope, *yes, please call him, have him come today.*

But then things got worse. For a long time Papá was unconscious, and we took turns sitting by his bed. Not long ago Saqui happened to be in the room when he saw Papá open his eyes and then blink a few times. But he didn't respond when Saqui exclaimed, *How are you, Papá?, How do you feel?* After a few minutes Saqui barely managed to hear a faint whisper, *waaaater.* Saqui suddenly realized that he had to let somebody know. *He's talking, he's talking, somebody help!,* and Dr. Guzman appeared, an intern just out of school, a pretty woman with long hair and big eyes full of curiosity, *How are you, Don Simón?,* as she put the stethoscope in her ears and listened to his chest. Papá gestured toward the water, and she took the glass and bent the straw toward him, holding it until he took a sip; half the water dripped onto his gown and the other half moistened his mouth. *You finally woke up. You're going to be fine, Don Simón, just take it easy and we'll get you out of here soon.*

Mourning for Papá

When Musa offered to stay the night, the rest of us immediately agreed, relieved because for days we hadn't been able to sleep and we hadn't even seen our children, *well, are you sure? You stayed two days ago and tonight it's David's turn.* Papá looked at us in a daze, barely able to mumble a single word. Our sister-in-law Ceci had begun to feel angry, *incredible, now nobody comes anymore! The first few days the room was full, sometimes you couldn't even move.* But for some of the family members it had become a burden to come every day and not even get to talk to Papá, who lay silently on the bed. *He's held on so long,* they'd say, *I didn't think he was going to last a month and now look, he's been suffering for two years, poor Simón.*

It was a month later when Dr. Constantino offered us a ray of hope, an incision to the brain to allow an antibiotic drip directly into the encephalic fluid; with advanced meningitis the treatment had to be aggressive. *Let's see how he reacts, he just might come out of the coma...* Earlier that year he had been unconscious for two months and then suddenly was awake saying, *you've got to be careful, watch out, don't go into the water at the Revolcadero,* like he used to tell us before a trip to Acapulco, when we were teenagers. But now things didn't look so good for Papá, with sores on his back, bruises on his legs, swollen feet, ingrown toenails, and his vacant gaze. We decided to discuss the operation in the next room. *Sorry, this room is for employees only,* said an attendant. But Beni was already halfway in, *what's it to you? we need to talk right now; here, take this five and buy yourself a coke, just give us half an hour.* Jaime calmly insisted, *we have to do everything we can, as long as there's hope, there's life.* Musa collapsed into an oversized chair, certain that the end was near. *This must be God's will, barukh hashem . He will take care of him.* Beni argued with Jaime, *why keep going? The doctors are just trying to get rich at our expense.* Jaime, who usually carried his wallet next to his heart, whirled around to face him and shouted, *How dare you talk about money at a time like this? Besides, I already spoke with the insurance company and he's covered, so that's the least of our worries right now. What matters is that he pulls through, barukh hashem,* and he put two fingers to his lips, gave them a hint of a kiss, and then raised them to his forehead, just like Papá used to do for him with a big smile, *a'aris, hijo,* he'd say.

Mamá was thinking about a different time, a Sunday evening. *Simón, give me my money for the week, you're already three weeks behind; I haven't paid the kids' tuition, they won't give me any more credit at the grocery store, and I have to pay the electricity bill or they'll shut it off.* Papá always stalled, *I'll give it to you tomorrow, I don't have it now; my brother didn't pay me; he didn't have enough for the whole payroll so he said he'd pay me next week.* We all knew that Mamá was wise to him, *what makes you think I'll swallow that line? Yesterday you were dipping your beak into the finest brandy at Gitanerías and I heard Salomón played dumb when the bill came, and you paid in cash. You're not fooling me, Simón!* Finally Papá gave in a little, *okay, you win, take a hundred for now and I'll bring you more, later.* Then Mamá flew into a rage, *oh, no you don't! You owe me a lot more, I want all that you owe me.* With no more excuses to offer, he launched the final offensive to cover his retreat, *That's enough!, leave me alone!* and he stomped off, slamming the door as he left. Bang! Startled, Mamá had to face the reality of the hospital again; she couldn't stand to see him like that, rotting away before her eyes, *the handsomest guy in town, what the years have done to him!*

Saqui, who didn't want to see him suffer any more, agreed with Beni and Musa. *Let God take him when He will, Jaime, but we should respect his body; look at him, he's had it. How much more should we make him suffer?* But it wasn't really up for discussion, *you shut your mouth, who do you think you are? You're not hashem to be making decisions!* As David left the room for a run to the coke machine, his wife Ceci approached him, *what happened, honey? what did you decide?* Mamá came out and saw the attendant, *hey, do me a favor and get me an ashtray,* but then she remembered that smoking was no longer allowed in the hospital, and the young man protested, *por favor, señora, you all have to get out of that room, you're not supposed to be in there, it's just for staff...* We were all shaking with laughter because Beni had been imitating him behind his back. *Okay, we're out of here.*

Later, after Papá came back from having his head punctured, he was completely out of it, oblivious to our concern; the doctors looked in on him now and then, *no change, he's not responding.* A few days later he finally opened his eyes; Dr. Constantino came with Dr. Charabati, *Don Simón,* they shouted, *¿can you hear me?* And they shone a flashlight in his eyes, but Papá never answered. We could hear his labored breathing, and see his green eyes just staring into space. Within a week he began to move his eyes in response to sound. *You see, it was worth it,* Jaime said joyfully, *in two days we'll have him up and we'll take him home, barukh hashem .*

Saqui stayed there at night and talked to Papá until three or four in the morning. Papá was like his baby who didn't speak, he just looked at him once in a while, but didn't answer. *Simoncito is learning to read in English, I'll teach him in Spanish later. The other day I took him to a baseball game and it reminded me of going to that stadium with you, so many years ago. I remember the señor who went running up and down the steps selling sandwiches, "tortas, tortas, tortas!" Jaime, Abram, Fule and I were there with you; it was the ninth inning with the bases loaded and the Diablos Rojos were about to tie or win the game and I couldn't hold it any longer, "I have to pee, Papá." And you, totally absorbed in the game, told Abram, "take Saqui to the bathroom, but don't let him out of your sight, and come right back." And Abram, pissed off 'cause he didn't want to miss a thing, "come on Saqui, can't you hold it?" was walking backwards waiting for the batter to swing and hit a home run, but no luck, we heard the umpire yell, "Ball One!" When we got to the bottom of the stairs I saw the sign that said* RESTROOM *and I ran for it. I made it to the urinal and just as I was relieving myself with a big sigh, I heard the crowd roar. When I turned around, a lot of men were coming into the bathroom and Abram had disappeared. As I fought my way out of the bathroom and into the corridor I saw hordes of people running to the bathroom, no, I was wrong, they were rushing to the exit, the game was over. I suddenly realized that I couldn't see you anywhere, not you, or Abram or Jaime or Fule. I stood frozen waiting for you to come until everybody had gone, there was just garbage everywhere, tickets, programs, candy wrappers and empty potato chip bags. A cleaning woman was gathering things up when she noticed me crying, wiping my tears and snot on my sleeve; I was afraid and didn't know whether to answer when she asked me where I lived. I finally worked up my courage and blurted out, "on Alvaro Obregón 210-9 and my phone number is 25-55-48." I calmed down when we found a pay phone, but the line was busy, busy, busy. It was almost dark. We went to see the man who sold tortas and the lady asked him to lend her three or four pesos, "I'll take you home myself, son." I saw cars speeding by; we finally saw a cab and she gestured with her hand. "How much to Alvaro Obregón?"; that's when I saw you, Papá, half a block away. I ran like crazy, and so did you. I saw the policemen looking at us, "I found him," you shouted, "here, have a few beers on me, muchas gracias." We got home and Mamá gave me so many kisses that she made my face red. And you pinched my cheek once and then hugged me and hugged me and wouldn't let go.*

Saqui's thoughts returned to the hospital, and he longed for another gentle pinch on the cheek. *Are you listening?, just make a face to let me know,* but all he could see was the white patch on his head and the little tube underneath. A nurse with hair like a broom came in, *you have to leave for a minute, I'm going to give him his medicine; Patricia, would you help me in 324, por favor?* Outside the room Saqui began to hallucinate, *I would like to get into your head through that syringe, get into your eyes, see myself again and hear you say, "Saqui, come back home, hijo, move in again, we miss you so much, look at me, you're all alone there in the U.S., tell me, who do you celebrate the holidays with?, what knis do you go to?, remember your family, what good is so much studying?"* Then the nurse with stiff hair came out and said, *you can go back in, we're finished.* Now Papá's head was reddish purple, with a white bandage that was shiny in spite of the stains. *Your eyes suddenly turned, and I shivered, but then there was nothing.*

Saqui stayed awake long hours contemplating the light from the streetlamp and listening to the city's silence, disturbed only by occasional ambulances. *How did he sleep?*, Jaime had arrived very early, dressed in a suit and tie. *Has Constantino been in?* Saqui stumbled over to the sunlight, feeling drugged, stammering as he tried to answer. *What do you mean you don't know? that's what matters, you gotta be on the ball, mano, that's why you're here.* And then Jaime looked at the chart, HOSPITAL PERSONNEL ONLY, disappointed, STABLE, CONTINUE SAME DOSAGE, CHARABATI. *Carajo, I missed him again,* Jaime sputtered; *listen, Saqui, we have to ask him how long before the medicine kicks in, and if that staring is a good sign, before he didn't even move his eyes; if you want to, write it down, I have to go to work. Do you want some coffee? It tastes like shit, but that's all there is; when Fule gets here have him take a turn and you can go to the cafeteria.*

Jaime felt depressed and irritated. People had been on our case for months, *you guys should get a private nurse for your papá, buy him a portable oxygen tank so he can go to the club and see his buddies, give your old man a few bucks, at least enough to pay the cab fare so he can live a little,* the gossip was everywhere. He was fed up with all the talk, *my cousin Adela told me that people are saying you don't give your papá any money, and he's really bad off.* The attacks came from all sides, but Jaime felt that he had done his part. *Let's see them go visit him every day, let them go all the way across the city to re-charge the oxygen tank three times a week, let them spend their money on medicine; I don't even have time to see my own kids!* But now, as he sipped his cappuccino, he was thinking, *what if he really leaves us? No... may hashem forgive me, but I did everything I could. Papá, hang in there, give it all you've got... échale ganas.* That's what Papá told him, he remembered, going back to the recently inaugurated Estadio Azteca, when he was ten and his team had been picked as part of a youth soccer exhibition before the América match. And Papá was shouting, *échale ganas, get in there, run hard, watch the ball, don't let it past you; watch out for number 11, keep your eye on him.* And there he was, in uniform posing for the photo, with a skinny body like Papá's, the smallest one on the team. Papá was so proud of him. And then with the stadium packed, the América team, led by their star players from Brazil, came out on the field and scattered across the green splendor of the newly mown grass.

When Jaime came back to reality, he heard a group of women speaking in low voices, *how is Adela Micha's new baby?, where will the celebration be? Tell her that if they want to do it at home, I can recommend Señora Atri; she caters the breakfast, and brings everything: pastries, tahini, eggs, chilaquiles, whatever you want.* Jaime wasn't in the mood to listen to gossip about the Michas. He was overwhelmed once more with memories of the café in the Colonia Roma. Every afternoon, Papá was there. *Go get your papá out of the café, it's late already, and if he doesn't want to come, tell him to send me twenty pesos.* Papá, as usual, welcomed us with kisses. *Here comes the gang; come, say hello to my friends.* But the domino players were impatient with the distraction, *come on, Simón, make your move, we don't have time to waste like you do.* Papá slapped his domino piece down on the table and grumbled at the man sitting across from him, *you jackass! can't you see what I've got?* Then in a calmer voice he said to us, *you guys have a coke and then be careful on your way home.*

Fule spoke up to convey the message, *Mamá said that she needs twenty pesos to pay the guy who delivers the pita bread.* But Papá, evasive as always, answered with a counter-request, *tell your mother to send Concha to buy two or three bottles of mineral water.* And so we went back home, but as soon as we got there, Mamá sent us to collect money from the Behar cousins who had a tailor shop called Paris. They owed us for some sewing machines they had rented from Mamá after she inherited them; *every little bit helps.* When we got there we found the cousins, with cigarettes hanging from their lips, seated behind piles of bills and receipts, crunching numbers on the new electric calculator as the roll of white paper cascaded over the other side like ticker tape. *Listen, Jaime, give these thirty pesos to your mamá and tell her that I'll send her the rest next week.* Their sister Estrella appeared, grabbed Jaime's shoulder and led him to the shelves in the back, *have some cookies, primo,* and we all left, happy to have two cookies each. That night Mamá and Papá were screaming at each other about money again; finally things calmed down and their attention turned to a favorite television program and the busy routine of frying eggs for dinner.

Jaime's reverie was interrupted by a sudden flood of visitors to the hospital. Someone from the Kalach family had been brought in, and the waiting room was crammed with people. *Hey, amigo, what kind of surgery is he having?* A friend answered, *his heart is in bad shape, they're taking a vein from his leg, barukh hashem, and hope for the best.* Another friend who was there to visit an uncle, commented, *those Kalaches are loaded, but you know, what good is money now?* Jaime was transported back to the day he went to work for the Swed brothers. He could hear a tape of his mother's voice being played in the back of his head: *You're crazy if you think I'm going to let you work with your father for Tío León; I already spoke with my sister Raquel and she told me her brother-in-law Elías*

Swed needs someone he can trust to keep an eye on things. When he arrived at the factory at six o'clock, Elías' brother Salomón was already working at full steam as he shuffled through orders and other paperwork. *Look, Jaime, you're going to open the factory every day at six sharp; when Elías gets here, you can watch the cutting table and make sure they don't steal any fabric.* The Sweds liked Jaime's advice, because he took time to analyze the personnel: *Salo, I think we should have Lupe handle the orders because she's really sharp; Tere is best at fastening the elastic.* Until one day the Swed brothers realized that they had to promote Jaime, *we want you to be the production manager, that idiot Marcos didn't work out. And meanwhile, Papá,* Jaime said to himself, *I was waiting for you to get a break so we could start a business together, for Tío León to give you some money, but it never happened, you kept driving around picking up furniture to be reupholstered; you had to answer the customers, sí, señora, I'll have them back in two days, guaranteed. And you carried the heavy sofas up and down those narrow stairs!*

Jaime could imagine Tío León giving Papá instructions in a loud, imperious voice, *make sure you get it straight: first you go to San Antonio Abad to make a delivery to Señora Gómez, but she has to pay you in cash, if she doesn't, don´t make the delivery; don't screw up, Simón. Are you listening to me? Then, get to la Condesa as fast as you can, on Nuevo León Street, to pick up an easy chair; get a deposit for half the cost; you know where it is, don't you?, it's on the corner with Michoacán, apartment 4. From there, go to Colonia Roma, Chihuahua Street number 46, apartment 7, their check bounced again; don't let them off the hook, and don't leave there without the dough. Since you will be in the neighborhood, go pay the electric bill for my house. And when you're done, call me, you hear, call me and I'll tell you if you need to come back or run another errand. Figure out the best route and take Pedro, he'll help you since Juanito didn't show up again today. Allah ma'ak, and don't forget to call me. So that's how your whole day went, Papá; you were always upset because Tío León was constantly yelling at you, "Damn it, why didn´t you check with me, mano? I'm sitting here all day like an idiot, waiting for you to call;" and you always answered honestly, "all the phones were out of order, León, I swear."* But Tío León was never satisfied, *well, get with it, mano, you should have asked to use someone's phone, don't be an idiot.* And when the day was over, you realized that you were starving, you had grabbed a bite to eat at Doña Leonor's place, but barely had time to swallow it.

I saved almost everything I earned with the Swed brothers, except the few pesos that I would give Mamá every week, until one day I added it all up and convinced Fule to leave his job with the Romanos. Mamá managed to find us a good deal on an empty loft where we could set up our own business. But you insisted on staying with Tío León. We had a hard time at first, we suffered a lot. Elías and Salo Swed were ticked off so they made up the story that I was stealing merchandise from them. Mamá had to call the tías and ask them to intervene with the textile distributor so he would give us credit. And it was hard to attract customers, since the Sweds had blackballed us with the big stores. I had to borrow money from a buddy of mine, so I could buy a pearl necklace and give it to the purchasing agent at La Super Venta, and only then would she buy from us, "we'll start with a small order, send me twenty briefs in each size and if they sell, I'll order some more." That same night we went to Doña Yunta's taco place to celebrate with Mamá, Fule, Saqui, David and Beni. You came along, even though you'd rather have pita bread than tacos. Mamá didn't tell you anything about the business; when we came home, her answers to your questions were always vague, "how did it go?", "so-so," "how were the sales?", "so-so." Until finally you'd get mad, "I'm your husband, not some idiot, I deserve some respect." Then you waited until we all went to sleep to eat your tacos, "Concha, warm them up for me, por favorcito, and make me some Turkish coffee; I'm going to bed, bring me the whole pot with my cup and leave it on the table." And you'd lie on your bed, taking deep drags off your cigarette, with your arm resting over your head, going over and over the day until you sank into a stupor.

Now, at the hospital on Rosh Hashanah, Tías Rosa and Pola said to Jaime, *we're not leaving here until León arrives, he'll be here any minute.* They had been waiting anxiously; every time someone approached the hospital room they felt their hearts thump in their chests, and they began to cry, but when they realized that it was a false alarm, just another sister-in-law or someone coming back from smoking, their tears subsided. *David, do me a favor, roḥi, and lend me your cell phone. I already told that bitch of a sister-in-law, but she probably didn't tell León.* And Tía Rosa, on pins and needles, dialed the number again, *Hello, let me speak to León. What? He already left? Didn't you give him my message?!* And she stomped the floor with all her might. Furious, she explained to her sister, *León doesn't know anything, he went to the knis like nothing happened. The housekeeper told me that Terri didn't let him know, that bitch!* There was a bitter scowl on Tía Rosa's face, delineated by a streak of mascara that ran down her left cheek. She was the one who kept the family together: her job was to settle all the fights that happened or that were going to happen. Six months after losing his wife, Tío León couldn't stand being alone any more. Terri was working as a secretary in the office of his friend Paco; he gave her an offhand compliment, *My, my, you're looking pretty today,* and to his surprise the secretary answered, *Is León just a name, or does it mean you're really a lion?* He took her dancing and after two or three drinks they went to a hotel. By then Tío León had tired of saying the kaddish every day, so he gave up on the mourning rituals just two weeks after his wife Alicia died. At about three a.m. he felt uneasy in bed with Terri. He had told his children that he was staying late at the office to work on the books. He was getting up to go home, but Terri wouldn't let him leave. *Where are you going?, don't leave so soon, let's get in the jacuzzi and have some more fun.* And they went back and forth from the hot tub to the bed until dawn.

At eight in the morning, with breakfast on the table, he called Papá, *listen up, Simón. If you talk to my children, tell them we were working together all night long.* And Papá, always the nice guy, replied, *anything you say, mano.* Within two weeks Terri had an apartment in Polanco and a car in the garage. When Tía Rosa found out, it was too late. *Rosa, this is Terri. We're going to get married in two months at the reform synagogue because the one on Querétaro Street is booked until next year.* Tía Rosa knew exactly what that meant. Terri was a goy and the only place she could be converted so fast was the temple in Las Lomas. Tía Rosa tried to talk to León in private, but Terri always answered the phone with her saccharine-sweet voice, *León's not here, Rosita, but I'll tell him you called, don't worry.* Weeks passed before Tío León finally called Rosa, *hey, you haven't called me since I've been seeing Terri. Come have dinner with us.* That night Terri protested, *why Rosita, I'm so jealous because León loves you more than me!,* and she didn't leave them alone for a minute. The last straw was when Tía Rosa went to León's office early in the morning; she was just about to give up because it was almost eleven o'clock, when he appeared with Terri. *You should have let us know, Rosita, and we wouldn't have made you wait; but we've got to run: we have an appointment with the notary and then León is going to take me shopping to buy some clothes.* Exasperated, Tía Rosa sputtered, *León, could I talk to you alone?,* but he felt uncomfortable with Terri there, *no, Rosita, whatever you want to say, just say it in front of Terri, I don't keep anything from her. What a bitch,* said Tía Rosa to herself. *He's not obligated to observe mourning for the whole year, but his children are. Poor things! That wench didn't let them fulfill their duty to their mother.* León and Terri had a huge party in the Camino Real Hotel, the trendiest spot for a celebration, and he forced his children to go. *We will always hold your mother in our hearts,* León said to them, *but I need to start a new life and you have to be there for me.* When his youngest daughter tried to protest, they stuck her with a babysitter who was more like a drill sergeant than a nanny, and controlled her every move.

In spite of our reluctance, all of us went, thought Tía Rosa, *except Simón's wife and sons.* She remembered that argument quite well. Papá got to the knis out of sorts, just when the bride and groom were about to walk down the aisle. This was the first time in his life that Papá had been to a reform temple. He was shocked that there were no kippahs, so he quickly took his handkerchief from his pocket and covered his head. His confusion increased when he noticed that the men and women were sitting together. He just stood there paralyzed, unable to respond to Tía Rosa's gesture to sit with her. *Come on over, we can sit together here, like civilized people, everyone with their family.* Papá had cut himself shaving and had put a small piece of tissue on his cheek to stop the bleeding. *I'm fed up with Rebeca, Rosa. She's not coming, and my sons aren't, either. She went on and on about León's lack of respect for poor Alicia. "Not only is he marrying a goy, but he doesn't even have the decency to wait until the year of mourning has passed". And you know how stubborn she is, I couldn't get her to budge on this. Look at me, I even cut myself, I was so worked up.* During the ceremony Papá was quiet for a while, observing what was going on. He noticed that nobody was speaking, and that they played organ music. *This sounds like a church, doesn't it?* He missed the traditional, out-of-tune, children's choir that sang at the community's weddings. The bride and groom had entered alone, and the rabbi was saying the blessings in Hebrew, translating them immediately into Spanish. Papá had never heard Spanish in a knis. He and Tía Rosa thought it was a shame that so few people attended. *León spent a lot of money on the banquet!*

But his doubts faded when they reached the Camino Real and half the tables were already occupied. Terri's family, after driving around and around looking for the synagogue, had given up and gone directly to the fiesta. Bitterly, Tía Rosa recalled the wedding, and now she was waiting like a fool for León to come see their dead brother. But Tío León was probably wearing his blue suit, sitting next to Terri in the reform temple. *I like the celebrations there better. They sing so beautifully, Ashkenazi style. And a lot of gringos go there.* Then Tía Rosa thought about Terri's reaction when she heard that Papá had died. *Simón died? That's good, he can finally rest. Can you imagine being sick for months and months... Look, León's on his way home from the office, I'll tell him, Rosa, don't worry. Let his sons take care of everything, okay?*

Jaime remembered Dr. Charabati telling him, *your papá has improved a bit, but we have to continue the treatment. We'll wait two more days, to see if he responds.* And Jaime, always the optimist, insisted, *but I saw him move his eyes. That's a good sign, isn't it?* The doctor didn't offer any hope, *we don't know if he'll be paralyzed or if there will be side effects later on. Medicine has its limits.* Jaime tried to encourage the rest of the family, *he'll be up in two days, and then we're out of here,* but his enthusiasm was not contagious. With his long face, it was clear that Musa didn't buy it. The day arrived when we were preparing for Rosh Hashanah. *Go take a shower, I'll stay,* said Musa, since he wasn't very interested in going to the knis without Papá. At four in the afternoon Papá became agitated so they gave him a breathing treatment that usually calmed him down, but this time it had no effect: they listened to his lungs, which were very tight, and they increased the dose of albuterol. The young resident with long hair told Musa to call Mamá. *And in a flash we were all here, Papá, we were just about to go to the knis to pray to hashem that you would get better during these holy days.* Just then he had a heart attack and nobody could stop it. Twenty minutes before the doors of heaven opened, Papá was in line, ready to enter. By now everybody would be at the knis.

With heavy hearts, we abandoned Papá in the hospital. *We've been taking care of him for so long, how can we leave him now, when he's most alone? You guys go, I'm staying by this door to keep him company tonight,* declared Musa, who couldn't pull himself away from Papá's body. One of the guards allowed him to sit on a wooden chair, in the middle of the cold mortuary. Luckily, Papá was the only dead person in that basement room. Musa began to cough convulsively, spitting up phlegm.

Upon arriving home, we mournfully contemplated the beautiful holy day table that was set for Rosh Hashanah. There was a huge platter of fresh fruit and a lovely bouquet of flowers that Fule had sent, which now looked offensive. Jaime ordered the flowers to be tossed in the garbage at once. With our stomachs tied up in knots, a dinner was the farthest thing from our minds. A few minutes later the phone rang and we realized that Musa wasn't there; Jaime lost his temper and shouted at Saqui: *I told you to get him out of there; you go over to the hospital this instant and bring him home. A nurse just called me and said she saw him crumpled on the floor and felt sorry for him. Take Beni with you...and wear your kippahs.* When they arrived they found Musa sitting on the cold flagstones of the basement floor, his eyes red and weepy. *Come on Musa, come home with us, we'll be back tomorrow.*

2

1 Tishrei 5757 (Shabbat) Rosh Hashanah
14 September 1996 (Saturday)

THE ONEN CANNOT JOIN NINE OTHER PEOPLE TO COMPLETE THE MINYAN AND RECITE A PRAYER, SINCE HE IS EXEMPT FROM THE MITZVOT. THE ONEN CANNOT SAY KADDISH UNLESS THERE IS NOBODY ELSE TO SAY IT FOR SOME OF HIS RELATIVES. BEFORE THE BURIAL, HE IS ALLOWED TO LEAVE HIS HOUSE TO MAKE FUNERAL ARRANGEMENTS.

Musa, Saqui, Abram and Mamá spent the night at home. We got up without a clue about what we were supposed to do. Musa hadn't slept at all and had spent most of the night coughing and shivering. Abram, Saqui and Mamá had stayed up talking until three in the morning. Jaime called at eight o'clock, *we have to go to the knis and look for Teófilo Buzali; he'll tell us when we can take Papá to be buried at the bet haḥaim. We can't do anything today because it's Rosh Hashanah.* Mamá wasn't listening. She couldn't believe that Papá had left us just when the high holy days had begun. She dreaded going to the knis and had no desire to see the sefer.

What should she wear? How should she carry herself? How could she greet people, knowing they'd be whispering about her as soon as she turned her back? *I'm not going! You boys go if you want to*, she managed to stammer. It never would have occurred to us that she would give us permission to skip services on Rosh Hashanah. A short while later Jaime, Fule, David and Beni arrived with their wives. Jaime had been given strict instructions that Papá's body was to remain in the hospital. They didn't even know yet if he could be buried the next day. Teófilo Buzali had consulted with several rabbis in the community, without reaching any conclusion.

Our tías Rosa and Pola showed up later, anxious to find out if their brother León had called. Nobody knew. Just then the phone rang and Tía Rosa answered; she heard her brother's voice. *I found out last night at the knis, but I couldn't reach anybody. I called your house, but you weren't there.* All the emotions of the night before overwhelmed Tía Rosa, and tears flowed down her cheeks, keeping her from speaking; the more she struggled to talk, the louder her sobs became. He had to wait until she caught her breath. *You should come here first, León. Don't offend the boys,* Tía Rosa said when she heard that her brother was planning to go straight to the knis. There was a brief pause; he had covered the mouthpiece with his hand to talk with Terri, who was reminding him of the incident with his nephews. *Remember, León, how they insulted you. Don't risk it. Don't go to that house; you won't be welcome...* León flashed back to that rainy December night when he and Simón stood proudly looking around the newly remodeled furniture store, illuminated by two long rows of fluorescent lights. Simón mentioned that perhaps now he could convince Jaime to come work with him. Just then Jaime, Abram, Fule, Saqui and Mamá arrived. Before León could say anything, Jaime, noting Papá's hesitation, stepped forward, *tío, we think it's about time you give Papá a business. We're here to ask you to give him the furniture store,* but León wasn't at all receptive; he was thinking about his expansion plan, which didn't include giving away this newly opened store to his younger brother. He had five furniture stores: the first one with Terri in charge, and four more, each one managed by one of his sons; this was number six, to be run by Simón. After all, it was a promotion. He would no longer have to carry heavy furniture up and down stairs. Now he would run the show, giving instructions to the agents, creating routes for the drivers -- he'd have everything on a silver platter-- and besides, he could teach his sons the business. Jaime could be the driver and agent, and after a while they could set up a new store... *You're crazy, I put up all the money, I found the building, I paid for the move, I had all these lights put in, I ordered all the merchandise. Your papá can be a partner at ten percent,* we heard him say. Mamá tried to counter his arguments, telling him to consider his brother and the rest of his family, but Tío León had dug in his heels, *absolutely not, Rebeca, I can't do that; the plan wasn't for Simón to be on his own, we were supposed to work as a team...* As he listened, Jaime's simmering fury began to intensify until he reached the boiling point and shouted, *Who broke his hand when a sofa got stuck on the stairs?! Who had to have a hernia operation? Who gave you his World Cup tickets because his hemorrhoids flared up and he couldn't go?!* Papá was so embarrassed he didn't know where to look and Tío León was obviously shocked by Jaime's outburst, *My God, Simón, how dare your son talk to me that way?, I'm his uncle! Do something, man!* Saqui started to protest, but Abram intervened and said it would be better for us to leave.

We went to Doña Yunta's taco stand, a place we had frequented since we were kids; it was a make-shift operation with two tables set up in the entranceway of an old building on a dark street in the center of town, next to a neighborhood bar. Sometimes drunks would stagger in, hoping to cure their hangover with the small tacos covered in a spicy chilpotle sauce. As for us, we competed to see who could eat the most. Doña Yunta always listened patiently to Mamá's complaints while she prepared our food. That night we laughed like maniacs, remembering our tío's incredulous face.

León, still holding the phone, was brought back to the present by Terri's voice, *remember, don't give them a chance to offend you again...* But his conscience began to bother him: he remembered their mother hugging him and Simón, insisting that brothers must always stick together. *I'm going over there,* he finally said to his sister Rosa on the phone, *tell the boys I'm on my way.* He said it reluctantly, knowing that Terri was going to give him a hard time about it, but realizing that there was no other way out, he had to be with his nephews, otherwise people would talk... Rosa felt satisfied as she hung up, *León will be right over,* expecting us to show some interest, but we didn't even look up. We still hadn't decided if we were going to the knis or not. Buzali had insisted that it was our duty, but Musa, Saqui and David couldn't imagine celebrating the holy day when we hadn't even buried Papá yet.

It was already nine o'clock when our cousin Elías Hanono showed up and announced in a decisive voice, *primos, you have to follow the customs, it's your duty to go to the knis; you don't have a choice, especially since today is not only Rosh Hashanah, but also Shabbat.* Jaime was convinced and began to give us instructions, *Beni, you take Musa, Saqui and Abram; Fule can take David and Mamá, and Ceci can take the other sisters-in-law. We're going to the knis on Querétaro Street.* Suddenly he realized that he had forgotten Tía Rosa and Tía Pola, and quickly tried to arrange for their ride. Tía Rosa insisted that we wait for Tío León, but Jaime countered, *Tía, we have to get there by the time they take out the sefer, we can't wait for him...*We were going down the stairs when León showed up alone. For a moment nobody knew what to say, but then Tía Rosa started crying and threw her arms around him. Solemnly, and without saying a word, we each greeted him with a hug and a few pats on the back. Tío León's face was strained, but he remained calm. Someone broke the silence and told him we were going to the knis. He said he would follow us and quickly motioned for Tía Rosa and Pola to get in his car. Somebody shouted to Musa to go with them. On the way there, we saw many booths with Mexican flags; firecrackers were already starting to explode in the streets, anticipating Independence Day. Luckily the traffic wasn't too bad since many people were off for the three-day weekend, taking advantage of Independence Day falling on a Monday. Tía Rosa asked her brother why Terri hadn't come, and he made up a flimsy excuse.

We arrived at the knis just when they were getting ready to take out the sefer and the rabbi's assistant hustled over to us. *Sit in the back, boys,* the shammash said. *When the ḥakham comes you can ask him all the questions you want. Don't say kaddish, just pray normally. Shafalkon, may you see no evil.* But we weren't convinced. *Jaime, I think we should say kaddish, what's with them? Are we in mourning or not?,* insisted Saqui, but Jaime wanted to do everything by the book. *No, wait. Salomón Amiga will be here any minute now and he'll know what to do; just hold on.* And up front, the cantor continued singing. Everybody was entering the knis and looking at us, *ḥazitos, their father just died.* And they didn't know if they could approach us, or greet us from a distance, or if they were allowed to embrace an onen. Because everyone knew that you can't hug an avel, it's bad luck, but we weren't avelim yet, and only a few people knew the rules for the onen. Even so, a lot of people came over and said *shafalkon, mano.* Others noticed our tormented faces, our swollen eyes, the shadows on our chins after one day without shaving. *Oye, who died? El papá, el papá. Lower your voice, they're going to hear you,* we heard them say two rows ahead of us. And everyone in the knis was watching, *I wonder what they're going to do, it's almost time for the kaddish, let's see if they say it or not.* One of us stepped forward and began to recite *yitgadal veyitkadash...* but right away someone shouted *No David, no David, you can't.* And the shammash rushed over to scold us, *Didn't I already tell you that you can't say kaddish?, listen to me! You've got to do as I say!*

David couldn't handle being silenced, and his eyes welled up with tears. He regretted missing the birthday celebration a month ago. Musa had wanted to take Papá out for lunch, give him one last fling, take him to the Caballo Bayo, *we should at least bring him a trio and have them sing for a while, make him happy just for one day.* That morning Papá wasn't in the mood, he had shouted at the top of his shaky voice that he wanted to be left alone. But he appreciated Musa's attention, and was pleased to know that Tía Rosa was coming to visit him. He was also excited about seeing his niece Mago, who had always danced salsa with him. It was his last chance. Musa remembered Papá out on the dance floor, moving his hips and gesturing with his hands. He was the master of moves and charm, no one could compete with him. Everyone liked to see him and admired his joyful, carefree style, *that Simón really knows how to live; he can gamble, drink, dance and do anything he wants, you name it.* Musa was sweating, trying to be as gentle as possible as he put his father's boxers on him, trying not to twist the urinary catheter. *And what about the bag?,* he would have to cover it somehow. But then he wondered, *what can I do about the smell? I already used the strongest shampoo I could find and the Yardley that he likes so much.* He remembered as a child the pleasant smell of his father recently shaved and bathed, and his ability to make him shake with laughter. But now the stench was unbearable. That's why when anyone came to visit the house, they didn't go upstairs to greet him, which made Musa's blood boil, *go on up, Tío; Papá is awake, he'll be glad to see you.* But they always beat a hasty retreat, *no, let him rest, just tell him I was here and brought some chocolates, and we're waiting for him at the club, all the guys miss him.* Papá was alone. The only one who could cheer him up even a little was Tía Rosa, who would quietly smuggle in an occasional cigarette, *What the hell, who cares, just be happy for a little while and Allah ma'ak.*

Musa went for the socks next; he chose the best he could find, some black ones that felt like wool. *Would it be bad for him to get all worked up?* He turned to the closet and found the shirt that he had given him a year ago. He had never worn it. *Papá, what about this one?, It's brand new...* But Papá was gone, either asleep or unconscious. *Papá! Papá!...* A drop of sweat fell from Papá's haggard face and he began to pant frantically. *Papá, calm down, calm down.* And then he had to stop everything and wait until Papá's breathing became more regular. Musa recalled when he had said that we should consider ending Papá's suffering in the hospital, no more heroics, and then at the Shabbat dinner, Jaime shouted, *who do you think you are? how are you going to know more than hashem? He's in God's hands. And don't spoil him by spoonfeeding him; he can do it himself.* Musa didn't care what Jaime said, because he was the only one who saw him every day. Sometimes he would play his trumpet, blowing his soul out the flared end of the horn along with the notes, and then he'd pound out the rhythm of his anguished heart on the piano. Music gave him courage; it helped him endure. He practiced desperately, as if Papá's fate hung on the perfection of each note. His days had no rhyme or reason. Sometimes he got up at two in the morning and they talked for hours, and Papá seemed fine, not suffering from anything, but the next day his vacant look returned, with the oxygen tanks that had left his nose raw, and the sudden, suffocating spells. Musa liked to spoonfeed him; he prepared scrambled eggs and took them up to his room at any hour. Papá accepted them with grateful pleasure. Musa would go to bed and wake up early, then run his daily fifteen kilometers in the Desierto de los Leones.

That day, however, he had planned everything carefully; he had called us all, but nobody believed him. *You're crazy, Papá can't go out. He doesn't like to be seen like this. He has his dignity, you know. Besides, Doctor Charabati told us that we have to keep him very calm; anything unusual could provoke an attack.* Musa wasn't worried about that. He was concentrating on trying to get the new silk shirt on Papá. He was almost finished when he realized that he hadn't called David. Maybe he could convince him. He quickly explained, *Papá, I'll be right back; hold on, I'm going for a glass of water and your heart medicine.* But he had really gone to another room to make a phone call. *Hello, put David on the phone please. No, tell him it's his brother Musa and to call me right away*! As he talked he saw himself reflected in the mirror and behind him hung his parents' wedding picture. They looked so much alike: thick lips; long, thin bodies; olive skin; the same green eyes. Musa was determined to plan everything so Papá could have a good time. It was almost impossible to get the wheelchair upstairs to his room. Papá was indignant, *no way, hijo, you're crazy. I'm not going that way; you'd have to kill me first, and even then I wouldn't go.* They started to struggle, and Papá resisted with surprising energy. *Papá, calm down; don't get all worked up, you're going to have an attack!* The whistling sound that came from Papá's lungs scared Musa; any minute now he might suffocate. Musa gave in for a moment. Then his salvation arrived. It was Mago with her laughter and grace that captivated everyone. From the moment he smelled his niece's perfume Papá was powerless to resist. She approached the room singing, *where is my salsa dancer?, where is my handsome man?* Musa was smiling now, seeing Papá straightening up, alert, and ready for the entrance of the queen: Mago at the doorway, a low-cut dress showing off a body that a woman twenty years her junior would have envied. *Vámonos tío, we're going to paint the town!*

Musa went to the closet for a tie, but then changed his mind. He envisioned Papá with his fitted grey-striped suit that he had bought at a boutique in the upscale neighborhood of *Zona Rosa*, greeting the captain of the ship on the Caribbean Cruise, feeling like a king, *all the martinis I can drink.* He imagined Papá in the bar like Humphrey Bogart, smoking a cigar and leaning on the piano. Then he thought of the trips to Acapulco and Papá's athletic body, lying in the sun all day until his skin became dark and sleek. Papá loved hotels with bars in the pool, where he could drink his rum in a coconut. Musa recalled the black-and-white honeymoon photos of Mamá and Papá, and he thought of their skin shining with tropical oil and how Papá showed off his body in La Quebrada, Puerto Marqués, or in the intimacy of Las Brisas. Musa could hear Papá's voice clearly, *bring me a piña colada, with an extra shot, and tell the boy to bring me a pack of Raleigh's non-filters.* And he could imagine him basking in the sun all day, sipping his drink as though entering a trance, closing his eyes, breathing in smoke and holding it in his lungs until he was about to burst, turning to gaze at Mamá feasting on a shrimp cocktail loaded with hot sauce, until she beckoned *Hey, Simón, that's enough, come into the shade where it's cool.* And then he pictured Papá getting up, covering himself with a towel and gesturing to Mamá, *let's go into the water, it looks so warm and calm, it's calling to us.* And he could see the photo of Mamá, slender for the last time, and he thought about how they played in the water, until Mamá protested, *stop, Simón, not here, stop it, Simón, I mean it.* But the rocking of the waves and the fresh flavor of coconut made them dizzy and Mamá surrendered to the pleasure and no longer worried about the vendors who were walking along the beach. Musa imagined how Mamá pressed her body up against Papá's and tasted the salt in his mouth as she gave him a long, lingering kiss, and how she must have thought triumphantly, *I stole him from Estrella Cababie, they were about to get married but there wasn't any dowry and Mamá, who was quick on the draw, offered to throw in the shop downtown in La Lagunilla, which stalled the engagement long enough for the groom to change his mind. And so I snagged the handsomest man in the community, el más guapo. If he doesn't know how to work, he can learn. Pretty soon he'll open another store and another and another. Just look at Carlos Meta, he hasn't stopped and now he has six. And I'll give him all the children he wants, we've got it made. Simón is so easy on the eyes, such a great dancer, he's got all the girls dreaming about him. If I don't watch out, the Cohab girl will steal him from me and her family has money and they'll set up a factory for him, and then that shop will look like small potatoes.*

Musa caught a whiff of Papá's stench and was startled out of his reverie, still holding the tie. *Musa, snap to it, get his feet up on the footrests and let's go, we're wasting time and I don't have all day,* Mago snapped at him, but Musa was staring at the tie and his eyes suddenly got watery so Mago took over, *let an expert do it.* Musa handed her the tie and she stood in front of Papá, but his grin was frozen on his face, and he didn't react. So Mago, in an exasperated voice, ordered, *go tell your brothers that we're leaving, and find out who's going.* David got the message at the store, *your brother Musa says that he'll meet you at the Caballo Bayo, he's taking your father to lunch and don't be late.* But David couldn't get away, *the idiot who brings me dresses hasn't arrived yet and if I don't wait for him he's going to leave me with nothing and his styles sell the best.* He now ran the store that Papá was given as a dowry. Papá had gone bankrupt and we had to make some changes; the dresses with the lace-lined collars didn't sell anymore, not even with all Lucha's tricks, and she could sell anything! *And now it's up to me,* thought David, *not one customer gets past me: I give the best prices. Look, I'll show you the latest styles; I've got photos, too, and I can make anything you like, you just choose one and we'll make a deal, no problem.*

Everybody turned to look when Papá crossed the threshold of the restaurant. The waiters were probably shocked by Papá's withered body, all skin and bones, *Don Simón, please come in, we'll set up your favorite table for you.* Musa had asked for the best table in the Caballo Bayo, even though he knew Papá would be humiliated because they would have to carry him, wheelchair and all, up the stairs. Musa noticed the waiters tearing up; they turned their heads to catch their breath and wiped their eyes with linen napkins taken from an empty table. Even though Papá looked dejected, he had recovered some of his energy. Mago ordered him a martini and Musa happily told the waiter, *we're celebrating my father's birthday; bring me a double tequila.* When they brought quesadillas and melted cheese with spicy sausage, their hearts sank because they realized that Papá's stomach couldn't handle his favorite foods. They didn't feel like eating either, even though it was three thirty in the afternoon. The trio came over without being called, and began to play "*Las Mañanitas.*" Tears rolled down Papá's face, but he didn't make a sound. Obviously choked up, the musicians struggled to clear their voices and, without invitation or consultation, they sang three songs that Papá had always requested. Musa saw Papá getting more and more upset, so he quickly dismissed the trio. They refused the tip that Musa offered them and reluctantly walked away after saying to Papá, *you'll get better, Don Simón, don't worry. We'll be waiting for you here.* Suddenly Papá turned to look at Musa and motioned to him to get close. Musa thought Papá wanted to tell him something so he gave him his ear. Papá clumsily raised his hand and rested it on Musa's shoulder. Musa looked at him and felt that Papá had made one last effort to give him a kiss.

And now we were standing here in the knis, on Rosh Hashanah, waiting to see the open doors of heaven, and David didn't know how to ask for forgiveness, but he decided that he had to pray the kaddish no matter what. They were just reciting the amidah. Jaime approached ḥakham Rayek, *we need to say kaddish, but the shammash says we can't. We don't know what to do.* The rabbi looked at us for an instant and replied, *yes, yes you can. It's not written anywhere that you can't. If you feel like saying it, then you should say it.* Everyone in the knis was listening to the conversation. *No, it is forbidden! That ḥakham is too modern!,* someone whispered. The words of the rabbi had been a relief to all of us, especially David, who started off with the rest of the mourners, even though he stumbled through the prayer and got confused, not knowing how to pronounce some of the words. And that made him remember the kiddush of Shabbat, and how Papá stood at the head of the table, painstakingly looking for the right page in the prayer book... *yom hashishi vayekhulu ha... shamayim ve'haaretz vekhol tzeva-am...* He heard that trembling voice, hesitating and stammering through each part of the prayer, until Papá finally gave up and said to Fule, *you do it, hijo, por favor.* And now David is Papá. We are all Papá. But now our Papá isn't here and we're saying kaddish (with our own trembling, stammering voices), even though everyone is looking at us in disbelief, this New Year's Day, while Papá's body waits for us in the basement of a hospital: *yitgadal veyitkadash sheme rabbah. Amen!...*

When the prayers ended that morning, we waited for Mamá on the stairs of the women's section, but we didn't see her anywhere. Ceci told us that Mamá had decided to stay home. Jaime felt guilty for having left her alone, *so who stayed with her?!* he shouted desperately. Bella calmed him down, saying that Fule's wife, Elena, was with her. Tío León said he would see us later and he left without waiting for us to invite him to our house to eat. We didn't see Teófilo Buzali anywhere. *Which knis did he say he was going to?,* Fule asked Jaime; *we need to see him right away.* And Jaime tried to encourage us, *I think Papá can be buried tomorrow, but I'm not sure. We'll call Buzali as soon as we get home.* We felt abandoned and vulnerable. *Who's going in what car?*, we asked, knowing that nobody should go alone. But since we still weren't avelim, no relatives had made the effort to accompany us.

David drove through the streets of the Colonia Roma instinctively, not noticing what street he was on or where he needed to turn. Musa observed the arched entranceway to a building on Alvaro Obregón Street and counted three floors up to spot the window that had been his look-out point as a child. He did a mental tour of the small apartment and recalled jumping on the bed and as we bounced up we could see Papá parking the furniture-store truck on the street below. He thought of Papá kissing him and pinching his cheeks; and then, while Papá drank his Turkish coffee, he would sit on his lap and let himself be tickled until breaking into uncontrollable laughter and falling on the floor. Musa looked up at the clear sky and wondered exactly where his father's spirit was lingering right then.

Concha had already prepared the meal when we got home. Jaime told her not to serve kibbe because we couldn't eat meat, according to what somebody told him at the knis. Mamá was sitting on the sofa with a lost look on her face. *Why did you stay home? It's haraam, Mamá!, you should have gone to the knis,* Jaime reproached her. Abram appeared with Beni and Saqui. The sisters-in-law went straight to the kitchen. They had left the children at home, so Ceci called to see how Simoncito was, after having a fever all night. Nobody felt like doing anything, but they managed to prepare some cheese fritatta; one of the sisters-in-law had brought yogurt. They made a meal with pita bread and a salad of lettuce, tomato, carrots and avocado, which we ate in silence, sniffling and wiping our tears. Saqui went to the upstairs bathroom, where he unloaded some tiny turds that floated like islands in an oval sea.

In the afternoon our cousin Elías Hanono arrived with his new wife, Bella Cohab. Even though Mamá couldn't stand the Cohab woman, she wasn't in the mood to protest. They were served Turkish coffee and roscas, but not even our cousin knew if he could say the berakha, so he said the blessing in a hushed voice, just in case. Afterward he took a small piece of paper out of his pocket, *here, I got you Teófilo Buzali's cell phone number; call him right away.* Strangely, at that very moment the phone rang and it was Buzali himself. *Hello, roḥi, I went to Bet Yosef and didn't see you, because you went to Querétaro, right?, but as I said, today we can't do anything. I already consulted with the ḥakhamim. Come to my house tonight and we'll make the arrangements. You can't talk to anybody; remember that these are holy days and we shouldn't even make phone calls, especially since it's Shabbat; but, well, this is an emergency, what can we do? Tell Beni to bring me the death certificate; I'm going to need it. And I'll call the hospital next.* Jaime asked him anxiously, *but, Teófilo, when can we take him to the bet haḥaim?* Buzali evaded the question; *we'll talk about it at my house. Did you write down my address? I live in Bosques...* Jaime hung up and announced that we would go see Buzali at eight or nine o'clock that evening.

Our primo Elías stood looking at the picture of Mamá and Papá that hung in the living room. He had taken it himself twenty years ago in Gitanerías, back when he was still married to Fortuna. Papá didn't care that Tío León shouted at him, insisting that he stay until ten o'clock to help close the store, or that Fule had a fever. Who knows what magic he used to get Mamá to go with him. When they walked in the door, someone had just cancelled a reservation and the captain, feeling a good tip being slipped into his hand, gave them the center table. They felt important. Mamá recognized a soap-opera actress at the next table, and Elías told them that the man at that other table was the assistant secretary of Foreign Affairs. Mamá went over to see the actress, and blurted out to her that she was prettier on television. Papá was so embarrassed that he didn't know where to look. *Why did you insult her, Rebeca?* But Fortuna was shaking with laughter, *that's why I love you, Tía, you're such a character.*

Papá soon forgot his anger when the music started and the flamenco dancers came out. He already knew them very well, since he had been there so many times. The one he liked the most was Mari Tere, especially when she danced intensely, tracing small circles with her graceful hands and tapping softly with her heels. Papá and Elías drank their cognac straight up and Mamá and Fortuna sipped theirs cut with coke, a drink called Paris de noche. Papá was captivated by the deep, mournful sounds of the cante jondo. He smoked one cigarette after another, paying no attention to the gossip that Fortuna was sharing with Mamá. Now and then his nephew extended his glass and toasted: *to your children, tío; may they give you joy, may you see them all married!* And Papá responded cheerfully, *the same to you, Elías, may you see them all married!* Elías returned to the present, still looking at the photo; he had never noticed that his ex-wife's slender arm was in the picture, next to Mamá. He shuddered as a bitter taste filled his mouth. He shifted his legs, repeating his usual, nervous habit. As he was about to leave, he tried to console Mamá, *Tía, please try to calm down. This is hashem's will. The poor man suffered so much and look what day he was taken.* Bella Cohab gestured at him to look at the clock and he saw that it was late. *So, I already told my mother and my brothers. Jaime, you'll tell me what you're going to do, right?* And he left without even taking a bite of the roscas.

Mamá went to wake up Abram, who had collapsed on his bed upstairs. *It's nine o'clock. Go with Jaime and your brothers to talk with Teófilo Buzali.* Abram got up and put on his shoes in a daze. We were on our way out when Beni asked if we should put on our kippahs or not.

Jaime didn't know what to say, but then he decided, *yes, everyone put one on.* We weren't used to wearing them outdoors and we felt strange; some young girls who were passing by stared at us. Since we didn't fit in one car, we had to take two. We identified Buzali's house by the black garage, just as he described it. *Hey, where did this guy get the money for such a mansion if he's with the Ḥevra?*, commented David to Fule. Jaime already knew the answer, *his brother has five shoe stores in San Juan de Letrán and I think they're partners; besides, everyone in the ḥevra has some business. The funeral work is all voluntary...* Buzali received us in the family room, *please sit down; you'll have to excuse me, since I'm planning to leave very soon. We're going to spend the second night of Rosh Hashanah with my brother-in-law Aarón; yesterday the whole family ate here. Delirios, please bring two more chairs.* We were all waiting impatiently. *Look, muchachos, we're going to bury him tomorrow. That's the decision I reached with ḥakham Yedid. It's haraam to do so on a holy day, but it's also a sin to not put the body to rest. The rabbi is allowing us to do it tomorrow because it is less haraam to have the burial on the second day. Please, boys, be discreet and don't tell anyone. Just you and those of the Ḥevra will go. Well, if you want to, you can tell your Tío León, but nobody else. Tomorrow we'll meet in the hospital at nine thirty; be sure to pay the bill so we don't get hung up. From there we'll go directly to Bet haḥaim.* Fule interrupted him brusquely, *Papá liked the knis in Querétaro a lot; couldn't we pass by there?* But Buzali very gently tried to calm him, *no, roḥi; no,... We can't go to the knis or even to his home, just straight to Bet haḥaim. It's haraam, roḥi. We can't ruin the holy day for others, do you understand?* Fule started crying and that upset David, whose shoulders started shaking as he held back the tears. Buzali asked for seven glasses of water; *God knows why he giveth, and why he taketh away, muchachos. Your father is going directly to heaven; today the gates are open. What a privilege, to die on Rosh Hashanah!*

The servant appeared at the door: *your wife says*

they are waiting for you at her brother's house... Well, said Buzali, *one more thing: your father has to be buried in line, like everybody else. And it's going to cost you seventy thousand pesos; that covers everything, including donations to charity.* Fule complained a bit, trying to bargain, *could you tell us, Teófilo, if that price is negotiable? I don't know if you heard that my father lost his business...* But Buzali didn't let him finish, *look, roḥi, thank God, barukh hashem, for you boys; it's a duty that you just have to do; like I said, it's a fixed price and you can't negotiate. If you prefer, you can make monthly payments. Talk to the community office in a couple of weeks. Ah, and before I forget, the headstone is up to you. I suggest that you order it as soon as possible, perhaps when the shiva is over. I'm sorry, boys, but they're waiting for me at my brother-in-law's house and my wife is getting impatient. I'll see you, God willing, at the hospital tomorrow.* As we left, we saw Buzali's black Cutlass disappear into the night. *Damn it! He didn't even let us get a word in edgewise!* commented David. Jaime was resigned to the situation, and to everybody's surprise he said, *you know how dignified Papá was; there's no other way, we'll just have to divide up the expenses and pay them as we can.* That night, on the eve of the burial, we all went to sleep with heavy hearts, haunted by doubts and fears.

3

2 Tishrei 5757 Rosh Hashanah
15 September 1996 (Sunday morning)

FOR THE SAKE OF THE DECEASED THE FUNERAL WILL TAKE PLACE AS SOON AS POSSIBLE; THEREFORE, THERE WILL BE NO WAITING FOR ANYBODY, EVEN AN IMPORTANT RELATIVE SUCH AS A SON OR DAUGHTER. IT IS CUSTOMARY FOR THE WOMEN NOT TO ATTEND THE BET HAḤAIM FOR THE FUNERAL; THOSE WHO ACCOMPANY THE DECEASED USUALLY WASH THEIR HANDS WITHOUT DRYING THEM AFTERWARDS, AND WITHOUT SAYING BERAKHA. AT THE MOMENT AT WHICH THE DECEASED BEGINS TO BE COVERED WITH DIRT IN THE TOMB, THE ONEN MAY SAY THE BERAKHOT OF SHEMA AND TEFILAH AND THUS THE LAWS OF AVELUT (MOURNING) BEGIN TO BE IN EFFECT.

Musa woke up Abram and Saqui. Jaime, Fule, David and Beni were already downstairs, waiting nervously. We put on the same clothes as yesterday, and hastily sipped some Turkish coffee before leaving. *Rápido. Get in the car.* Musa began to cough repeatedly, until he finally had to spit an enormous glob of phlegm out of the car window. He had forgotten his kippah, but to his surprise, Fule told him that there was an extra one in the glove compartment. As he drove, Jaime was saying, *right now, Abram, you're the calmest one, so you should take care of telling Tío León that Azra is not welcome in our home... we don't allow thieves...* That set Fule off, who shouted, *And his wife better not set foot in the house either!* Saqui tried to be reasonable, *put yourself in our uncle's shoes, Fule, she's his daughter.* But Fule was up in arms, *no, she's not his daughter, she's his stepdaughter, and I wouldn't give a damn, even if she were his daughter. Don't you remember how she would hang up the phone on Papá?! don't you remember how she gave him the run-around?! and don't you remember how Terri slammed the door in our faces every time we went to collect our money from that ratero?!*

In the parking lot at the Hospital we saw Tío León kissing his wife good-bye. Saqui tried to remember seeing Papá and Mamá kiss each other on the lips, but he couldn't recall that ever happening. Only in their honeymoon picture, in Acapulco, he thought. On Shabbat, the most they did was shake hands. Jaime was inspecting the hospital bill. *Carajo,* he said furiously, *they charge you for every breath you take.* After complaining bitterly to the cashier for charging forty pesos apiece for four adult diapers, he had to summon the manager to approve the discount they had been promised when Papá registered.

Suddenly, people from the Ḥevra began to arrive: five tall, stocky men, with enormous mustaches and bellies, all wearing white shirts with the sleeves rolled up. They greeted us one by one, *shafalkon, shafalkon.* One of them told us that Teófilo Buzali was already at the bet haḥaim; he had sent a car for the body, and we should join him as soon as the discharge papers were in order.

Musa, Saqui and Abram rushed to the basement of the hospital. Four of the men from the Ḥevra brought in a simple, pine coffin, along with a blue cloth with the star of David. Saqui tried to help, but they stopped him, *take it easy, muchachos, you better wait for us outside. Beto Mochón is out there. He'll tell you what you have to do.*

They turned the cars' headlights on even though it was midday. Beto Mochón told us to drive slowly in single file without trying to pass. The men from the Ḥevra accompanied Papá in a navy-blue van; Fule followed closely in his olive-green car, then came David's red Celebrity and at the end, the other three men from the Ḥevra in a Celebrity just like David's, but brown. Fule, Jaime, Abram and Beni were wondering who those men were. *I think the tallest one is a Syrian Argentinian who is married to one of the Zaga sisters. The bald guy is a cousin of Vicki Meta, the wife of Zequíe Mustri's brother-in-law. And the chubby one is Rubén Chayo, remember? the one who always brought ham tortas to school, until the principal caught him and expelled him for three days. Look at him now, who would have guessed? You know how you get paid for this job? They open the doors of heaven for you! Just imagine what a mitzvah that would be!* Fule was driving like a bodyguard, right on the tail of the car carrying the coffin. When Jaime and Fule realized that Tío León was riding in David's car with Saqui and Musa, they hoped their brothers would remember to make things clear to him. Saqui seemed to get the message telepathically, since he began to insinuate to Tío Leon that his son-in-law was not well liked by the brothers, *tío, even though this isn't the right time to talk about problems, remember that Azra treated my papá horribly...*Tío León already knew where Saqui was headed and he cut him off, *por favor, don't talk to me about this now when we are all suffering, we're going to the bet haḥaim, don't complicate my life.* Musa flinched as if he had been poked in an open wound, shouting, *A complicated life was what my papá had! Don't forget that* *my papá lent him all of his savings in good faith, and he responded by stealing it from him, depriving him of his dignity, which was all he had left. He better not dare come to our door!* And Saqui added, *that goes for his wife, too, tío.* He said it slowly, as if it just slipped out. Now it was their uncle who got angry, *but, you guys are crazy, she's my daughter! All I can say is if you treat her with disrespect, I'll march out of your house and there will be a big scandal...*Just then we arrived at the bet haḥaim. Jaime got out of Fule's car and gestured to David to leave his car with two boys who had offered to watch it. *Give them a good tip, this is a really bad neighborhood.*

We looked with curiosity at the Monte Sinai logo on the iron gate at the entrance. We stood there, paralyzed. Rubén Chayo had to push us inside, *it's dangerous to stay out here, go on in.* Teófilo Buzali was waiting for us. *Shafalkon, muchachos. From now on may you see no evil and may we be together on joyous occasions. Listen, Beto Mochón and the others are going to take your papá to prepare him, to perform the Taharah, the purification and the washing.* Four of them took the coffin out of the car and carried it into a small building, closing the door behind themselves immediately. They didn't allow any of us to get close. Tío León went to get a kippah, entering the building through the main door. Saqui followed him, wondering where he was going. Once inside, he realized that although the building looked like a knis from the outside, the interior was cold and desolate: there was a large empty space, with benches on the sides. Rubén came at once to tell them to go outside. While we were waiting, we read the inscriptions on the closest tombs and on one of them we found the name of a great uncle, *Papá always spoke of him with great respect, he was one of the founders of the community,* said Jaime, confirming a legacy that would make them proud. There lay the mysterious past: that uncle had been one of the first to make the voyage to Mexico from Damascus. *First he encouraged his brothers to come and then he brought his parents and sister.* Papá had told us how his uncle supported the family for a long time until Papá and Tío León grew up and began to work. Now, with an eerie feeling, we contemplated the tomb of an uncle that no one remembered. Without Papá's memory, our uncle was erased from the face of the earth.

Abram, Jaime, Fule and Saqui had been at the bet haḥaim twenty-five years before. They hardly remembered anything. The voices of Papá and Mamá haunted them: *it's just not done, you can't go to the bet haḥaim as long as your parents are alive.* At that time, Papá and Mamá had taken Musa, David and Beni to Disneyland, Las Vegas and San Francisco, to celebrate Musa's bar mitzvah and while there, to buy the bateh, the gifts for Jaime's fiancée. They were all excited because it was going to be the first wedding for one of us. The families got along very well. Our brother Abram and Salomón Saad, who were inseparable buddies, had served as matchmakers. Sara, the future bride, was gracious and affectionate, almost like the daughter that Mamá always wanted. Furthermore, her mother, Elena Saad, had the same opinions and preferences as Mamá. But one weekend, all was lost. Sara drank some contaminated water from a river in Cuernavaca and in less than a day she died, while the doctors were still trying to figure out what happened to her. They had operated on her without knowing if it was appendicitis or an internal hemorrhage. Saqui closed the store even though the sales clerk told him that they only closed for the death of a family member. The four brothers, horrified by her premature death, went to the bet haḥaim without giving it a second thought. During the funeral, Abram embraced his inconsolable friend Salomón, while Saqui tried to comfort Jaime. Saqui still had a vivid memory of Salomón asking to kiss his dead sister's hand before she was laid to rest in the tomb. The next day, Papá and

Mamá returned triumphantly from their trip to the United States, loaded with presents for the bride and wondrous stories to tell of the marvelous places they had visited. When Abram told them in the airport that Sara had died, they cried out in disbelief and began to wail, oblivious to the crowd that had gathered to greet the arriving planes. Some people formed a semicircle around us, trying to figure out what was going on. From then on, Saqui suffered from flashbacks of the funeral at night, but he had completely forgotten what the bet haḥaim looked like.

In the patio by the entrance, we were left waiting for a ritual that was completely unknown to us. Minutes passed, but we didn't look at our watches. We obeyed the men of the Ḥevra, convinced that the only thing to do was to respect the legendary customs of the community. Buzali approached us to ask if Papá had worn dentures. We told him no, Papá had become accustomed to chewing with the few teeth he had left.

Beto Mochón appeared at the door and gestured to Teófilo Buzali. We all rushed over there, hoping to get instructions about what we should do. Buzali took a deep drag on his cigar. As he exhaled the smoke he began to explain, *muchachos, you're going to enter one by one -from the oldest to the youngest—to say good-bye to your papá, we'll let you know when it's your turn.* Buzali took his post outside the door, where Mochón soon appeared and motioned to Jaime. They closed the door after him and we heard a soft moan. Soon they called to Abram. When it was his turn, Saqui saw Papá wrapped in a white shroud, with his hand exposed. Beto Mochón indicated that he should kiss the hand and say mehila. Saqui stood rooted to the spot, not understanding. Mochón explained, *you have to ask for mehila, forgiveness.* But Saqui just stood there, not knowing how to react. Rubén Chayo became impatient, *come on, Saqui, this is how it goes, you just have to say mehila, that's the custom.*

Don't think it over, just say it. Saqui snapped out of his trance and touched his lips to the cold skin. He trembled as he felt the flaccid hand. He remembered the prayer of the Shabbat, when he kissed Papá's hand, but the memory disappeared in an instant. They had already called Musa when Saqui turned and asked Mochón to let him see Papá's face. *No, you can't do that, it's haraam.* Saqui pleaded with him, arguing that he hadn't been able to see him before he died. He insisted so much that they called Buzali so he could decide what to do. Buzali nodded his approval. When Beto Mochón uncovered Papá's face, Saqui immediately realized his mistake, as he looked with horror at the countenance of death. In preparation for the burial, they had filled his nostrils and ears with a blue substance. His eyes were covered with dirt, leaving his face void of any expression. They also had put a wad of gauze in his jaw. Saqui contemplated the dirt in his eye cavities, terrified by the effacement of Papá's features. He anxiously confirmed that Papá was not breathing: without eyes and with no respiratory movement, Papá's body had ceased to be Papá; it had become a corpse. Saqui scarcely noticed that his body had begun to shake. He was surprised by Mochón's strength as he held him up and curtailed the motion of his hands. *Calm down! You can't touch him.* With Mochón on one side and Chayo on the other, the two of them managed to overcome Saqui's feeble resistance and lead him out of the room. Jaime and Fule were waiting anxiously. *¿Qué pasó? What's going on?* While Saqui caught his breath, Musa took his turn, then David and finally Beni. Teófilo Buzali gestured to Tío León to go in. We remembered Mamá's words: *your papá loves him more than life itself; he would do anything for him. He pays more attention to his brother than to his own sons.* It was true, Papá adored him. *Look, for Papá's sake we're going to have to put up with Tío León. Just one week and then ciao! I bet it's the end of the family,* Beni said to Abram.

They brought out Papá's body in a coffin that seemed wider and deeper. We rushed over to carry it, but we quickly realized that the coffin was embedded in a cart with wheels. Buzali, Mochón, Chayo and another man from the ḥevra whose name we didn't know began to push the cart from behind. We lined up on each side, placing our hands on the coffin but not making any effort to carry it. We walked in a straight line, looking all around, trying to read the names on the nearby tombs. Since Buzali was aware that we didn't know the rules, he explained, *the red line is for the kohanim, the descendents of the first priest, Aaron. They cannot walk along the pathways between the tombs, especially if the deceased is not a close relative. That is why the corners are reserved for them... Pay attention, muchachos, we have precise instructions from the ḥakhamim: we're not going to perform an ordinary funeral. You should be praying at the knis, since it is Rosh Hashanah. It is up to us to bury your papá, but we're supposed to be doing it secretly so as not to desecrate the holy day.* We weren't listening; we were sobbing and wailing, replaying the images of Papá unconscious with oxygen tubes in his nose, lying on his bed. Out of the corner of his eye Saqui noticed our paternal grandfather's name on a corner tomb. The men of the Ḥevra rolled the cart with excruciating deliberation, as if they were on a very busy street. Jaime remembered Dr. Charabati's explanation, *imagine that your papá's blood is circulating on the freeway, on a Friday afternoon payday, with bumper to bumper traffic, pouring rain and an accident to slow things down even more; the only way to make it circulate is to draw half a liter every month so it will thin out and flow more easily. I can't promise you a gringo highway, but at least an arterial street.*

The cemetery was narrow at the entrance but widened as we walked further in; thus the pathway that separated the men's from the women's tombs divided and angled out toward each side. The men of the Ḥevra turned for the first time toward the right, following a path that led to another section. Suddenly we spotted three workers who were digging dirt out of a deep hole. They were being supervised by another man from the Ḥevra. *Have you finished yet, Moni?* Abram recognized Moni from middle school. He was surprised to see him there, helping the workers. *That Moni used to hang out at the Tizoncito, eating tacos. He liked to pick up girls in the Zona Rosa. How in the world did he end up dealing with dead people?* Abram noticed that at the bottom of the grave there was a kind of internal step on each side, narrowing the hole, but not perfectly formed yet. Buzali told Moni that the bottom wasn't big enough. Moni took the shovel himself and started to dig, trying to make the sides straighter. He didn't rest until he was satisfied with his work. Buzali took the opportunity to instruct one of the workers, *be careful, Nacho, show Moni how it should be, with a step on each side that goes down about sixteen inches.* From down in the grave, Moni looked at Abram and recognized him instantly, making a gesture that reminded them of their adolescence. Without prayers or speeches or protocol of any kind, Beto Mochón and Rubén Chayo took the corpse out of the coffin. Now Papá's body was only a bundle wrapped in a white sheet. Teófilo Buzali got down by Moni to receive it. They both stood with their legs spread, their feet on the earthen steps, one behind the other. We watched as they very gently lowered Papá's body, taking precautions so the corpse would not get hit or mistreated in any way. They placed him delicately in the deepest and narrowest part of the burial chamber, which was only large enough to hold the body and nothing else. There was Papá, shrouded in a white sheet and at the bottom of a deep, strange and asphyxiating hole. They had placed him with his head toward the interior of the cemetery and his feet toward the entrance gate. Buzali asked them to pass him the stones: the three large rocks were wide, solid, and heavy. It took two men to carry each one. Abram finally understood the logic in the way they had dug the grave, since the rocks were placed on the two steps that served as a platform, and they were able to cover Papá's body without touching it. Once the stones were in place, the white shroud was no longer visible. We embraced each other, holding on tightly while wailing and crying. Buzali and Moni climbed out of the grave. The men of the Ḥevra glanced back and forth, not knowing what to do, waiting for Buzali to give them instructions. Mochón grabbed a shovel and threw some dirt on the stones. Fule tried to do the same, but Chayo gently stopped him, *not you, mano.* Fule was determined, so he ignored Chayo and plunged the shovel into the moist earth that was piled on the edge of the hole. Soon the rest of us, including Tío León, began to take turns shoveling dirt into Papá's grave.

When we finished, Buzali told us that it would be better to say kaddish at home with the evening prayers, because they would do the keriah for us then, and after that ritual tearing of our shirts, we would be considered avelim. But David answered him almost shouting that no, we were going to say it even if he didn't approve. And we started reciting it, stumbling over the words because several of us didn't know the prayer by heart; we repeated some phrases that had been drilled into us as children, and the rest we muttered or stammered, striving to say them in unison, but failing. The workers waited as we said our prayer and then hurried to fill the hole as quickly as possible. Since they were all young and slender, we were surprised by their strength and the speed of their work. Musa gazed at the empty coffin and wondered if it would be used again.

Saqui asked to see our sister's tomb, but the men of the Ḥevra immediately refused, *we are definitely not going to permit that. When you come back in a week, which will coincide with the eve of Yom Kippur, you can visit any grave you wish.* As we were leaving the cemetery Saqui saw our grandfather's name again and asked, *Teófilo, if my grandfather wasn't one of the kohanim, why is he in a corner?* Buzali gave him an evasive answer, *I don't know, he was lucky, being in a corner is a great privilege. People used to pay a lot of money to be given a corner, but we don't allow that anymore. You can be the richest man in the community, but your tomb will be the next one in line. That's the only way to make sure that we are all equal in death, from the greatest ḥakham to the most wretched bum. Hashem is the only one who decides whether our soul will go up to heaven. Just last week we brought in Señor Jacobo Masri. That guy was a multimillionaire and there's his tomb, still fresh, right next to your papá's. What's money worth? Your true home is with God. We're only here a little while, right?* As we listened to him we watched the sun peek between the heavy, black clouds. Upon reaching the exit we saw two sinks on the wall near the gate. Mochón warned us, *wash your hands without saying berakha and without drying them. Those drops of water are your tears that will never dry.* Jaime told us to tear off a branch from a tree, *as you leave the bet haḥaim throw it backwards without looking, as a sign that we won't ever have to return.*

4

2/3 Tishrei 5757

15 September 1996 (Sunday afternoon and evening)

KERIAH. THE KERIAH (TEARING THE SHIRT OR DRESS) SHALL BE PERFORMED ON THE DECEASED'S CHILDREN ON THE LEFT HAND SIDE OF THE GARMENT, OVER THE HEART; FOR ALL OTHER RELATIVES, IT SHALL BE ON THE RIGHT SIDE. BEFORE THE KERIAH, THE AVELIM SHALL STAND UP AND SAY THE FOLLOWING PRAYER: BARUKH ATAH ADONAI ELOHENU MELEKH HAOLAM DAYAN HAEMET (BLESSED ART THOU, O LORD OUR GOD, KING OF THE UNIVERSE, JUDGE OF ALL TRUTH). THE LEADER OF THE ḤEVRA SHALL START THE KERIAH WITH A KNIFE AND THE AVEL SHALL CONTINUE IT WITH HIS OWN HANDS FOR A MINIMUM OF THREE INCHES LENGTHWISE (NOT ACROSS THE GARMENT).

AFTER THE KERIAH, THE AVELIM SHALL TAKE OFF THEIR LEATHER SHOES AND SIT ON THE FLOOR AND THUS THEY SHALL REMAIN THROUGHOUT THE SEVEN DAYS. ALL THE MIRRORS OF THE HOUSE SHALL BE COVERED, AND DECORATIONS SHALL BE REMOVED FROM THE PLACE OF PRAYER.

We had stretched out on our beds to wait for the afternoon. Our sisters-in-law were bustling around diligently in the kitchen. Fule's wife Elena had agreed to negociate with Señor Salame so he would handle things, *don't worry, I'll take care of everything, I'll send you chairs, dishes and silverware. I'll also send you a cook for the breakfasts, and a waiter. Let me know if you need anything else.* They hadn't allowed Mamá to get involved, but since she wasn't used to sitting on her hands, she was already getting impatient. Bella had been calling the relatives; Ceci was in charge of covering the mirrors and taking down the decorations. Fortuna made sure there was enough toilet paper and that the kitchen was well stocked.

The men of the Ḥevra arrived at about five o'clock in the afternoon. They brought a basket full of kippahs and about forty prayer books, which they placed on two folding chairs at the entrance to the house. Jaime, Fule and David carried the sofas out to the garage. A waiter arranged the chairs in seven rows with seven chairs in each row, as if they were in a small theater. The sofa cushions were placed on the floor against one of the walls of the living room, facing the chairs. Bella went up to the bedrooms to look for pillows because she realized that there weren't enough cushions for all the avelim. Beto Mochón brought four large pieces of paper that he posted on the living and dining room walls with masking tape. David went over to read:

Mourning for Papá

LEILUY NISHMAT
SHIMON BEN RAḤEL

PASTRIES, CRACKERS, BREAD WITH ANISE:
BARUKH ATAH ADONAI ELOHENU MELEKH
HAOLAM BOREH MINEH MEZONOT.
LIQUIDS, CHEESES:
BARUKH ATAH ADONAI ELOHENU MELEKH
HAOLAM SHEAKOL NIHIYAH BIDBAROH.
VEGETABLES AND FRUITS OF THE EARTH:
BARUKH ATAH ADONAI ELOHENU MELEKH
HAOLAM BOREH PERIH HAADAMAH.
DRIED FRUITS FROM THE TREE:
BARUKH ATAH ADONAI ELOHENU MELEKH
HAOLAM BOREH PERIH HAETS.
WE REQUEST THAT YOU NOT SHAKE HANDS
WITH THE AVELIM. THANK YOU.
SCHEDULE FOR THE PRAYERS:
SHACHARIT: 7:30
MINḤAH: 18:30
ARVIT:
AS YOU TAKE LEAVE OF THE AVELIM YOU SAY:
'TENUHAMU MIN HASHAMAYIM'.

A short while later Mamá's sisters arrived: Tías Jasibe, Raquel and Zequíe. Tía Raquel was accompanied by two of her seven daughters, Rosa and Sofía; Tía Jasibe had her daughter Alegra with her, as usual. Tía Zequíe told Mamá that her children would be there soon. Mamá went up to tell Abram, Saqui, Musa and Beni that they had to come down because people were arriving. David remembered the wedding of Tío León's daughter, Raquel. At that time, the house belonged to Tío León. Papá, Mamá and the seven of us squeezed into a Volkswagen to ride over there. It was the first wedding in the family, and Raquel glided down a stairway with suspended steps in the middle of the living room, provoking exclamations and cheers. Now we descended the same stairs, our bodies clammy with sweat and chins itchy from unshaven beards. The house was packed with people. David began to go down the list with Fule: all of Mamá sisters were there, but not their children or spouses. On Papá's side there were Tío León and Tías Rosa and Pola, but the eldest, Tía Sara, wasn't there yet. David assumed that our cousin Jaime Behar would have his chauffeur bring her. They had told us that Tía Sara was in a wheelchair so maybe it wasn't a good idea to break the news to her.

Fule also saw two of Tío León's sons. David commented with relief that he hadn't seen the ratero or his wife. Three of Tía Raquel's sons-in-law were talking to Jaime, explaining something about the ritual. Fule approached them to ask, *Jaime, didn't Buzali tell you who was coming? It's getting late, and no ḥakham has shown up yet. What time is minḥah supposed to begin?* Tía Raquel's sons-in-law –Abud Nehmad, Salomón Tuachi and Nissim Entebi— answered almost in unison that minḥah had to start at six-thirty in the evening. The heat began to accumulate in the house as more and more people arrived. Tía Zequíe's daughters Sara and Alegra were lighting one cigarette after another, and a thick haze of smoke obscured the living and dining rooms. It was six fifteen when Teófilo Buzali arrived with some blue pamphlets entitled "Beginning of Wisdom. Reverence of G'd." In smaller print were the acknowledgements of those who paid for the edition: "In memory of Rubén Abadi. Courtesy of the Señora Olga Jafif, widow of Abadi, and their children." He gave one to each of us. Tío León requested one, too. The booklet had the following sections: "At the father's tomb," "At the mother's tomb," "At the husband's tomb," "At a child's tomb," "At a brother's or sister's tomb," and a "Prayer during times of misfortune or pain." It also included the entire prayer of the shema and the amidah, with transliteration from the Hebrew. And at the end, also with transliteration, was the Kiddush of Shabbat and the Kaddish.

The men of the Ḥevra had realized that we didn't know many of the prayers and they wanted to help us with the basics. *The kaddish is on the last page. Por favor, it's very important that you say all of the words clearly and in unison, without getting ahead or behind. You say three versions throughout the service. The longest and most complete is the one you have in the pamphlet. We're going to call that one number three; it's the one that includes the paragraph that begins with "To Israel"; when we indicate number one, read only the first two paragraphs; number two is the same as three, but without the "To Israel" paragraph. Understood?* We felt confused; Musa was writing numbers in his booklet with a pen. David told him it was haraam to mark up the prayer books, but Nissim Entebi, who was listening to the conversation, butted in to say that it was okay because the pamphlet wasn't in Hebrew. Jaime asked Buzali why no ḥakham had arrived. He hastened to explain that Rosh Hashanah was ending that afternoon and all the rabbis were busy with the holy day. *But tomorrow morning Rabbi Mizrahi is going to come, roḥi. We're also going to send you Isaac Helfón so he can be reciting the tehilim all day. Right now I'm going to perform the keriah, and Nissim will be in charge of leading the prayers.* We were surprised that Buzali already had arranged with Raquel's son-in-law to preside over the service. *And how could he know that Nissim was going to be here? What if nobody had known how to do it? I bet Buzali doesn't even know how to lead the service.*

At exactly six thirty, Salomón Tuachi began to hit his prayer book with an open hand. With the unexpected silence, Buzali dryly announced that we would begin minḥah, *por favor, the señoras should go to the dining room; there are books at the door for the señores. Take your places.* He had us sit in the first row. They set up some chairs on the side for Mamá and Tías Rosa and Pola. Tío León sat in the second row, but one of his sons brought another chair for him so he could sit with us. Nissim began to pray in a loud voice and at such a fast pace that most of us had trouble staying on the right page. Every two or three minutes we'd look over at Fule to see where we were supposed to be. When we came to the first kaddish, Tuachi gestured to us to keep silent. We were still confused. Tuachi, Entebi and Nehmad had all been informed about the episode in the knis the day before, when one of the ḥakhamim had given us permission to say the kaddish even though we were onenim. They thought that could only happen with a rabbi from the Shami community, because no one from the Ḥalabis would have allowed it to happen. When minḥah was over, it was just getting dark outside.

Teófilo Buzali grabbed a small bag out of his pant's pocket, which contained a short blade. He called to Mamá and the people gathered around him. Buzali cut Mamá's blouse on the right side and asked her to continue the tear vertically. Afterwards, he had her repeat the prayer *barukh atah Adonai elohenu melekh haolam dayan haemet.* It took a long time because Mamá cried as she pronounced each of the words. Tuachi, Nehmad and Entebi wondered if they were going to do the keriah for Abram and Tío León. In the knis they weren't allowed to go up to the sefer or receive any religious honors. Abram, for his part, wasn't interested in going to the knis, even though he had separated from his wife. We didn't know if Buzali had been informed of this, so Mamá gave him a heads-up when he arrived, *Abram is living at home now; his girlfriend will be here soon, she's Jewish, her name is Guite Zyman, do you know her?* Tía Raquel's sons-in-law had a fit when they saw Buzali proceed to perform the keriah for each one of us, including Abram, Tío León and even Tía Pola. When Buzali made the short cut on the left side of his shirt, asking him to tear downwards, Abram yanked on his shirt with so much fury that he tore the cloth too far, knowing that they were watching him and wondering if any of his relatives would dare to offer a reproach. We were crying so hard that our cheeks began to sting. Buzali asked for the pita bread and the hard-boiled eggs that he had ordered when he arrived. We sat down on the cushions. *Eat, roḥi, eat.* And when he saw one of us choking on the bread, he ordered *water, por favor, so he can swallow.* Bufali ended with the obligatory phrases, *may you see no evil, may we see each other in celebrations and in joy, may you live to be a hundred and twenty. Shafalkon to you all.*

Almost immediately we began the prayer of Arvit. Nissim gestured to Abud Nehmad to take charge of the reading. Fortunately, Nehmad read more slowly and, even though he exaggerated the intonation, it was easier for us to follow. When we got to the first kaddish, they pointed to number one. Once again, even though we had the transliteration, we stumbled over some words as we recited, falling out of sync or simply remaining silent when we couldn't follow the rest. Only Fule had decided to skip the blue book and recite the entire prayer in Hebrew. When Arvit was finished, Salomón Tuachi came over to see how he could help us with the kaddish. *Listen, you have to say the kaddish with all of the words pronounced carefully, but without shouting...* Saqui interrupted him, *but they race through the prayers and I can't even keep up. Besides, Amiga pronounces the words differently. Here in the little blue book it says "Bealma di berah kiruteh..." and I hear everyone saying "khiruteh."* Tuachi looked perplexed. *That's how it's pronounced, say "khiruteh." Besides, when they say "veḥayekhon" you turn to the left, and on "uyomekhon" to the right. Then when you say "veimruh amen," you have to wait for them to answer "Yehe sheme rabah..."; you should wait for us to say a whole sentence and then you repeat it.* With thinly disguised indignation, Tuachi asked if we hadn't learned to read in Hebrew. Abram and Jaime answered, *of course we have, but we don't spend all our time in the knis.* Tuachi noticed our irritation and turned to talk to one of his in-laws. David commented, *He's a show-off, one of those conservative religious types who pound their chests and then go around looking for someone to screw. His wife gets the worst of it: he doesn't give her money to run the house, and he doesn't let her go anywhere alone.* The waiter passed by with a tray full of the small demi-tasse cups of Turkish coffee. Abram grabbed two of them. He looked at the words so he could say the correct lines before sipping the coffee. One of the Hanonos who was listening to the berakha answered *amen* and then he told Saqui, *you have to answer amen. If you listen to a berakha, it's your responsibility to respond with amen.* Our cousin decided to give us advice, *tomorrow is the fast of Gedaliah; it begins at five thirty in the morning (before dawn) and ends at dusk. It's a good idea for you to fast, now that your papá's soul is lingering in the house; you'll help him ascend...*

Four of us were sitting on the cushions on the floor; Tía Rosa, Tía Pola and Mago were questioning our cousin Salomón Behar, *Salo, isn't your mamá coming? Did they let her know? What did Jaime say?* Salomón explained very calmly, *Sí, tías, Jaime sent his chauffeur to pick her up. We told her that Tío Simón was very sick, but I don't know if she knows the whole truth.* Just then Jaime Behar entered, giving instructions to two people who were carrying Tía Sara's wheelchair. They managed to fit the chair between the cushions on the floor and the living room stairs. When we all went over to give her a kiss, she began to cry. She couldn't keep us straight: Fule she called Beni, and David she called Saqui. Then she asked, *Where is Simoncito? Where is my Simón, so I can give him a kiss?* We didn't know how to react. Jaime Behar answered her almost shouting, pausing at each syllable, *your brother Simón passed away, Mamá, his soul is in heaven now...* But Tía Sara paid no attention to him, and insisted, *where did you leave him, León?*

Tía Sara was seventeen years older than Papá. Now she was probably eighty-seven. She was the only one of Papá's siblings who was born in Damascus. Tía Rosa told us once that there had been two other sisters, but they died in Syria before they could make the trip to Mexico. *They were very poor and most likely they were caught in an epidemic. Infant mortality was very high; that's why they had a lot of children, because some never reached adulthood. Sara was the second child. When my parents came to Mexico, she was about eleven or twelve years old. So León, your papá, and I were born in Mexico, and then, finally, Pola. When Sara got married, we were still children. Pola hadn't even been born; your papá would have been about two years old. Jacobo, Sara's eldest son, is almost the same age as Pola; they grew up together almost like brother and sister, even though she was his tía. Then Sara's husband died. He used to travel around the nearby pueblos to sell things; he would leave at dawn with two suitcases full of underwear, socks, ties, stockings and handkerchiefs. He didn't come home until he had sold them all. The next day he would go to a different pueblo, with two more suitcases. One day someone tried to take away his suitcases. While they were struggling, the thief took out a knife and stabbed him in the stomach. He was taken to the nearest hospital and treated, but he had already lost too much blood. Sara was left with four children and no money. The leader of our community gave her money for rent and my tíos helped her a little, too. They got by eating lentils and rice every day. Who would guess that Jaime Behar was so poor as a child? He doesn't want anybody to suffer; he supports his mother and pays for her nurse, and maid. He also gives money to his mother-in-law, to his brother-in-law, and to his brother Salomón. He even sends a few dollars to his brother Jacobo, who lives in Miami. He gives me some money now and then, too. He's such a kind man!* Abram thought about the time when he was working for his cousin Jaime at Mueblemex. He used to dump all the difficult customers on Abram, and they would usually give him a hard time before going off to buy cheaper, low-quality furniture from another store. Jaime's brother Salo, on the other hand, got all the clients with deep pockets who wanted to furnish their luxury homes in Las Lomas or San Angel. The best customers were government officials because they never wanted to haggle and they trusted Salo's good taste (and he always managed to sell them the most expensive furniture). He remembered the day when Salo sold the Secretary of the Treasury some furniture imported from Paris, which was transported by boat in a huge container. Later, the Secretary decided to ask him to supply all the furniture for the office building they had just inaugurated.

Jaime liked to go for a walk at night. He would say to Abram, *Keep me company, mano, and then dinner's on me.* So they rushed along the streets of Tecamachalco, traversing the entire Avenida de los Bosques. Jaime chattered endlessly, as if nobody were listening. He carried a cane that could give electric shocks, in case they were attacked by a stray dog or a thief. Abram could scarcely keep up. For years he had wondered why he ever kept working at his cousin's store for so long. *He hated being alone and he used me as his shadow. One day*

I didn't go back. I realized that there was no reason to keep paying homage to Jaime Behar. But apparently nobody agreed with Abram. Now, during the mourning, no one asked why he had arrived so late, why he didn't pray, or why he hadn't said anything to console us for the death of Papá. Everybody was thrilled to see him and have a chance to cozy up to him a bit, *Jaime, would you like some coffee? some roscas? Are you comfortable in that chair?* Tía Rosa loved to listen to Jaime, *Sí, tía, every day a violinist and a pianist come to play while I eat; Doctor Pablo de Lejada, the expert in Greco-Latin mythology, gives me private classes on Tuesdays and Thursdays, and the sensei Yamamoto (the greatest sensei in all of Mexico) comes on Wednesdays for karate lessons. Last month I invited him to accompany me to Japan. This week the chef from the restaurant Maxims is coming to cook for me. He's the toast of the town and he comes straight from Paris, tía. The poet Luciano Guerra and his wife, the painter Dulce Campos, have been my guests. Do you know them? I've just bought one of her paintings that was being shown in New York, in the Mary Ann Art Gallery...* And Jaime kept blabbing on and on, but Abram had gone to the other side of the room to smoke a cigarette.

Saqui had been looking through the blue pamphlet, searching for words that might serve as consolation to him. On the first page he read a text that reminded him again of the morning in the cemetery, "At the father's grave."

Lisa went to ask him what he wanted for dinner, but Saqui didn't turn around. He was staring at the candelabra on the cover of the booklet and hoping that if he imagined it with all the candles lit, he could focus on an image that would overlay the void for a while and allow him to sleep that night. He felt a stabbing pain and squeezed his buttocks.

After a while one of the Hanonos showed up with some other pamphlets that he distributed among us immediately. It was a longer text, with the title

"Avelim's Manual." *Look, primos, everything is clearly explained in here. Por favor, read it so you understand what you have to do.* Tuachi and Nehmad, who had been chatting in the third row, rejoiced at Hanono's arrival. *It's great that you brought the manual! These Shamis don't know anything. They need some instruction so they can learn to be decent Jews. What a joke, they don't even know how to recite the kaddish!* We skimmed through the booklet, but nobody was interested in learning any more rituals at that point. Soon Jaime Behar came over to say good-bye to us. We got up from the floor to give him a hug, one by one. He gave us each a kiss on the cheek. Tuachi, Nehmad and Entebi muttered, *this is a farce, not only do they shake hands, but they even receive kisses!!* They indicated to their wives that it was time to go. They all stood about twelve feet away from us so they wouldn't have to shake hands, and with one voice said *tenuhamu min hashamayim.* After they left, Tía Raquel turned to us and said, *get up now, muchachos, sit on the chairs. My sons-in-law are very religious, and sometimes insufferable.* Beni took the opportunity to make fun of them. *The three musketeers, Tacky, Nebbish, and Enteric, one for all and all for one, to fight for the honor of proving who is the biggest brown-noser of them all! Don't shake hands with the avelim, they say, but it's okay to give kisses, right?* Tía Raquel burst out laughing and her mirth was infectious. We weren't sure what was so hilarious, but we all were in stitches. Musa was the only one who kept quiet, thinking that it wasn't a good idea to laugh so much on the day we had buried Papá. *Are we making light of his memory? Are we giving him his due respect?* He suddenly sneezed as hard as he could. Mamá told Saqui to yank on his ear. While he was doing that, Mamá shouted, *Musa, David is calling you.* Intrigued, Abram asked why it was necessary to pull his ear. *It's the custom: if someone sneezes when you are talking about a dead person, his soul might depart with the deceased; that's why you pull his ear so he doesn't go away and he stays here with the living.*

Before going home to sleep, Jaime asked if we were going to fast. We all said yes. *You can get up early to eat if you want, before dawn. Tomorrow the prayers start at seven-thirty sharp.* But afterwards, when Jaime had left, Mamá said, *may God forgive me, but I'm not so religious. I'm not going to fast.* Saqui and Abram followed her lead, *if we've never done it, why start being so zealous now?*

Saqui, Lisa, Abram, Musa and Mamá went up to the bedrooms. Saqui and Lisa went into Papá's room. He stood there envisioning Papá lying on the bed wearing a white, sleeveless T-shirt, his left forearm resting on his head, smoking a cigarette and watching television, with a cup of Turkish coffee on the night table. *Sit down, hijo, sit here and keep me company.* So Saqui became a young boy again and sat on the edge of the bed and smelled Papá's sweat, but it didn't bother him. A sharp pain brought him back to reality. He ran to the bathroom, pushed with all of his might, but only expelled a thread of blood.

None of us remembered that the grand celebration of Mexico's Independence was happening that night.

5

3 Tishrei 5757. The Fast of Gedaliah / 4 Tishrei 5757

16 September 1996 (Monday)

THE AVEL SHALL NOT GREET, EMBRACE, OR KISS ANYBODY DURING THE FIRST THREE DAYS, OR EVEN RESPOND WHEN HE IS GREETED DURING THESE SAME DAYS; FROM THE THIRD TO THE SEVENTH DAYS HE SHALL NOT OFFER GREETINGS, BUT HE MAY RESPOND IF HE IS GREETED. ON SHABBAT, THE AVEL SHALL OFFER GREETINGS, SAYING SHABBAT SHALOM. THE AVEL SHALL NOT LEAVE THE HOUSE WHERE THEY ARE SITTING DURING THE SEVEN DAYS, UNLESS IT IS NECESSARY (FOR EXAMPLE, TO GO HOME TO SLEEP AT NIGHT), IN WHICH CASE HE SHALL BE ACCOMPANIED AND WEAR A SHAWL ON HIS SHOULDERS.

ONE SHOULD NOT CRY IN EXCESS FOR A DECEASED PERSON. OUR RABBIS COMMAND US TO BEHAVE AS FOLLOWS: THE FIRST THREE DAYS ARE FOR CRYING, SEVEN DAYS FOR SADNESS AND LAMENTING, AND THIRTY DAYS WITHOUT CUTTING ONE'S HAIR. DURING THE FIRST SEVEN DAYS, THE AVEL SHALL NOT PERFORM ANY WORK OR DO ANY BUSINESS BY MEANS OF ANOTHER PERSON, EVEN IF THIS PERSON IS NOT JEWISH. THE AVEL WHO HAS A BUSINESS IN SOCIETY SHOULD CONSULT THE RABBI OF THE COMMUNITY. THE AVEL SHALL NOT BATHE HIS

ENTIRE BODY, NOT EVEN WITH COLD WATER; HE SHALL WASH ONLY HIS FACE, HANDS AND FEET WITH COLD WATER; WOMEN SHALL NOT WEAR MAKE-UP. THE AVEL SHALL NOT REMOVE HIS TORN CLOTHING, NOR SHALL HE CHANGE HIS OTHER GARMENTS. CONJUGAL RELATIONS SHALL NOT BE MAINTAINED; A WOMAN IN MOURNING SHALL NOT ATTEND THE PURIFICATION RITUAL DURING THIS TIME. THE AVEL SHALL NOT STUDY THE TORAH.

Fule already had gone up and down the stairs three times, but he hadn't managed to rouse Abram and Saqui. *Get up! Rabbi Mizrahi is here. Shaḥarit is going to start. We can't miss the morning prayers. Get up!* Musa was downstairs with the others, looking for a tefillin. He asked Jaime if he had an extra one for him. David intervened to tell him to look for Papá's in the closet. Five minutes later Isaac Helfón arrived, carrying several tefillins and tallits. Musa was relieved because he hadn't been able to find Papá's velvet bag with the prayer shawls anywhere. Abram wanted to take a shower to wake up, but Jaime told him he couldn't. Saqui got out of bed, thinking about the lit candelabra that he had dreamed about all night. Abram and Saqui sipped the coffee that Concha had brought up to them, savoring the thick, liquid warmth as if it were an elixir that would tame the shooting pains in their heads. They knew that the fast of Gedaliah had begun, but they told themselves that right then the most important thing was to diminish the body's complaints.

Isaac Helfón had begun to pray out loud. Two of Tía Jasibe's sons-in-law tiptoed in without saying a word. They put on a tallit and tefillin as they whispered the berakha. We didn't remember seeing them yesterday during the keriah, but with all those people and as quiet as they were, perhaps they had been there. With those two, Rabbi Mizrahi, Isaac Helfón and the seven of us, we had the number required for minyan. But we didn't have to worry about having enough people, since relatives, friends, and even strangers kept showing up. The house quickly became the prayer room of a knis and, for a moment, we felt as if we, too, were visitors. Fule was the only one who knew what to do during the prayers: when to reply, when to stand up or sit down. When we were kids, one day he said to Mamá that he was tired of the Colegio del Río and he wanted to study at the yeshivah. Mamá didn't know how to react. On one hand, she was pleased that one of her sons wanted to study Torah, but on the other hand, the teachers at Del Río adored us and treated us like kings. *And what if he becomes a ḥakhamito, demanding that everything be kosher? That would be a real hassle.* Fule attended the yeshivah for two years and, as could be expected, he began to pressure us all about religion. Mamá resisted his requests, saying that Saturday was the best day to sell at La Lagunilla; besides, installing a second sink in the kitchen would be very expensive. The kitchen itself was quite small and even if we had enough money for a second set of dishes, there would be nowhere to store it. Not to mention the two extra sets of dishes for Pesaḥ. In spite of Fule's tender age –he was only about twelve— he insisted stubbornly that it was time to change and follow the path of hashem. Mamá made up excuses and put him off, saying, *pretty soon, Fule, on the day of Ekha.* We all chuckled at that phrase because we figured the day of Ekha was something like "el día de la Chingada" (when hell freezes over). Every night when we were in bed, supposedly falling asleep, Abram would tease Fule, chanting *we're all going to become ḥakhamitos on the day of Ekha, it's coming soon, the day of Ekha.* Fule was aching to give Abram a good thumping but he was still too small to take him on, so he had to put up with the taunts.

Many years later we learned that the day of Ekha actually existed. We were at Tía Raquel's house when somebody mentioned *Tuesday is Ekha, you have to fast, go to the knis, and you can't bathe or shave.* We were dumbfounded. *What is commemorated on Ekha?*, one of us asked. *A lot of calamities, especially the destruction of the Temple and the beginning of the diaspora. It's as if we're all in mourning; people sit on the floor in the knis and the lights are turned off; it's a very solemn, ominous day. The mourning begins on the seventeenth of Tamuz and ends on the day of Ekha, the ninth of Av. During this period you should not cut your hair, shave, go to fiestas, or buy new clothing or luxury items; also there can be no weddings.* Later we reproached Mamá, *The day of Ekha exists!* She smiled and said *Of course! I never said it didn't; I was always tempted to give in to Fule, and every Ekha my conscience bothered me.* Even though we had never been in the knis on the day of Ekha, we realized during this fast of Gedaliah that Ekha had finally arrived for us. The bitterness of centuries descended upon us, as if the Temple had just been destroyed. We all prayed reverently, expressing our repentance, repeating the kaddish over and over, reafirming the glory of God. All of us, except Abram and Saqui, had decided to fast, even though this fast was not one of the most important of the year. *Let's follow the rules of mourning to the letter. May Papá's soul be elevated to heaven, may he feel proud of us, and may God allow him to enter Paradise!*, exclaimed Fule, convinced that such was our duty. Jaime's pride was at stake and he was determined to show that we were capable of carrying out the customs. By the second or third kaddish of the morning, we were all in sync, without missing a word, and with voices so loud that nobody outdid us. Our cousins Hanono were impressed that in one night we had learned the prayers perfectly. Following Fule's lead, we had abandoned the blue booklets; we read the Hebrew directly because it was obvious that the transliteration was full of typos. *That never happens with a book in Hebrew because the rabbis proofread it a thousand times before it's published; if there's a mistake they have to do it all over,* Fule explained. Our Hebrew was coming back to us; we recognized that ḥakham Saal's lessons had been worthwhile. No Ḥalabi could make fun of us; every time we had to say the kaddish, we opened our mouths and spit out the words with bitterness. Some of the cousins looked at us out of the corner of their eyes, probably because of the fulminating odor of our breath that was wafting into their nostrils.

There were about thirty or forty men praying. Some of their wives had gathered in the kitchen or the dining room to chat. Mamá and Tías Rosa and Pola were sitting with us on the cushions. Tío León had arrived late and was covered with sweat. Fule commented to Jaime, *we've already finished two kaddishes; just think, if that's how he arrives on the first day, how will he be showing his respect for the rest of the week?* Tío León was panting as he put on the tefillin. He had to sit on a chair because it was hard for him to get up over and over again from the floor. Terri had been sitting by herself in the dining room, watching him attentively, not missing a flinch. After about ten minutes, she walked over to him and said, *León, don't torture yourself, you don't have to sit on the floor, just take a chair!* Rabbi Mizrahi didn't even wince. When shaḥarit was over he gestured for us to approach. All the avelim made a semicircle around him. He recited a long prayer, at the end of which he evoked Papá's name, Shimon ben Raḥel. As is customary, after mentioning the name of the deceased, we rose up on tiptoes two or three times to indicate that Papá's soul was still going up toward heaven, as if he were an angel.

Most of the visitors knew that it was the fast of Gedaliah. We only heard a few disoriented folks who complained that the table was not set. One or two went into the kitchen to ask for coffee. Isaac Helfón sat in a corner near the window and began to recite psalms. *The community pays him to pray all day,* Jaime told us. Rabbi Mizrahi asked us to sit on the cushions. He started to speak, but the noise from the dining room and kitchen drowned out his words. Elena, Fule's wife, had to go hush the cousins. *Por favor, the rabbi wants to talk to the avelim, por favor.* The women lowered their voices, but their incessant buzzing accompanied our entire conversation with the rabbi. *In general, there is confusion about mourning. Some believe that the restrictions imposed this week are a kind of torture. And that is a complete misconception because in reality, any kind of suffering that one inflicts upon oneself is forbidden and condemned. So, why are the rules of mourning so strict? One must realize that our religion focuses on avoiding indifference or a lack of respect for the deceased person. If life just went on as usual, including listening to music, for example, that would show a lack of respect. That's why there are restrictions: they are rules to avoid everything that is luxurious, comfortable or pleasurable. But everything that can be considered routine is permitted. In the old days, it was considered a luxury to sit in a comfortable chair; that's why it's forbidden, not to make you suffer. It is our duty to give consolation to those who are in mourning. One must help the avelim to overcome their anxiety. But you shouldn't try to escape reality. Some might think that to get over their suffering they need to work or do something else, to keep busy so they can forget. That's not appropriate or healthy, either. If you need to vent your feelings, you should do so.* David interrupted him to ask, *what should I do with my children, if they want to laugh, go out for a walk, or play?* Addressing David directly, the rabbi answered, *you have to use your own judgment. Children, gracias a Dios, do not have to mourn. They have to keep up their normal life and you can't restrict them in any way. It's not right to impose your anguish on them. However, you do need to make it clear that you are in mourning; for example, if they want to listen to music they should go to their room and close the door so you don't hear it; if they want to go to a fiesta, well, they should find a friend to take them. Basically, just use your judgment and try to maintain your mourning and give due respect to your Papá's memory, without upsetting your children.* When the rabbi paused Abram took the opportunity to ask, *but, how do we define pleasure? I take great pleasure in food...* For the rabbi the distinction was obvious, *eating is a pleasure and going out dancing is a pleasure. But one is a necessity and the other shows a lack of respect. The difference is clear: if you don't eat, you don't live; if you don't dance, nothing happens to you.* Now it was Musa who had a question, as he thought about how he had missed playing his trumpet this morning, *and if you earn your living by playing music?* The question made our cousins Zonana quiet down for a moment to listen to the rabbi's response. They thought Musa's playing the trumpet was very strange, they couldn't understand why Papá and Mamá had permitted it. *That Musa is crazy,* they would say when they talked about us at their home. The rabbi turned toward the dining room, as if he guessed that the women were interested in his answer, *if that is your profession, then you should do it. If you are a musician, then you can play your instrument; if you are an actor, even in a comedy, you're doing your job. That's not for pleasure or for fun, but to earn a living.* Musa wasn't satisfied with the answer, *sí, rabbi, I understand, but it gives me a lot of pleasure to play the trumpet, even though it's my job.* We all noticed that the rabbi was becoming impatient. *The question that you have to ask yourself is very clear: are you behaving with indifference toward your father's death, or are you earning money with your regular, daily activity?* The rabbi had raised his voice somewhat with the last answer, so Musa decided that he'd better not ask anything more. Without waiting for any further questions, the rabbi continued speaking, *there are some erroneous customs in our society. For example, many believe that a widow should wear black while she's in mourning, and not leave the house. People feel pressured to conform to that custom, even though it goes against our philosophy. That's something that needs to be changed. It is not written anywhere that one must wear black; that concept comes from the society in which we live, and we have been influenced by it, but the idea does not belong to us and we should eliminate it.* Mamá was listening to him, but was not convinced. When her mamá had died, for a long time she wore black, navy blue or dark brown skirts. She didn't wear make-up or go anywhere besides her store in the Lagunilla. *This rabbi is crazy,* she thought, *wearing colorful clothing is a lack of respect!*

The rabbi began to go down the list of rules for mourning. *All of our rules and customs have their foundation in the Torah or the Tanaḥ. For example, the shiva is based on the Book of Bereshit, Genesis, when Jacob dies and Joseph orders seven days of mourning after the burial. Or in the Book of Job, where it says, "Veyishvu itoh la'aretz shivat yamim veshivat leilot... They sat with him on the ground for seven days and seven nights, ve'ein dover elav davar ki rahuh ki gadol ha'keev meod, and nobody spoke a word to him because they saw his pain was great" (2:13). This explains the ancient custom of not greeting the avelim. There are people who make the awkward mistake of asking "how are you?" or "what's happening?" or "how's it going?" What are the avelim supposed to answer? Could they say "fine, thanks"? Rather than help alleviate their pain, those questions can aggravate it. Consolation should be found in the reaffirmation of the glory of hashem, that's why we say the kaddish. The kaddish is a proclamation of faith. It is an explanation of the verse hashem natan, hashem lakakh, yeḥih shem hashem meborakh: the Lord giveth and the Lord taketh away, blessed be the name of the Lord. Even when the Lord takes one of our most beloved relatives, we should reaffirm our absolute faith and submission to the judgment and will of the Creator. Yitgadal veyitkadash sheme rabbah, May his great name be glorified and sanctified.* Patiently, the rabbi continued to translate each verse of the kaddish for us: *In the world that was created by his will, and that is governed by his reign, may his redemption be forthwith and may the arrival of his Messiah be near. May he be in your lives and in your days, and in the life of the entire house of Israel, without delay, and say all amen. May his great name be blessed throughout all generations. Praised, exalted, glorified, extolled, elevated, majestic, sublime, and acclaimed may his sacred name be, blessed is He (amen). And may He be above all the blessings, songs, praise and consolations that are expressed in the world, amen. May a great peace be conceded by the heavens. May life, abundance, salvation, consolation, protection, healing, redemption, pardon and expiation benefit and liberate us and all the people of Israel, amen. May the one who makes peace in the heavens, make peace among us and among all the people of Israel, amen.*

The rabbi paused to take a breath. We were trying to listen to the translation of the kaddish with great interest, but we were constantly interrupted by the loud voices of the women in the dining room. Encouraged by our interest, the rabbi continued, *it is necessary to make the avelim see that hashem is the one who decides everything in life, including death. Therefore, one must always remember the phrase from the Book of Bereshit, Genesis: "ashes to ashes, dust to dust" (3:19). Afterwards, this saying should be elucidated with another sentence that comes from Ecclesiastes: "Dust returns to dust, but the spirit returns to God, since it was given to us by Him" (12:7). What is the soul? It is the mind, the conscience, knowledge, memory; the soul is composed of all these abstracts. And it doesn't die. It goes up to heaven, to Olam haba, and it remains connected to you, his children and grandchildren. Now then, why do you cover the mirrors in the house of the avelim? That is because mirrors are symbols of human vanity, and that is not allowed in the house of mourning. There was an ancient belief that the soul exists also in a person's reflection in the mirror; therefore, they cover the mirrors to prevent the souls of the living from accompanying the deceased. But the true explanation is that in a house of prayer there can be no mirrors because there can be no images; it is forbidden to pray in front of a mirror. hashem is an abstraction that can not take the human form. That is the simple and correct explanation.*

We were all startled when Ruth Mustri, the daughter of Tía Jasibe, began to shout into the telephone. Mamá got up and rushed over to find out what was going on. Rabbi Mizrahi realized that he had lost our attention; he bid us farewell from the door, saying, *may the Lord console you among the descendents of Zion and Jerusalem.* Mamá returned from the kitchen to tell us that Ruth's outburst wasn't about anything important. *What was she shouting about then?*, asked Tía Rosa. *Nothing*, she answered, *her son was throwing water balloons off the balcony. Just nonsense, Rosita.*

Saqui and Abram took advantage of the fact that the ḥakham had left, and went to eat breakfast in the kitchen with Mamá trailing after them. It was ten o'clock in the morning. The house was almost empty; there were only a few women left: some of our cousins and Mamá's sisters. Most of us brothers went upstairs to lie down. Beni was getting phone calls from Samuel Levin every now and then with questions about the business. Beni had met Samuel, the owner of an enormous chain of paint stores, in the Deportivo, playing soccer. Samuel enjoyed Beni's competitive and aggressive spirit, which was reflected in every play he made. One day Beni committed a flagrant foul on Samuel, who, instead of getting up to fight, thought immediately that Beni would be ideal in his business, so he offered him a job. At that time, Samuel had only four stores, but in five years, Levin's Paints had increased by twenty times, and he now had eighty branches. Beni was crucial to his success because he was able to get huge discounts from the suppliers. Samuel made him one of his executive managers, in charge of purchasing. Jaime was miffed that Samuel wasn't respecting our mourning, *oye, mano, tell him you can't answer his calls, you can't be working!* Beni wasn't sure that talking on the phone could be considered working. *I'm only answering his questions. For example, just now he wanted to know if I had already placed the orders for the branches in Tijuana, Ciudad Juárez and Monterrey, so I told him yes, I had placed the orders last week and they would certainly be filled by next week. Is that working? Samuel needs that information so he knows what's going on in the business.* Although the argument was convincing, Jaime insisted, *that's fine, but he calls you every five minutes. Tell him to respect us, por favor! He should write down all his questions and make just one phone call. Besides, today's a holiday, so why does he need to know right now?* Beni didn't want to keep arguing with Jaime. He knew very well that if he didn't answer Samuel's calls, it could cost him his job. He remembered hearing that our religion prohibited risking one's job, so he felt at ease with his conscience.

Almost all of us were in Papá's room, some lying on the beds and others sitting on the sofa that faced the window. Saqui recalled coming to visit the house at a time when most of us had moved out. Musa was the only one left, and his strangely-shaped room was in the corner of the house, with each wall a different size. Mamá slept in the bedroom that had belonged to David and Beni, so everyone had his own room. As Saqui went up the stairs that night he could hear Mamá saying, *come up here, Saqui, what do you want for dinner? I'll tell Concha to make your tacos just the way you like them with Arabic sausage, coriander, onion, avocado and hot pepper.* Saqui sat down with Mamá and they chatted with the murmur of a soap opera in the background. At eleven o'clock, when Concha came in with the dinner tray, Papá called to Saqui from his room, *hijo, don't you want to see the soccer game? They're showing the finals for the Italian League.* Saqui made up an excuse to leave

Mamá's room and cross the hall; from the doorway he could see Papá in bed with his oxygen tank on one side, smoking a cigarette, inhaling deeply. The television was on full blast. Saqui sat down on the empty bed next to Papá's (which had been Mamá's) and watched soccer while munching on the spicy sausage tacos. Concha came back soon with another tray. Papá ate his tacos with Pita bread instead of tortillas. Saqui could hear his agitated breathing with each bite; once in a while he also could hear his teeth grinding. Saqui prepared a dose of albuterol for him, which Papá inhaled with a mask covering his nose and mouth. The machine made a lot of noise during the breathing treatment and they couldn't even talk. Saqui counted the cigarette butts in the ashtray and observed the ashen color of Papá's face; the hairs in his ears were so overgrown that it seemed like that was the reason Papá was going deaf. And then at a few minutes before midnight Musa came up, *I'm trying to master a concert for trumpet by Miles Davis, but it's taking a lot of work.* It was already past midnight when Papá turned to Saqui and implored, *un cafecito, Saqui, por favor, just make a little coffee...* And Saqui looked at him with compassion and even though he was falling asleep, he dragged himself to the kitchen and put a pot on the stove. While he waited for the water to boil, he chatted with his brother, asking him if he had found someone to go out with, and Musa answered, *someone gave me the phone number of a girl named Tere Romano, but she wanted me to take her to see a show at the Sheraton, right off the bat. I don't even know her, and I don't know yet if she's fat or ugly, but she wants me to spend an arm and a leg on a show that I won't even like, so I told her to go to hell. All of the blind dates I get want me to take them to luxurious restaurants, they don't like jazz, only Luis Miguel, Emmanuel, and other pop superstars. Just imagine, if I married one of them she wouldn't even let me practice the trumpet. When I tell them I play in a symphonic band and I'm going to play for*

Catholic masses, they are shocked and they think I'm crazy. Saqui countered, *the problem is you're limiting yourself to the girls your friends find for you; you ought to join a social group that is interested in classical music and jazz. There's probably something like that at the Deportivo, so take the initiative and seek out people who are more like you.* Musa always stuck to the same routine: jogging in the Desierto de los Leones, doing scales on the trumpet and piano, going to practice with the symphonic band, coming home, playing some pieces on the trumpet, listening to jazz in bed until he got groggy and then sleeping with the music on all night. He kept his visits to the Hare-Krishna temple an absolute secret. Saqui went upstairs with the cup of coffee and saw Papá staring at the television. Finally Papá looked up and said, *gracias, papi, gracias.* Saqui enjoyed being called papi; so much affection was expressed with that one word.

We had been standing there looking at the mattress on Papá's bed and we were perplexed to see that it was sagging in the middle. Jaime sat down on it, *for crying out loud, this mattress is totally ruined, you can feel the springs.* He told Musa, *as soon as the shiva is over, throw this mattress in the garbage. Give all the clothes to the community for the poor, except for the shoes.* Saqui wondered why they couldn't give away the shoes. Abram commented, *maybe it's an ancient superstition that it's bad luck to walk in the shoes of a dead person.*

When we went down at around noon, the living room was full of people again. We asked Jaime or Fule to help us identify some people we didn't know. Tía Rosa called us, *come here, muchachos, I want to introduce Alegra Smeke; she's my first cousin; her papá and my mamá were brother and sister.* We were surprised at the family resemblance, the same eyes and the same smile as Papá. She hugged and kissed us effusively. To Musa she exclaimed, *incredible! you're a spitting image of your papá! He and I grew up together. We're almost like twins, I was born two days before him. In my house they doted on him because he was so obedient and not spoiled, like my brothers. One day we went to the fair and snuck onto most of the rides. We didn't notice how late it was getting, and we arrived home after dark. We were only about twelve years old. Since my parents realized that I adored Simón, they thought it was dangerous and decided to forbid me to see him again. I could only see him on Pesaḥ or Rosh Hashanah when the whole family got together. I remember once when we hid in a closet and your papá gave me my first kiss. For years I dreamed about that kiss and about your papá.* Abram interrupted her, *but why didn't they let you go out with Papá? they could have arranged for you to get married, what was the problem?* A faint smile crossed Alegra Smeke's face, *sí, hijo, there were many marriages between cousins back then, but my parents didn't like your grandfather much because he was Turkish, and he was a bit unconventional. My papá was president of Monte Sinai and wanted me to marry the son of his friend, Moi Zetune.* We were astonished that the señora would tell us these intimate details. Jaime knew several of the Zetunes because he played squash with them in the Deportivo, but he had never imagined that they were connected to the family. *And did you marry him?* Alegra Smeke hesitated, then began to cry. Tía Rosa embraced her and said, *why are you telling all this to the boys? why put yourself through this?* She couldn't get out an answer. Tía Rosa gestured to us to leave them alone for a while. She asked for water. Fule was intrigued so he went to ask Mamá, *what happened to Papá's cousin, that señora who is sitting with Tía Rosa?* Mamá told us sadly, *she ran away with a fellow from Mexico City; they went to live in the province so nobody would bother them. It was a big scandal, just imagine, her poor papá was the president of the community; he had to set an example, so he had them perform the keriah on him and he never saw his daughter again. It didn't go well for her. One day her husband left her and nobody from the community wanted to marry her. That young woman with her is her daughter. She's about thirty, but who would want to marry her?* Saqui intervened to say, *according to the most orthodox rabbis, if the mother is Jewish, her children are Jewish, no matter who the father is.* We all knew the rule, but Mamá answered very confidently, *they can say whatever they want, but in my opinion, she's half 'n half.* We hadn't been aware of the young woman's presence because she had been sitting in back, not talking to anybody. She got up from the chair to get some kleenex. She was slender and sensual, with full lips, enormous eyes, and thick, black hair that cascaded down her back almost to her waist. In spite of being thin, she had ample hips; she was wearing tight pants that revealed athletic legs. Musa heard Beni whisper, *she's gorgeous, if we weren't in mourning I'd tell you to go after her right now. If you want, later on I'll get her phone number from Tía Rosa.* But Musa told him not to bother. After a while they came over to say good-bye, *forgive me, muchachos, for giving you such an earful, but I adored Simón and you remind me so much of him...that brought back many memories...* We all took the opportunity to give her daughter a kiss. Beni told Señora Smeke, *I hope you can come again; we'd like you to tell us stories about Papá.* She was pleased at the request, and said she would return. Mamá commented that it was not customary to visit the house of mourning twice, *either they come once, or three times.*

By two in the afternoon the majority of the people had gone home to eat. Our heads ached from fasting. Fule complained about not being able to drink coffee. Once again, Saqui, Abram and Mamá went into the kitchen to eat something with the sisters-in-law and Tías Rosa and Pola. Isaac Helfón told us that he was going out for a walk but he'd be back soon. David commented, *I bet he went to grab a bite to eat. I don't think he's very religious, but he's probably embarrassed to eat here in our house.* Tía Zequíe remarked that Isaac was a diehard gambler. *He loves to go to the racetrack, and to bet on jai-alai games, too. His wife can't stand it because he loses everything, even his shorts. He had to sell his store to pay off a big debt. He went to Las Vegas and after winning twenty thousand dollars in one hand, thought he was going to become a multimillionaire. The idiot not only lost the twenty thousand, but also another thirty thousand that he didn't have. The community members took pity on him and that's why he goes from house to house praying for the dead. Don't think he's a ḥakhamito; he knows the prayers, but he doesn't keep Shabbat or anything.* Mamá reacted by saying in a mocking tone, *well you should have told me and I would have invited him to eat, poor fellow!* Helfón came back at about four o'clock. His face was animated. Abram laughed and said, *the heart is happy when the stomach is full.* Helfón went back to his corner to recite some psalms.

It was five o'clock and most of us were sitting on the cushions, some actually lying down. David and Fule had fallen asleep in the living room, in spite of the chattering and the hubbub of people coming and going. Saqui and Jaime were conversing with one of the Hanonos. Tío León came in and sat on a cushion in the corner, almost underneath the stairway. Saqui noticed that Terri had entered through the kitchen door, followed by her daughter. They sat in the dining room without saying anything, intent on following every movement that Tío León made. Saqui turned to say to Jaime, *look, there's the ratero's wife, what should we do?* Jaime didn't know how to react. We thought our warnings had been enough to keep our uncle from bringing Dorotea. Saqui insisted, *Jaime, if Mamá sees her she could have a heart attack, remember she told us that by no means should we let her enter our house.* David and Fule reacted as if they had been awake. Fule asked Saqui where Mamá was. We started getting worked up. Tío León was watching us to gage our reaction, but he hadn't heard any of our conversation yet. Fule got up and said to Jaime, *We've got to do something, we can't wait.* He had raised his voice so much that people looked over at us. Even though he had been caught off guard, David stood up to face the two women and said directly to Dorotea, *please have the courtesy to leave this house.* Tío León looked at us with disbelief, *are you crazy or what? She's my daughter, how dare you throw her out?* Fule responded immediately, almost shouting, *in the first place, she's your stepdaughter; in the second place, she's the wife of a thief.* Tío León shook his head and spoke to Terri, *vámonos, I'm not going to put up with this nonsense, we're out of here, and that's it, I've had it!* And then he ordered his sisters, *you come, too, we're not going to put up with being insulted in front of everybody!* He was shouting so loudly that Abram, Musa and Beni, who were upstairs, came running down. Mamá came too, from the kitchen. Abram tried to stop Tío León, *wait, tío, let's work things out.* Still sitting on his cushion on the floor, Saqui hollered, *that woman and her husband stole money from Papá; that's why he died, because they took away his dignity, which was all he had. Rateros!!* Tías Rosa and Pola were crying in the back of the room, not knowing what to do. Saqui turned to look at Tía Rosa, *tell them, tía, how my papá suffered, tell them, you know very well how they hung up on him when he called and they made up excuses over and over again.* Tío León was grabbing his chest. Terri was alarmed, *vámonos, León, before you have a heart attack!* Abram made one last attempt to stop him, but failed. Before leaving, Terri lamented, *poor Simón, his sons are so rude.* And then she fired at us, *you're all dead for me.* Tía Zequíe, who had been paying close attention, shouted when Terri crossed the threshold, *Sharmuta! you're a Sharmuta! just a gold-digging whore!* Tías Rosa and Pola left also, sobbing as they went out. Tío León instructed his sisters, *follow us, we'll go to my house.* Terri took off as fast as she could. Mamá followed them out the door, trying to dissuade Tía Rosa, *it's haraam, don't leave, you should stay until the prayers are over.* Mago, Tía Rosa's daughter, opened the car door. They got into the front seats, but Mamá kept them from closing the door. *Let me go, Rebeca, I have to accompany my brother. He's the only brother I have left.* But Mamá didn't give up, *at least hold on until the week is over, you can't let Simón's soul suffer. He adored you!*

Inside the house we all were trembling with rage. Musa noticed that nobody from Papá's family had stayed. Tía Zequíe approached Saqui, *well you sure did a great job of telling them off!* One of Tía Jasibe's sons came over to ask us how much money they had stolen from Papá, and how was it possible that we hadn't been able to get them to pay. David decided to tell them everything, in detail.

Papá had a furniture store in partnership with Tío León, or at least that's what he said. The store was in a good location in the Zona Rosa and, barukh hashem, they were doing well. Three years after the earthquake of '85, the owners of the building where their store was situated decided to sell it to a company that had a chain of banks. The new owners wanted to put the bank on the first floor and the offices on the upper floors, but they knew that Papá was going to charge them a lot for the transference because he had been there for more than twenty years. It occurred to some of the bank executives that it would be easier to evict Papá from the premises. Since the building had been slightly damaged by the earthquake, they used a remodeling project as a pretext. They went to see the commissioner, gave him a significant bribe, and delivered an eviction notice to Papá, who could not believe his eyes when he opened the envelope. Immediately after the quake they had replaced the windows and reinforced the main supports. Since Tío León was vacationing in Europe, only the accountant was around to offer his useless advice. Jaime tried to help, *defend yourself, Papá. Get a court order and they won't be able to touch you for at least two years.* But Papá didn't listen to Jaime, or to Mamá, either; he asked his nephew's lawyer to look into the matter. *Look, Don Simón, this situation is very difficult. Don't try to fight with these monsters. They have loads of money and if it comes down to bribes, they're going to win. I recommend that you work with them and try to arrange some kind of indemnity.* Papá was never interested in fighting, and now less than ever, since he could imagine constant trips to the courthouse, hours of waiting, and entire weeks lost in the bureaucracy of the government. After much effort, he managed to contact a low-ranking bank employee, who promised to try to obtain a fair indemnity for him. Papá left the meeting in a good mood; he thought he could finally retire and spend his afternoons playing dominoes, basking in the sun and his newfound serenity. According to the eviction notice, he had to be out of the building in two weeks, so he decided to transfer all the furniture that he had on display to the store belonging to his nephew Morris, another of Tío León's sons. Jaime asked him if the person from the bank had signed any paper for him, and of course his father was furious. *No, hijo, you have to trust people. This is a large company, and very respected.* All Mamá could do was sigh with resignation. *Your papá is an idiot, he's going to end up on the street!* None of us knew if Papá had been saving anything throughout the years. Mamá supposed that he spent all of his money, without putting a dime in the bank. *And you know what else,* she warned, *pretty soon he'll want you to support him.* We all went to observe the transfer of the furniture to our cousin Morris's store. When his locale was completely empty, we could see the anguish on Papá's face, as he looked at us in bewilderment. He invited us to eat at Rafaello's. It seemed ironic that on the day he became unemployed, we went to eat at an expensive restaurant. We had celebrated several family birthdays there, but it never would have occurred to us to go out to eat on a sad occasion. Papá drank so many martinis that we practically had to carry him out. Afterwards, when Papá tried to collect his compensation, the customer service manager laughed at his naïveté. However, we found out that Papá had some savings. During the first weeks after closing his business Papá would get up late, then take Tía Rosa or Mago or one of his friends to eat in a good restaurant, and from there he would go to the Deportivo to play dominoes. He would arrive home, as he always had, after dark. Musa commented that he didn't even notice that Papá was unemployed.

One day Jaime called a meeting of the brothers and announced that we urgently needed to help Papá find a locale to set up another furniture store. We all agreed that he was right, it would be best for Papá to keep working; however, nobody went to look for places with him. Mamá told us that Papá read the newspaper like somebody looking for work and praying to God that he wouldn't find anything. Papá was only sixty-three years old, but he acted like he was ninety. One day his car wouldn't start; the mechanic told him it would need a major overhaul. Papá told us he wasn't going to buy another car because he didn't need one and he preferred to take a taxi to the Deportivo. That same day Fule was surprised to notice that Papá's suit was frayed. Musa was concerned when he realized that Papá had to catch his breath as he was climbing the stairs. *He doesn't want another car because he gets tired when he drives; besides, if he wants a drink with lunch, he doesn't have to worry.* During that same time period David and Beni both got married. Mamá took the opportunity to move into their empty room. Papá and Mamá had fought for years, but they had never decided to separate. Mamá informed us, *I always have to fight with him to be able to watch my soap operas, so now I want to have my own room.* Papá said he wanted to move to a small apartment in Polanco. He tried to convince Mamá to sell the house so they each could have half the money, but she replied sarcastically, *not even in your dreams, Simón, this is my house and you'll only get me out of here when I'm dead.* They went for months without speaking to each other. Musa entertained himself playing the trumpet in the storage space in the garage, and only came up to his room to sleep. During Sunday dinners, Papá would drink half a bottle of cognac by himself. Then he'd fall asleep in his easychair, with his grandchildren bouncing around him.

Several months later, they called Musa from the Deportivo to come get Papá. He was in the infirmary; they had just given him a breathing treatment with oxygen. *Your father is ill. Haven't you taken him to see a doctor?* Since Papá didn't complain, none of us had bothered to watch over him. Dr. Charabati, a renowned pulmonologist, informed us that the pulmonary emphysema was already advanced. Papá didn't seem affected by the news; he convinced Saqui and Musa to accompany him to Dorotea's wedding, that very weekend. She was marrying Azra Arditi, one of Saqui's former classmates in middle school at Monte Sinai. Papá remarked that his brother had given an incredible dowry to the groom, to compensate for the fact that his stepdaughter had been a devout Catholic for the first twelve years of her life. Tío León bought them a furnished home in Bosques de las Lomas and set Azra up in a real estate business, besides paying for a sumptuous banquet at the luxurious Hotel Camino Real. Azra was known for being a womanizer since high school. He had been expelled several times for smoking marijuana in the bathroom or masturbating with pornographic magazines. Saqui had a very bad memory of him because two days before final exams his backpack had been stolen during recess. He knew Azra and Nissim Penhos were responsible for the theft because they repeated his notes word for word in their exam booklets. However, since Saqui didn't have any proof, the principal didn't do anything to punish the guilty parties. Azra, nevertheless, didn't finish school; he got a job as a clerk in a men's clothing store. He was fired after two years because the owners realized that he wasn't reporting all the sales.

We lost track of him for a while, but now and then we would hear about another incident in which he was involved. Since he had burned his bridges with the women of the community, we were surprised when Papá told us that Dorotea was going out with him. Apparently Tío León was adamantly opposed, but Terri knew that only someone like Azra would marry her daughter. Terri was so persuasive that Tío León was finally convinced that with a good dowry Azra would be a good son-in-law. Besides, Tío León was pleased that one of Azra's cousins was the second-in-command in the committee of religious affairs; they might even be able to have the wedding in Monte Sinai. Naturally that was just a pipedream; Tío León had a black mark by his name in the books of the community and any request for a religious ceremony would be immediately rejected. Azra's mother was happy that her son was getting married, so she had no objection to the wedding taking place in the knis of Las Lomas. During the banquet, Azra began calling Papá "tío" and, soon they were getting drunk together, competing to see who could drink the most tequila in one swig. Perhaps that was the last time that Saqui and Musa saw Papá happy and lively. After the fiesta, he couldn't get out of bed for three days. Azra came to visit him when he returned from the honeymoon, when nobody else was home. *Listen, tío, I want to buy a piece of land in the new residential district of La Herradura; we're going to build a complex of eight houses. I already have the architect's blueprints and getting the permit will be a snap because the guy in charge is a buddy of mine. The houses are going to sell as soon as the ground is broken. I just have to round up some investors so I can buy the land and get the construction started. The rest will be smooth sailing. My father-in-law already put up half the money; my brothers-in-law are going to divvy up 10% each. It would be a great investment for you, tío. In one year I'll triple your money. Besides, I'm willing to give you a monthly payment, which would be deducted at the end of the year, so you won't be needing anything.* Papá loved the idea: tripling his money, without lifting a finger! That very night he called Tío León, *what do you think, mano?, I'm really tempted, but I'm afraid of losing my only capital.* Tío León clinched the deal, *Don't worry about a thing, Simón, I'll be the guarantor. If for some reason the enterprise doesn't work, I'll pay you back. In fact, I was the one who suggested to Azra that he invite you to invest in this, because I know it's going to benefit you. And you can't count on your sons.*

Musa wondered why Azra was visiting the house almost every day. He left with Papá at lunchtime and brought him back at around six in the afternoon. Judging by the smell, Musa guessed that Papá was drinking heavily again. One day, while Musa was helping him get undressed and into bed, Papá said that, gracias a Dios, there was no need to worry about him in his old age anymore. *Azra is going to build some houses in La Herradura and I'm going to triple the money I have.* Musa couldn't resist telling Mamá and the rest of us. Jaime was alarmed, *that Azra has a bad reputation in the community, he's going to steal his money!* But Mamá stayed out of it, *don't get me involved in this, I'm tired of fighting.* Jaime and Fule went to talk to Papá, *be careful, everyone says that Azra is not to be trusted. Beto Nacach told me that last year they almost threw him in the slammer because he was laundering money. He was incredibly lucky because they nailed his partner but they couldn't pin anything on him.* Papá looked panicked as he stammered, *too late, hijo. Today I went with Azra to the bank to make the transfer.* Jaime pressured Papá to tell him how much money he had lent Azra, but Papá wouldn't be specific. *It doesn't matter, hijo. When I get my money back in triplicate, I won't have to worry for the rest of my life.* Then Mamá, Fule, Jaime and David tried to guess the amount. *How much money does he need for the rest of his life?,* asked David. *One and a half million? If so, then Papá lent him 500,000 pesos.* Fule countered, *why would he need so much money? For taking taxis and eating in restaurants? The house is paid off and Papá only pays for electricity, gas and property taxes. Add it up and you'll see that Papá only needs three thousand a month. With about six or seven hundred thousand pesos he would have more than enough to live comfortably for twenty years.* They averaged their estimates and settled on an intermediate sum; the loan was probably for about three hundred thousand pesos, but they still had their doubts.

For the first four months after the transfer, Azra came to the house and gave Papá the monthly payment as agreed. Papá began to complain after that because Azra would give him half and say he'd pay him the rest next month. At the end of the year Papá was very anxious; he called Azra about twenty times. Dorotea would answer and say, *don't worry, tío, I'll give him the message; he'll be back soon. He'll call you right away.* But days passed and Azra didn't ever call, and the monthly payments ceased altogether. After three months of calling him daily, Papá complained to Tío León, *Azra hasn't given me anything for three months and by now he was supposed to have sold the houses.* But Tío León was in a foul mood, *and how do you think I feel? I invested seven times more than you did!* Papá tried to get his brother to explain what had happened with the houses, but he would only say, *Azra has had terrible luck, everything has gone wrong, the blueprints were poorly designed, the construction workers are slow and disorganized and, to make it all worse, he has been mugged three times.* Papá didn't know what to do. He must have had a few pesos left since he didn't ask us for anything. His health continued to decline. The doctor had ordered him to use the oxygen every night. Since Mamá wasn't in the room anymore, he just left the television on all the time. Sometimes Musa got up in the middle of the night to lower the volume on the television set, and he would be startled to find Papá with his eyes wide open. We realized that things were going from bad to worse when Papá came downstairs one Sunday wearing some striped pants that reminded us of our childhood. Mamá reproached him, *you've got good clothes, why do you have to wear those old trousers?* But Papá didn't answer her, he just said to Musa, *be a good boy and buy me some cigarettes at the pharmacy.* Musa had become accustomed to not charging Papá; without telling anybody, he would leave packs of cigarettes on the night table as if they had fallen from the sky.

Another three months passed, and Jaime arrived at the house with a radiant smile, *I got the inside scoop from Beto Bucay! Beto is a close friend of Azra's brother and he told him that they just began to sell the houses. Call him up right now!* Papá was calling all night. The first two or three times Dorotea answered, but when she heard Papá's voice she hung up immediately. Later they left the phone off the hook so they wouldn't have to answer. Papá banged the receiver against the wall and became more and more agitated. In desperation he asked Jaime and Beni to accompany him to demand his money. They knocked on the door of Azra's house and to their surprise, Terri opened it, but she blocked the doorway with her body and didn't allow them to enter, *nobody's home, Simón, I just came to get the dog.* Jaime insisted, *we urgently need to talk to Azra, but it's been impossible by phone.* Terri played dumb, *Dorotea and Azra are vacationing in Cancún. I think that's why you haven't been able to reach them.* They were already back in the car when Jaime caught a glimpse of Dorotea peeking out between the curtains. Jaime asked Papá what Azra had signed for him. His mouth dropped open when he heard the answer, *nothing, nothing, I only have the bank receipt from the transfer.* From that day on, Papá was submerged in a terrible depression. The doctor prescribed oxygen 24 hours a day. Papá stopped going to the Deportivo and became increasingly lethargic. He saw no need to bathe, dress, or even get out of bed. On Sundays we had to almost carry him downstairs. His eyes were sunken, and he had dark blotches on his cheeks. His grandchildren avoided him because they didn't want to be scratched by his poorly shaven beard. Tío León had forbidden him to talk about the deal with Azra, *that's between you two, don't get me involved.* Between coughs, Papá managed to protest softly, *it was all I had, León; I'm not asking him for double or triple the amount, I just want him to give back my money, without interest or anything.* Nonetheless, Tío León stubbornly protected his son-in-law, *we all lost money, Azra had to auction off the houses, it was a bad enterprise. Just let him recuperate and he'll pay you back.* Papá knew his money was lost. Once Fule had told him that he saw Dorotea in a Mercedes, with a chauffeur, *you've been fleeced, Papá. They're living it up while you're stuck here without a cent to your name.* That was the day Papá went to the hospital for the first time; he got so agitated that he couldn't breathe and he lost consciousness. Using the bank receipt as evidence, Jaime filed a lawsuit against Azra, but Papá didn't show any signs of taking heart. He refused to ask us for money and when we offered it to him he would feel so offended that he'd start to cry. Jaime resorted to stuffing pesos in his pockets when he fell asleep on Sunday afternoons.

Now we were all there, thinking how Dorotea had a lot of nerve, she never should have come to our house after making Papá suffer so much. *At least,* we told ourselves, *we humiliated her in front of everybody. She can drive around with her chauffeur in the Mercedes, but here she was put to shame.* Mamá was really upset about the fight, but she radiated satisfaction, *I've been putting up with my brother-in-law for years and years! I thank God, barukh hashem, that my sons finally told him off.* Musa, however, thought that Papá's soul was suffering terribly. He spent his whole life with his back to the wall, and now his siblings had left the house of mourning. Would God take pity on him because of the fight? After a while Isaac Helfón announced in a loud voice, *señores, we're going to begin minḥah; please, señoras, go to the dining room, we're going to start.* Restlessness still rippled around the room, as the incident was recounted over and over. We relived it time and time again as we laughed and celebrated Terri's and Dorotea's reaction. Mamá said with a broad smile, *you have to kiss Tía Jasibe's hand for calling that wench Terri a sharmuta.* Abram commented sarcastically, *we sure gave new meaning to the phrase "DON'T GREET THE AVELIM", which here could be interpreted as "BEWARE OF THE DOGS".* With nervous laughter still lingering in the air, Helfón led the prayers of minḥah and arvit. Meanwhile, Tía Sara appeared in her wheelchair; her sons Jaime and Salomón Behar showed up at about the same time. Rather than join the prayer group, Jaime spent time chatting with some guy we didn't know, and he left before we finished arvit. Later we found out that the guy was a brother of the woman married to Morris, Tío León's son. He had decided not to leave because he thought it was haraam to abandon a house of mourning without participating in the prayers.

When arvit was finished, Helfón said that it was okay to eat. We didn't even remember the fast: we asked for camomile tea and roscas; Fule asked for broth with shredded chicken. Soon we were eating hard-boiled eggs with lime and salt, Pita bread with yogurt, and borekas. With our stomachs upset by the argument, we couldn't eat the more substantial dishes that had been prepared for us. Salomón Behar came over to talk to us, *What happened with Tío León? how could you have thrown him out of your house? He's getting on in years, you should be considerate...* Fule jumped right in to explain, *we didn't ask him to leave, we asked his stepdaughter to leave, because she's the wife of the ratero who stole all of Papá's money.* His tone was emphatic and challenging. Salomón didn't dare respond because he saw the fury in our eyes. For the first time Helfón participated in the conversation, *that Azra is a con man. At least you sent him a message with his wife.* David replied, *Sí, señor, let them rot in hell.* Abud Nehmad and Nissim Entebi turned to look at us disapprovingly. We heard one of them say, *what a lack of respect, for avelim to be saying vulgarities during the shiva.* Fule looked at them and began to thump his chest with his fist. Nehmad and Entebi felt offended and decided to go outside.

Jaime Behar came back at ten-thirty that night. Almost everybody had left and we were sitting on cushions on the floor, still going over the details of the scene that afternoon. Jaime sat on a chair in the first row, facing the cushions. *What a lack of respect, throwing out Tío León, primos! I've just been to his house and he's very offended and he flatly refuses to return to the shiva. Under these circumstances, we should all be together. Tío León loved his brother a lot, but now you are keeping him from praying for his soul. You should call him and ask forgiveness and allow his daughter to come. It's his daughter, primos, and she has the right to come express her condolences to her papá.* We listened to Jaime Behar, thinking about how everybody always fawned upon him because he's a millionaire. Saqui decided to interrupt him, *excuse me, Jaime, but I think you don't understand what happened. That woman and her husband made my papá suffer...* Jaime Behar didn't let him finish, *let's skip the bullshit, your papá was killed by cigarettes, he died from pulmonary emphysema, nobody murdered him. I can't believe that you guys, who are so intelligent and educated, refuse to face reality!* Abram was getting fired up, *you're a fool, Jaime, if you think we're going to open our doors to the miserable wretches who stole Papá's dignity!* Certainly it had been years since anyone had dared to call Jaime Behar a fool. He looked around to see who was in the house, as if searching for somebody to bear witness to the great offense that he had just suffered. But hardly anyone was there. Mamá was talking with two of her sisters, Tías Zequíe and Raquel, and one of the Hanonos was engrossed in an argument with Helfón about whether or not the government was planning to devalue the peso soon. Jaime Behar had no choice but to defend himself alone, *you know of course that I care about you and your brothers, Abram, but what you have just done is offensive to me. Money is the least of our worries. Why make such a fuss? How much are we talking about? You should have told me and we would have taken up a collection to make sure that Tío Simón got his money and that would've been the end of it, primos. It could have been that simple.* David managed to interject, *and why don't you reproach the ratero, Jaime?, he didn't return one cent to my papá!, why don't you rebuke Tío León, since he had agreed to be the guarantor?, why should we suffer humiliation and stifle our rage?* Jaime Behar realized that we were too worked up and any argument that he might offer would not be enough to convince us. *Caramba, primos, if that's all it's about, I would have put up the money.* He said it to wound us, as if he wanted to make us see that we were squabbling over a few pesos. *Caramba, Jaime!*, Musa answered scornfully, *you should have shown up two years ago, and everything would have been resolved!* Suspecting that Jaime would go back to Tío León's house, Saqui decided to send a message: *One thing I can say, Jaime, is that those scumbags will not enter this house. The ḥakham told us that the darush will take place on Thursday in the knis. We can't keep anybody from going to the knis, so if they decide to go to the memorial, they can, but let that ratero know that if there's the slightest provocation, we'll break his nose, or rather, we'll knock the snout off that swine.*

Jaime Behar's cellphone interrupted the conversation. He covered the mouthpiece and whispered that it was his girlfriend. Jaime had divorced his first wife because he found her in bed with their chauffeur. After that he hadn't dared to commit to anyone, since he was afraid of being deceived again. While he was talking in the kitchen, Beni began to imitate him; the parody amused us so much that we all began to laugh like lunatics. When Jaime Behar returned, he couldn't understand how our mood could have changed so abruptly. Not knowing that we were making fun of him, he laughed with us and began to talk about his girlfriend. *I'm going out with Denise Cohen; she's a great girl, and very pretty, too. I met her through a friend, Moni Zetune, who has a jewelry store downtown. Denise waits on the customers who have loads of money. She was widowed two years ago when her husband was in an accident on the highway to Toluca. She has a daughter who's ten years old. Last month I took her to Europe; we went to Paris and several cities in Italy.* Mamá, who had been listening from a distance, came over to ask him, *so when are you going to get married, Jaime?* Our cousin smiled, *For the time being, we're very happy just as we are. Denise visits me almost every day or I visit her; it's almost like we're married, right?* Mamá thought that only Jaime Behar could live such a life without anybody criticizing him. And nobody would go near the poor girl, if they ever separated.

When Jaime Behar left, we realized that we were exhausted. Jaime said, *we have to get up early, remember, we start at seven thirty.* Saqui and Abram agreed reluctantly, resigned to having to fulfill their duties as avelim. Abram was beginning to notice some pain in his back; he had a hard time finding a comfortable position to sleep. Saqui's stabbing pains returned in the middle of the night. Sitting in the bathroom, he thought that he probably had inherited the hemorrhoids from Papá. Every morning, Papá spent an hour in the bathroom, plagued by hemorrhoids and a nicotine hangover, which has the same aftereffects as a drinking binge. Papá would cough and cough until his body convulsed and he vomited the mucous from his lungs. It was disgusting, but we all accepted it as an everyday occurrence to which we had become accustomed. Saqui stared at the blood-soaked toilet paper, and was convinced that Papá had been through the same thing thousands of times. He squeezed his buttocks and tried to relax so he could go to sleep, but the pain wouldn't let him. After a while, Mamá came to the door to ask what was going on. Saqui replied with panic in his voice, *I urgently need to take a bath in a tub, but it is forbidden and the week is just beginning.* Mamá took pity on him and replied that in our religion, good health is a priority. *Since there's no bathtub here, tomorrow after morning prayers, go to one of your brother's homes and take a bath.* But Saqui's conscience bothered him, *no, I can't do that, it's haraam, I've read that in an emergency you can take a bath with cold water, but warm water is forbidden because it gives you pleasure.*

Mourning for Papá

6

4 Tishrei 5757
17 September 1996 (Tuesday)

GOD COMPENSATES THOSE WHO LIVE BY THE COMMANDMENTS OF THE TORAH THROUGH THEIR GOOD DEEDS, AND PUNISHES THOSE WHO DO NOT OBEY HIS ORDINANCES. THE GREATEST COMPENSATION IS ETERNAL LIFE IN THE OLAM HABA, AND THE WORST CONDEMNATION SHALL BE THE ELIMINATION OF THE SOUL WHICH SHALL BE REMOVED FROM LIFE. WE WHO KNOW THE WISDOM OF THE TORAH AND THE TRUE PHILOSOPHERS ARE AWARE THAT THE PLEASURE OF ANGELS AND STARS CONSISTS IN THE KNOWLEDGE OF GOD AND HIS TRUE ATTRIBUTES. THIS IS A PERMANENT PLEASURE WITHOUT INTERRUPTION.

GOD WILL SEND THE MESSIAH AND NO MATTER HOW LONG HE TAKES TO ARRIVE, WE SHALL ALWAYS WAIT FOR HIM. IN HIS TIME HE WILL INCREASE WISDOM AND DIVINE KNOWLEDGE, AND PEACE AND JUSTICE WILL REIGN OVER THE EARTH. WE AWAIT THIS TIME FOR THE SPIRITUAL ADVANTAGE WE SHALL GAIN AND NOT FOR THE PHYSICAL ADVANTAGE, AS SOME DULL AND CONFUSED PEOPLE IMAGINE. IN THE TIME OF THE MESSIAH, GOD WILL RESURRECT THE DEAD.

MAIMONIDES

Jaime was desperate because he couldn't rouse Abram and Saqui, *Shaḥarit begins in three minutes and the kaddish is right at the beginning. Get up!* Concha came upstairs with a pot of Turkish coffee. Musa was downstairs, putting on the tefillin. There was already minyan, so Helfón could begin the prayer at any moment. Jaime asked him to hold off for a couple of minutes. Helfón answered, *está bien, I'll wait, but we're starting in two minutes, whether or not they're here.* When he heard Helfón starting the prayer at the top of his voice, Saqui pulled on his smelly clothing as fast as he could and bounded down the stairs two by two. He barely managed to put on the tallit before saying the first kaddish. By this time, Jaime, Fule and David were saying it by memory. Saqui took a deep breath and flopped down on the cushion on the floor. An image flashed into his mind as he suddenly recalled Papá lying on his bed, struggling to breathe, and instead of putting on the tefillin, he began to cry. David put his arm around him and Saqui smelled his foul breath. He had to go to the bathroom to try to inhale other fragrances and keep from vomiting. We were all relieved to see Abram coming down the stairs. Fule reproached him, *you missed the first kaddish, mano...* Helfón glared at us and snorted, trying to make us be quiet. Nevertheless, Abram and Beni got into a brief exchange of words that ended in laughter. Rabbi Mizrahi arrived a few minutes later; with deliberate parsimony he put on the tefillin and started to pray on his own. When we got to the shema, we noticed that the rabbi had caught up to us, and was now on the same page.

While we were praying in the living room, there was constant hustle and bustle in the kitchen; Concha was chopping onions and the waiter that Señor Salame had hired was frying tortillas for the chilaquiles. Ceci was beating eggs and two servants were busy setting the table. The waiter had prepared about thirty dishes with each of the foods planned for breakfast: yogurt, black olives, guacamole and jalapeño peppers, olive oil, mixed spices, quesadillas, hummus, eggplant tahini, round bread sticks with sesame, and, of course, Pita bread cut in fourths to be dunked in each of the dips. Later, when he saw that we were about to finish praying, he filled huge platters with plain scrambled eggs, huevos rancheros, and chilaquiles. In the center of the table there was an enormous tray of fruit: cantaloupe, watermelon, papaya, prickly pear, mamey, mangos and tiny bananas.

Our cousins the Hanonos had put away their tefillins and tallits as we were saying the last kaddish of the morning. They were the first to rush to the dining room and sit down to eat. Soon more than twenty men had squeezed in around the table. The waiter circulated with a large pitcher of orange juice. Helfón reminded them all, *señores, por favor, it's very important to say a blessing in the name of the deceased.* After about fifteen minutes, the Hanonos were bidding us a hasty farewell, *we have to go open the factory, we're already late.* And then one by one, almost all of the men who had come to pray made their way out the door. Our sisters-in-law Ceci, Bella and Elena helped clear the table and urged us to come eat breakfast. We invited the rabbi to sit at the head of the table, and the women sat down with us, too. Since the rabbi noticed that Tío León wasn't there, and neither were Tías Rosa and Pola, he asked us what had happened. We were surprised that he hadn't heard anything. Beni responded that we had asked the wife of the thief who had stolen Papá's money to leave our house, *how can she have the nerve to show up at our house, after all that my papá suffered because of her miserable husband?* The rabbi wanted to know more. We all started explaining at once, raising our voices to make ourselves heard. After listening to us, the rabbi said in a low voice, *your father's soul is wandering about this house; surely he is suffering. Call your uncle and ask him to come pray.* There was a long silence. The rabbi's request had caught us by surprise because we thought he was going to understand that our actions were justifiable. *But ḥakham, we didn't offend him; we threw out his stepdaughter, but he was not the one offended,* Fule replied. The rabbi was not convinced, *what you have to ask yourselves is how your father would have reacted when his brother and sisters left the house. I do understand that he was hurt by his brother's son-in-law, but one must always consider how the deceased person might feel: that is the rule of respect that must be honored.* Jaime was the first to concede, *está bien. Beni, after breakfast, call Tío León and tell him to come to the house to pray this afternoon.*

Mamá had gone to the kitchen, stifling her rage. She unloaded on one of her nieces who had just hung up the phone, *This is incredible! Even after my husband's death, they're still tormenting me. Caramba! Even the ḥakham is on their side, and now he wants us to swallow our pride and ask* ***him*** *to forgive* ***us****! This is outrageous! I've had to put up with him for years, but this is the last straw.* The rabbi realized that many of us were still indignant. He calmly explained to us, *these are the most sacred days; the doors of heaven are open and we must reflect on the entire year. Soon it will be Yom Kippur, which is the culmination of the process of examining our souls. Don't regard this as a humiliation, but rather as a religious duty. One of the principles that are essential to our faith is the fifth commandment, which says: "Honor thy father and thy mother." The fact that hashem placed it in the middle is indicative of its importance. While the first tablet of the law (the first five commandments) deals with the relationship between man and hashem, the second tablet (the other five commandments) establishes the rules that should reign among men. For that reason, the rabbis have interpreted the fifth commandment as the one that connects men to their progenitors and, simultaneously, to hashem. That is to say, the interpretation that is given is that honoring your parents is like honoring hashem himself. And remember that this commandment never ends: you must continue honoring your parents even after they have passed away. You have the* *obligation to honor the memory of your father and behave in the same way you would if he were alive.* Nobody dared to reply. We looked at each other, not knowing how to react. Mamá could not contain her fury in the kitchen. Just then Tías Rosa and Pola entered the house. We rushed over to greet them, demonstrating to the rabbi our warmth toward our aunts. *We're glad you're here, tías! We missed you so much yesterday.* Tía Rosa explained, *León doesn't want to come because he feels very offended. But we believe it's haraam to not be here with you, so we're going to have to go back and forth between the two houses, there's no other way.* Although they had not changed their clothes nor put on make-up, it was obvious that the tías had bathed because they smelled so good. Jaime took heart and commented to the rabbi, *God willing, we will all be here, as we should be, to show due respect to my papá. Let's hope that by this afternoon our tío will be with us.* The rabbi nodded and took his leave. *I'll return this afternoon or tomorrow morning. Now I have to go visit another family.*

As soon as the rabbi was out the door, Mamá called Jaime to the kitchen and exclaimed, *I've been putting up with your miserable uncle for forty-four years; he's walked all over me ever since I married your papá. Have a little consideration. The ḥakham is out of line. Why should you humiliate yourselves if he was the one who encouraged your papá to lend his money to that lousy ratero?* Jaime didn't know how to respond to Mamá. Musa dared to comment, *if Papá were alive, he would be suffering.* In a flash Mamá retorted, *even if you don't want to believe it, your papá was furious with that con man and with Dorotea: he would have thrown her out himself!* But we all knew that wasn't true. Papá didn't like confrontations, especially with someone from his family.

The house had filled up with women: not only Mamá's nieces, but also our aunts' daughters-in-law, as well as sisters-in-law, second cousins, distant relatives, friends of friends. They were chatting at the top of their voices, almost shouting as they competed to make themselves heard. Tía Pola's only daughter arrived. *Come over here, muchachos, this is my daughter Beatriz and her daughter Laura.* The child hid behind her mother's skirt. Beatriz was a very slender woman, with light-brown hair that covered her shoulders. She had a combination of refined and coarse features: a narrow forehead and thin eyebrows, but oversized eyes with long lashes. Like all of us, she had fleshy lips, but her nose was short and narrow. We stood there trying to think of something to say to a cousin we didn't know. Tía Pola intervened, *Beatriz is a chemist who does research at the National University.* Rather than taking the hint to inquire about her experiments, David asked if the students' strike was affecting her salary. *No,* replied Beatriz, *we're receiving our checks, but we don't know if they've taken over our labs.* Beni addressed Tía Pola, *oye, tía, what do your other children do?* She was somewhat surprised by the question because we had never gone beyond a simple greeting. *Well, my eldest son Luis has a small bookbinding company; Beatriz is my second child; Miguel, my third, works for the Benito Juarez delegation as an event manager; and my youngest, Emilio, is studying cinematography at the university.* Jaime's curiosity was piqued, so he asked, *and who is doing the best economically, tía?* Pola answered tenderly, *they all get by the best they can, Jaime. Gracias a Dios, my daughter Beatriz and her family live in the same building as I do. Ever since my husband died, we always see each other and we have lunch together every day. I take care of little Laura while she goes to work. My other children come to see me quite often. The one who suffers a lot is Emilio because he's trying to raise loads of money to make his movie.* Saqui commented, *making movies is really expensive; in the United States, any picture, no matter how small the budget, takes at least a million dollars.* Fule turned to Saqui and inquired, *what do they spend the money on? the actors' salary? the cameras?* Saqui answered, *just pay attention to the credits at the end of the movie and you'll see how many people are involved, all the different teams and multiple areas of production.* Jaime offered his opinion, *well they might spend a million dollars, but then they earn ten times what they invested. That's Hollywood, hijo,* remarked Tía Pola, *in Mexico they never manage to recuperate the money.* Fule reacted as we all could have predicted, *so why do they make movies, tía, if they know they're going to lose money?* Pola felt that she wasn't the appropriate person to defend Mexican cinema, so she changed the subject, *Beatriz, tell your primos about your research on the contamination of the city's water supply.* Reluctantly, Beatriz responded in a petulant voice, *cousins, don't drink the tap water, always boil it first.* Jaime thought he didn't have to be a chemist to know the water wasn't potable.

Abram came down to the living room with greasy hair and wrinkled clothing, irritated because he was chafed on his butt and between his legs. He told Mamá that he could hardly walk. *Well, go to the bathroom and take a cold shower,* she answered him, not caring what the rest of us might say. Abram was used to deferring to Jaime and Fule verbally, but he always ended up doing whatever he felt like doing. Now, images of the past came flashing back to him. He asked himself when he had begun to fight with Papá and Mamá. Maybe his guilt complex was a result of Raquel's death. He was sick that day, with a cold and fever, so he decided not to go out with the family. When we came back and he realized that a tragedy had occurred, he thought that perhaps he could have prevented the accident if he had been watching out for Raquel, as he so often did during our sister's brief life. But the first serious fight he had with Papá was provoked when he was cast in a play performed at Monte Sinai school. Abram played the role of a drunken poet who went from cantina to cantina expressing his anguish over the atrocities of the modern world. Papá was so convinced by Abram's performance that at the end of the play he went directly to the dressing rooms and instead of congratulating him, he nearly hit him because he thought Abram had really been drinking. When he realized that Abram was sober, he was taken aback and didn't know what to say. The teacher who had directed the play gave Papá an enthusiastic hug and said joyfully, *your son Abram has a great future in the theater! Congratulations!* But rather than feel proud, Papá was afraid. When he got back home he told Mamá to take Abram out of the theater group immediately because his future was in danger. Mamá also had reservations, even though she was thrilled that Abram had the lead role and all her friends exclaimed, *congratulations, Rebeca, your son is quite the actor!* Jaime added his own two cents, *I didn't get the point of the play. Who cares about the words of a crazy drunk? What a bunch of bull!*

The word got around that the theater teacher wanted the high school students to become professional actors and pursue an artistic career. Within a month, almost all the parents had taken their children out of the theater class, and the teacher had no choice but to transfer to another school. Before he left he told Abram, *I would like you to perform in my next play, I'll call you.* He convinced a girl from another school to act in *The Lover,* a two-person play by Harold Pinter, and they rehearsed in a room on the university campus. Only Musa and Saqui knew about the opening night of the play, which was performed in a small studio at the College of Philosophy and Letters. Since the young teacher was enrolled as a student at the university, he invited all his classmates and the place was packed. Abram and the girl, Eugenia Marechal, put on an excellent show, in spite of their young age. Afterwards, Raúl Barba, one of the best known theater directors in Mexico, came up to Abram and said, *if you decide to continue in theater, come and see me.*

Mourning for Papá

One day, two Ashkenazi boys arrived at our school, trying to recruit people for the Shomer Hatzair, a Zionist organization with socialist ideals. Nobody paid any attention to them, except for Abram, who had an avid curiosity about other kinds of people. He assimilated quickly into their group and, after a couple of months, began to talk about going to Israel. One Friday, after Papá recited the prayer for Shabbat, Abram couldn't keep his secret any longer, *I'm going to Israel for a year with a group from the Shomer.* We all looked at him as if he were crazy. *What's this about the "Chomer"?, who gave you permission to go?, and where are you going to get the money for the trip?,* exclaimed Mamá, falling apart. Abram tried to explain it to us calmly. *It's going to be a super-cool experience; my plan is to go to a kibbutz to work the land. I won't need any money because on the kibbutz everything belongs to everybody: they don't pay you for your work, but they don't charge you for room and board, either. I'm going to study Hebrew four hours a day on an Ulpan and the other four hours I'm going to work in the fields. It's going to be incredible! I'll meet Jewish people from all over the world. The trip is being planned well in advance. First of all, the people from the Shomer are going to organize a meeting for the parents.* Papá thought Mamá was pretending not to understand anything. He gave her an inquiring look, but without even noticing his bewildered face, she began to cry, *we've given you everything, you insisted on studying and we supported you. And this is how you pay us back? Who put these ideas in your head? We won't allow you to go, so next week you go to that "Chomer" place and tell them to take you off the list. And you stay away from that blasted organization!* Abram tried to reason with Papá and Mamá, but it was impossible.

The next day Mamá called her sisters to find work for him. *That's what we get for letting him waste time! He just hangs out at school and doesn't answer to anybody. Find out if someone in your family needs a young fellow he can trust to manage his business.* After arguing for two straight weeks, Abram conceded to Mamá that he would leave the theater and the Shomer, if she allowed him to finish high school. Papá and Mamá were pleased, and thought they had been too flexible with us, so from now on they should be stricter. During Friday dinners we could relax because we knew there weren't going to be more fights. But none of us imagined that Abram would keep seeing his friends from the Shomer on Sundays, instead of Fridays. They had secretly organized various raffles to raise the money for Abram's plane ticket. Then Abram went to see the men of the Jewish agency and told them he wanted to be considered a new immigrant to Israel, so they would pay part of his expenses. He was only waiting for his eighteenth birthday so he could become independent. The dates would coordinate perfectly so he could travel to Israel with the group from the Shomer. One month before the journey, during another Shabbat dinner, Abram took the opportunity to announce, *well it looks like I'll be going to Israel with my friends from the Shomer after all. I already have my plane ticket and I've got everything organized. I don't want to fight or anything; since I'm going to be eighteen, I can make my own decisions.* Mamá began to wail and shout, *why, hijo?! what have we done to you? We've always treated you well. You've had everything you ever wanted; we let you study through high school.* Papá's face had frozen and he could hardly get the words out of his mouth, *look what you've done to your mother! Have you no heart?, who is brainwashing you?* Abram tried to reason with them, *it's not the end of the world. What's wrong with going to Israel? You should be happy for me!* Abram argued with them for hours, while the rest of us kept quiet, not daring to intervene.

The next day Tío Elías Zonana arrived, accompanied by two of his sons-in-law. *Listen, Abram, it's one thing to take a trip as a tourist, but going for a whole year is crazy. You're going to be an outcast, without your loved ones, with nobody to take care of you. Your parents only want what's best for you. Just imagine, what if you get sick, who's going to watch over you? Don't do this to your parents. I've talked it over with your papá and mamá and we would like to propose that you set up your own business. Half a block from your mamá's store they are selling a small locale. Your tíos and primos are going to pitch in so that by next week it will all be arranged. Later, when you earn a bit of money, you'll be able to afford some luxuries and travel as a tourist.* As hard as everyone tried, it was impossible to convince Abram, *no, tío, I'm not interested in money. What I want to do is go work the land in Israel, have the communal experience of a kibbutz, meet people from all over the world. Aren't you proud that I'm the first in the family to go to Israel?* Nobody convinced anybody. That week we had visitors every day, including Isaac Romano, Jaime Behar's friend who had a huge textile factory. *Listen to me, hijo, money is good for wiping your butt. What matters most is your family. Don't abandon them! You're supposed to leave your house, God willing, when you get married. I've already convinced your parents: if you decide to stay, they'll allow you to go to the university. They told me you're interested in physics. Are you going to be the next Einstein? Ha, ha, ha. God willing, hijo. Although I'd recommend that you get into medicine or business administration.* Abram was so determined that nobody managed to dissuade him. Papá and Mamá resigned themselves to the inevitable when they realized there were only two weeks left before the trip. They went to the Shomer for a parents' meeting in which they were given all kinds of advice. They didn't dare open their mouths. On the day of the send-off we all went to the airport. Before he entered the passengers-only area, Mamá kissed him over and over. We could tell that Abram was afraid because he looked like a lost child. Papá looked frightened and began to shout, even though Abram was right in front of him, *keep your eyes open, be very careful, don't do anything crazy, don't get into trouble, always think before you act; call us collect as soon as you get there, write to us, Allah ma'ak, Allah ma'ak.* Now that Papá was dead, Abram felt guilty for having made him suffer.

The trip to Israel was only the beginning of the problems he would have with Papá and Mamá. Mamá would cry every Saturday night at Doña Yunta's taco stand. *I haven't heard anything from my son, he hasn't written and he hasn't called,* Mamá complained as she ate the tacos seasoned with chilpotle sauce. Meanwhile, Abram was learning Hebrew and English and forgetting about us as he worked in the cantaloupe and watermelon fields. He was surprised to learn that the majority of the people in the kibbutz were atheists, so religious holidays were celebrated as if they were secular. For the first time since his bar mitzvah, he decided not to fast on Yom Kippur and nobody made him feel guilty. On the contrary, the religious people, who only numbered about six or seven out of the six hundred who lived on the kibbutz, were considered old-fashioned. He had an Israeli girlfriend who said they should enjoy life because they could die any day. Abram tried to separate himself from the group of Mexicans so he could assimilate better in the kibbutz; in the common dining hall, he would sit at the tables with volunteers from Holland, Sweden, or other European countries, who worked there for short periods of time. He also enjoyed hanging out with the people of the kibbutz; he had been assigned adoptive parents, Argentine immigrants who had been in Israel for ten years, but he almost never went to see them because he wanted to avoid speaking Spanish. He preferred to visit a couple of Holocaust survivors who had an excellent collection of jazz music. One afternoon, as he was drinking tea and speaking Hebrew, he felt that perhaps his destiny was to stay on the kibbutz for the rest of his life. That very night they came running to tell him that he had a phone call from Mexico. It was Mamá, who was crying so much she could hardly speak; Papá, on the other hand, was shouting at the top of his voice, *how are you?!, when are you coming back?!, Don't forget us! Remember that you have brothers and parents!* Even on the kibbutz, he had to put up with criticism. Gabriel Steiner, one of his friends from the Shomer, complained about everything and argued, *so if you stay on the kibbutz, how are you going to develop intellectually?, are you going to be a farm worker all your life?, don't you want your own home?, what if they kick you out when you're old, what will you live on?* He disregarded his friend's comments because Gabriel was so bourgeois; Abram preferred the idea that everyone is equal and nobody should have any privileges. *The best form of communism is the kibbutz,* the teacher from the Ulpan would say to them proudly.

Papá and Mamá were desperate because the muchachos from the Shomer were starting to return and Abram kept telling them, every time they talked on the phone, that any day now he would be back in Mexico. However, Abram had moved to the rooms for the volunteers inside the kibbutz. He broke up with his Israeli girlfriend and fairly soon he started a relationship with a Dutch girl named Tineke; gradually he had been solidifying his plan to travel around Europe visiting all of his friends that he had met at the kibbutz. So, when he met people he would ask them to indicate on the map their place of origin. Within three months he had planned his itinerary: he would visit the homes of thirty people who had offered to give him food and a place to sleep. He had a farewell party at the kibbutz and told himself that he might return with plans to stay there indefinitely. He bought a backpack and a sleeping bag and went by boat to Athens and then on to Brindisi, Italy. Since his funds were very limited, he decided to sleep in the train stations and hitchhike to the north. Upon arriving in Rome, he went in search of the house of Paola Aroeste, one of his classmates at the Ulpan. His mouth fell open when he saw the mansion. His friend's father regarded him as a smelly drug addict, but decided to drive him to a nearby hotel and pay for two nights in advance, with breakfast included. Rather than getting angry, Abram was happy because he was going to have a bath and something more to eat besides bread and cheese.

He let a month go by without calling Mexico. When he finally called, Mamá was furious, *hijo, call me collect once a week, come home now, we'll pay for your plane ticket. Don't make us suffer any more!* Papá just shouted, *keep your eyes open, take care of yourself, don't do anything foolish.* Abram was surprised to see the houses of the friends he had met in Israel; sometimes, those who had been really wild at the kibbutz greeted him coldly, saying their parents were very strict and he couldn't stay in their homes; in contrast, when he would go see some other acquaintances almost out of inertia, even though he didn't know them well, he would get treated like a king. That happened in Rotterdam when he went to visit Ivonne, a volunteer who was at the kibbutz for only two weeks. When he knocked on the door of her house, she greeted him enthusiastically and, since at the moment she was neither studying nor working, proceeded to show him around Rotterdam and several other nearby places. Abram spent two weeks there because Ivonne's mother insisted emphatically that he stay. After almost two months of going from house to house, Abram ran out of money. Instead of returning to Mexico, he decided to look for work so he could stay in Europe for a while longer. He managed to convince the owners of a hotel in Amsterdam to give him a job in the bar of the restaurant. Thus he was able to spend five more months in Holland. At home, Abram's absence was a cause for constant worry and anguish. During that period of time we moved to Polanco; we were almost the last of the community to leave the Roma neighborhood.

We all remembered the day when Abram came back from his long journey. He had a thick beard and very long, blond hair. We could hardly recognize him. *Did you dye your hair, or what? Of course not,* he replied, *the sun bleached it.* Abram was also looking at us as if we were strangers, *Caramba!, Fule is stronger than I am now, and Musa has shot up like a weed.* Even though he had spoken in Spanish, Abram sounded like a foreigner. *Who were you hanging out with, Venezuelans or Chileans or Argentinians? Have you forgotten your Mexican accent?* On the way home we told him about the new apartment in Polanco and how we had arranged the bedrooms. He would have to share a room with Jaime and Fule, but they would each have their own bed. In the other bedroom Musa slept with Saqui, and David with Beni. Papá and Mamá were very upset by Abram's beard, *for us the beard is a sign of mourning; gracias a Dios you still have parents; you have to shave tomorrow.* But Abram didn't pay any attention to them. In a few weeks, he said he was going to study physics at the university, but that month a strike broke out, so he had no choice but to give in to Mamá and go work for a while at the store in La Lagunilla with Fule. Papá begged him to go work with him at the furniture store, but Mamá had forbidden him to do that because she thought Tío León kept all the money for himself. At the store at La Lagunilla we sold some old-fashioned dresses for elderly ladies. We barely made enough money to cover the expenses. Abram grew impatient and bored because we never had any customers. Mamá would arrive in the afternoon and get angry because she'd see Abram lounging around in the back, Fule flipping coins with the pastry vender, and the employee twiddling her thumbs, *get moving!, you have to draw people in! Have you made your first sale today? Let's see, Lucha, sprinkle some water so our luck will change.* We never understood how Mamá did it or where she found some customers, but she always managed to sell something.

Abram was relieved when the strike at the university ended and he could finally start classes. Then, after a couple of weeks he realized that his life had changed so much that he was no longer interested in physics. In Israel he had learned to play a drum called the derbekeh, and now he thought that he could devote himself to music. He joined Kol Valev, a group of Israeli folkloric music and dance that practiced at the Deportivo, and soon he was performing all around the country. Mamá would say to him, *don't be a fool, you'll starve to death as a musician. If you like it so much, play music as a hobby at night, but during the day you should have a business.* Abram thought his destiny was to be an artist. Right about then we went to the wedding of our cousin Salomón Hanono. The Hanonos were doing better all the time and the event was an opportunity to show off their newfound wealth. They offered a banquet for more than five hundred people in the Hotel Presidente Chapultepec, with two orchestras. Mamá had been drinking heavily and every now and then she would ask her sister Zequíe to have them invite Abram to play the derbekeh. After all that pressure, Abram got up on stage and began to play without accompaniment; his music stirred up the whole family. A second cousin of the Hanonos grabbed another microphone and began to sing in Arabic. The musicians in the two orchestras were irritated because everybody forgot about them. According to Jaime, from then on all the orchestras felt compelled to learn some Arabic songs which became obligatory in all the weddings and bar mitzvahs, besides the typical "Mazal tov siman tov," "Havah naguila," and "Tzena." Since Papá loved Arabic music, he would ask Abram to play the derbekeh when his friends gathered for a game of cards. Rather than get angry, the neighbors would peer through the doorway, hoping that one of us would invite them to join us. Sometimes at two in the morning our apartment would be transformed into a crowded dancehall, with people shaking their hips and sweating. One night, the neighbors in apartment 301 called the police, but another neighbor greeted the patrolmen when they arrived, gave them a little spending money, and then invited them to come listen to the music. We all knew that joyful time wasn't going to last.

After about a year, Abram became bored and began to think about living independently again. He thought he could use his savings from his job in Holland. He informed Mamá, *I want to go live in the south part of the city and try to form a group to play Middle Eastern music.* Mamá reacted as if she had been doused with a bucket of cold water, *hijo, are you crazy, or what?!, what do you mean you're leaving?, I really don't understand you, what do you want?, what will you get out of living alone, like an animal?* A few days later when Abram was about to leave the apartment with his backpack slung over his shoulder, Papá blocked the door and said, *listen to your mother, don't leave, don't be a bad son, you should obey us.* Abram tried to reason with him, explaining that it was time for him to be on his own and find his own path in the world, but Papá didn't budge, *you're not getting out of here unless you knock me down.* Abram strode toward the door anyway, and to our surprise, Papá slugged him in the face. Nobody said anything. Abram sat on the floor with his nose bleeding and tears flowing down his cheeks. Mamá ran to the bathroom for paper and water; by the time she was back, Papá had begun to cry. Moments later, Abram got up from the floor. Papá moved away from the door and they hugged each other. Abram picked up his backpack and walked out the door, still sobbing.

Abram didn't want to tell Mamá where he was going to live, *I'll call you.* Mamá was very worried because she thought he was going to move in with a girl who wasn't Jewish, so she hired a detective to inform her about everything Abram did. *He's living in an apartment on the top floor of a building in the Narvarte district. He's sharing the apartment with a muchacho his same age. He works on the university campus selling books outside the College of Philosophy and Letters. At night he gets together with a group of musicians and they play until dawn.* Mamá felt a certain amount of relief. When Abram called to say hello and that he was alright, she told him to pass by the house for money and clothes. Little by little, Mamá managed to convince Abram to come to our house at least once a month for Shabbat dinner. When Papá greeted him, he overdid the kisses, perhaps feeling guilty about punching him, or maybe he missed him a lot. Jaime and Fule, on the other hand, were relieved because they didn't have to share their room with a third person.

A couple of years later, Abram had formed a group of musicians who played a variety of pieces from the Middle East. Two Lebanese brothers were in the group, one in charge of the wind instruments like the argul, the ney and the clarinet; the other was responsible for the strings, like the lute and the mandolin. Abram's specialty was the derbekeh, but he also had learned to play several other percussion instruments such as the Egyptian tabla, the triangles and the bells. They had found a singer who was trained in classical music at the National Conservatory and who had an aptitude for learning the tones and melodies quickly. Her name was Alicia Mercado; she had a sweet, smooth voice that enhanced the original melodies. The group had managed to play in university settings, although those gigs didn't provide enough money to subsist. After six months they gave up practicing every night and gradually the group dissolved completely.

However, the relationship between Abram and

Alicia had intensified throughout the months. Abram convinced Mamá to give him more money each month, which allowed him to move into a new apartment, with Alicia. Of course Mamá didn't know anything about that. Abram and Alicia lived together happily for six months. They decided to create an orchestra with the idea that they would play at fiestas. Abram thought that if he could get someone from the community to hire them, the rest would be easy. He was convinced that the Arabic component, besides all the conventional tunes, would give them a special appeal. Papá found out about Abram's orchestra from the fellows who played dominoes with him, *hey there, Simón, I've heard your son has a top-notch orchestra that can play Arabic music to beat the band. But he better be careful; the singer has the voice of an angel, but she's goy.* All the tíos and primos teased Mamá and Papá, *how did Abram turn out to have such strange ideas?, who does he take after?, why don't you put a leash on him?* Mamá recalled that during the family get-togethers her mother-in-law would turn the kitchen pots upside down and play them like drums. *He gets that from your mamá, Simón.* Papá bristled, *leave my mamá, may she rest in peace, out of this discussion! She always respected our customs; she has nothing to do with this.* Abram noticed that Alicia was pregnant because she couldn't fit into the skirt she usually wore for performances. The group kept playing for fiestas, but as time went by they had fewer and fewer bookings. One day, Abram reproached his friend Jacobo Mustri because he hadn't hired them for his wedding. Mustri replied, *you know how it is, you're a good buddy; it's nothing against you, but your singer has a bun in the oven and that doesn't look good on stage. Take my advice: get rid of her and find a sexy lead vocalist; you'll be getting invitations right and left.* As her waistline grew, Alicia became increasingly grumpy, *they're taking it out on you because you live with a woman who isn't Jewish and you don't dare confront them: you're a coward!* Fed up with her insecurity, Abram took the plunge, *I'll prove to you that I love you, let's get married as soon as possible.* He called Saqui and Musa and secretly invited them to the wedding. A year later, the gossip reached Mamá that Alicia had had a baby, *and they say he looks just like your son Abram.* Several years later when Abram separated from Alicia and moved back into our house with his young children, Papá became the same affectionate man with them that he had been with us, during our childhood.

Now, feeling dazed and uncomfortable with his sweaty, dirty body, Abram told himself that he had to put up with the grime in order to respect the mourning period. Around noon another rabbi appeared, whom we didn't know. Tía Zequíe had invited him to come, *it's his duty to come to the house of mourning; and it's also his duty to speak with the avelim and offer them words of consolation.* Our tía introduced him to all of us, *he is ḥakham Cherem, from Argentina.* The rabbi didn't greet us, but he gestured to us to sit down on the cushions. *May God comfort you and may your father's soul rise up to heaven during this week that is so sacred for all of us. I say to all of you, we have just celebrated Rosh Hashanah, the New Year, which literally means the head of the year. We should think carefully about the meaning of the phrase "rosh hashanah." Why "the head"? Think about it. Rosh Hashanah is the beginning of a serious and profound meditation. The ten days that go from Rosh Hashanah to Yom Kippur (Tishrei 1 through 10) are called "aseret ieme hateshuvah," the ten days of repentance. This is the time, señores, to do teshuvah to show your repentance and seek the path of the Torah. This is the key moment to change and search for something new. Many of us are accustomed to buying new clothes for the New Year; well, now it is important to put on the new clothes, move out of your house and inhabit the house of hashem. A spiritual exchange, señores, and not a monetary exchange!* Helfón chuckled, but the rabbi looked at him with reproach. *I implore you to consider making a small change in your lives. The rabbis tell us that the teshuvah is a process that takes time and adaptation. For example, you could start by making sure that your house is kosher; you have to start with something: change the house! Have two sets of dishes, one for meat and one for milk products, and follow the other Kosher rules to the letter. Then you can proceed to honor the Shabbat, our most sacred holiday. He who honors the restrictions of Shabbat is guaranteed a special place in his future life. Keep in mind, señores, we reside here for a very brief time; the true life is the one that follows, in the Olam haba. That is where we wish to have the best conditions because it is eternal life. Therefore we need to prepare ourselves in this life and do good deeds and be very respectful of our Torah and our laws. I request that during these sacred days you think about it seriously and decide to take the correct path and do teshuvah. Thus spoke Rambam, Maimonides; repentance will always be well received, but during these days the teshuvah will be even more readily accepted. May your father guide you and help you take this righteous path. Barukh hashem.* The rabbi said a blessing and took a sip of Turkish coffee with a rosca. He also ate some fruit and nuts with dried dates. He stayed for another five minutes talking to Jaime and then left, nodding his head in a sign of farewell.

Beni went upstairs to call Tío León on the phone. He had to dial several times because Terri kept answering. The tenth time, Tío León finally answered, *Bueno!! Who's calling?!* Beni told him very calmly, *hello, tío, this is Beni speaking.* Tío León was almost raving, *were you the one who kept calling?!* Beni chose his words carefully, *I have just dialed your number, tío; this morning ḥakham Mizrahi came and we had a little talk here at the house.* Hearing the rabbi's name piqued his curiosity. Terri was gesturing emphatically, drawing her finger across her throat so he would hang up. Beni continued speaking calmly. *The rabbi explained to us that Papá's soul is suffering at this time and we have to avoid conflict. He wouldn't be pleased that you are not reciting the kaddish with us. So in the name of my brothers and my mamá, I'm asking you to come to our house to pray.* Tío León took the chance to express his rage, *you boys threw me out by throwing out my daughter; and besides, you insulted my wife. I can't agree to go to a house where I am not respected. I'm giving you two conditions: one, my daughter is going to visit me and she has to be well received; two, you have to ask my wife's forgiveness in front of everybody.* Beni answered that he was going to talk it over with us, but after he hung up the receiver, he said, *we'd better forget this; does he really believe we're going to humiliate ourselves, apologizing to that bitch?* Musa was curious, *what did he say, exactly?* When Beni spelled out the two conditions, Jaime and Fule were furious, *no way are we going to agree to that. Beni's right, may Papá forgive us and may his soul go up to heaven, but our uncle's miserable stepdaughter is not setting foot in this house, and his wretched wife is not going to have the satisfaction of an apology from anyone!* Musa and Saqui had been hoping that Tío León would come back to the house to complete the week of mourning in peace, but they realized that it was useless to argue with the rest of us.

7

5 Tishrei 5757

18 September 1996 (Wednesday)

THE JEWISH TRADITION VALUES LIFE. THE TORAH WAS GIVEN TO THE PEOPLE OF ISRAEL SO THAT THEY COULD LIVE BY ITS TEACHINGS AND NOT DIE FOR THEM. RELIGIOUS LAWS AND PRACTICES REGARDING DEATH AND MOURNING ARE BASED ON TWO PRINCIPLES: 1) HONOR AND RESPECT DUE TO A HUMAN BEING WHO IS NO LONGER ALIVE; 2) MENTAL AND EMOTIONAL SUPPORT FOR THE RELATIVES OF THE DECEASED; THE OBLIGATION TO OFFER THEM COMPASSION AND CONSOLATION.

Each morning Abram found it more difficult to wake up and go downstairs for the prayers of Shaḥarit. Helfón, already wearing the tefillin, was looking anxiously at the clock about every sixty seconds, *this is outrageous, Jaime, you have to rein in your brothers. Shaḥarit has to begin at 7:30 on the dot; the ones living here haven't come downstairs yet, and your other brothers haven't even arrived yet.* Just then Fule, Beni and David appeared, sweaty and panting from the rush. *Sorry, but Fule got behind schedule,* they explained. Since there was minyan, Helfón started the prayers immediately. Saqui and

Abram came down right when it was time to say the first kaddish. When they had finished it, Jaime reproached them, *you guys are really screwing things up; all of us have to be here on time, out of respect for Papá.* Musa noticed that, with the exception of the real ḥakhamitos, each day different cousins showed up. *It's lucky we have more than fifty cousins, otherwise we'd have trouble getting minyan.* We all knew that it was the custom to visit the house of mourning either once or three times, since twice is bad luck. Those who came more than three times were the super-religious or the closest relatives, like Mamá's sisters, and some of their daughters who accompanied them everywhere. Today our second cousins, the Camhis, had come; we spent our childhood with them because they lived in the same building in the Roma neighborhood. We hadn't seen them for some time because we weren't such good friends anymore. Saqui was happy to see Salomón Camhi; they nodded to each other from a distance during the prayers. Afterwards, Salomón sat down to have breakfast with his brother Elías. Saqui was surprised that he didn't come over to greet him after not seeing each other for more than fifteen years, but he figured that Salomón was in a hurry to eat and he would come chat with him a while before leaving. As he sipped his Turkish coffee and talked with Musa, Saqui saw Salomón get up from the table and say good-bye to his brother. Before going out the door, he left his kippah in the basket at the entrance and looked at us out of the corner of his eye. Saqui felt hurt and irritated, *did you see that?, he didn't come over to say hello to me. We spent our whole childhood together, we were like Siamese twins, and now, in spite of what we're going through, he doesn't even offer me a hug. I'm sure he won't be back; who made him come, his mamá?* Musa tried to defend Salomón Camhi, *maybe he's a ḥakhamito and doesn't greet the avelim.* But Saqui countered, *if he's such a ḥakhamito, why did he have to grab a kippah at the door and put it back when he left? The tefillin that he wore was really small for him; it was probably the one he got for his bar mitzvah. Besides, if he were so pious, he wouldn't have been chatting all the time with his brother Elías during Shaḥarit. And he didn't even know the prayers of the berachot by heart! He had to read the sign in the dining room.*

Fule had been listening to Saqui and he intervened to explain, *didn't you know? Salomón went away with a lover to live in some small town. After a few years he came back to Mexico City, met a Jewish girl and married her. Two weeks ago his ex-lover showed up with two kids and denounced him to his new wife and there was a big argument with the in-laws, who didn't know anything about his past. Now he's separated from his Jewish wife, but she's pregnant. The bone of contention is that they gave him a huge dowry because the girl was 28 years old, already an old maid. With the furnished house, the banquet, the honeymoon and the factory set up for Salomón, they spent a fortune. But since they put everything in her name and in her father's name, they threw him out of the house and the factory, and that idiot Salomón was left with nothing. He wants to sue them. You think they'll pay attention to him, when they hear he has two children he never acknowledged? He'll be laughed out of court!* Saqui was still curious, *so why did he come to our house?* Jaime had an explanation, *he's desperate and he wants people to take pity on him, he's telling everybody that his wife and in-laws were perfectly aware of everything, but they had feigned ignorance to avoid gossip about them and the marriage.*

At ten o'clock Sofi Zonana arrived with a three-year-old girl, *primos, I want you to meet my granddaughter Raquel; my daughter had to go to the market and she left her with me all morning.* Sofi's granddaughter began to play on the living room stairway, using the suspended steps as a slide. Saqui approached and before he could say anything, the girl gave him a kiss and, while caressing his scratchy beard, asked him, *do you have any chocolates for me?* Sofi laughed at her granddaugher's candor, *she's quite clever, she knows how to get what she wants.* While Mamá went to look for the chocolates in one of the drawers of the dining room cabinet, the girl went up the steps so she could slide down again, but this time she lost her balance and fell off the side of the steps. We all ran to make sure she was alright. Saqui picked her up and realized that her knee was bleeding. As he held the girl in his arms, tears started rolling down Saqui's face. Sofi grabbed her away from him. *It's okay, Raquelita, it's just a scratch, roḥi.* Mamá noticed that Saqui was suffering from something else, and she whispered to him, *why are you crying, hijo, it's because of your sister Raquel, isn't it?* Saqui nodded and said he wanted to lie down for a while; Mamá went upstairs with him. For the first time since the tragedy, they decided to talk about Raquel. Saqui told Mamá, *seven years ago, thanks to Lisa, I wrote about what happened to Raquel. It helped me a lot and finally my nightmares went away. I think it's time to read it to you, so I can find out if it all happened the way I remember.* Mamá wasn't surprised to hear that Saqui was still obsessed with Raquel's death. He took some yellow pages out of his suitcase and began to read:

"Raquel died twenty-seven years ago and ever since then she appears to me everywhere and almost constantly. When I dream about angels I always discover Raquel among them. I see her happy, offering me a smile and some chocolates. However, it's not the dream, but insomnia that gives me vertigo. During the quiet hours of the night Raquel's image appears to me, motionless and silent. There we are, face to face, in an impossible dialogue. Perhaps some day, after so much repetition of the same speechless scene, she will manage to defy the boundaries of death.

"There's a photo hanging in my room. It's one of those old-fashioned portraits; even though it has faded somewhat, I can still make out the image. It was probably taken in a park in the Roma neighborhood. My sister is sitting on a swing; her small hands seem to caress the safety bar and her legs, still chubby with the remains of baby fat, are dangling beneath the seat. Her checkered dress has some delicate lacework on the front, whose graceful pattern is well captured by the photo. Raquel has a round face, short nose and fleshy lips, like the rest of us. If it weren't for the dress, I could confuse her with Abram or Fule. Mamá has asked me for that picture many times, but I always find a pretext to avoid giving it back to her. That photo is like the word itself. It's always there and I repeat her name under my breath, or resign myself to that endless dialogue of the eyes.

"Raquel was the next child after me; she was number five. Because she was the only girl in a family of boys, Mamá pampered her a lot. But she didn't act like a spoiled brat; on the contrary, she shared her allowance with us and avoided getting caught up in our fights. Mamá had taught us how to love her; she always hugged her tenderly and called her: my darling, my sweetheart, my princess.

"It was during the time we were all going to the Del Río school, except for Raquel, who stayed home because she was too young; I was in kindergarten. Since it was a small school, Miss Anita and Miss Sarita seemed like our second mamás. Every year there was a festival to celebrate Mother's Day, with medals for the best students. Abram always got loads of prizes: for discipline, hygiene, arithmetic, language, history. After the ceremony, we always had to take photos. I remember a picture of the four older brothers and Raquel: Jaime, Abram and Fule are standing in back; Raquel and I are in front. All of us boys were wearing bowties and matching outfits.

"We were living in a six-story building on Alvaro Obregón Street. Sometimes we'd go out to play on the island of grass that divided the avenue, and when we were lucky we'd get to go to the gazebo in the Ajusco park where we could rent bicycles and tricycles. Our best friends were our second cousins who lived in the same building. Some Italian neighbors used to challenge us: --You damn Jews, you're the ones who killed Christ!

"Then pretty soon the punches would be flying. I didn't want to leave the house, for fear of running into them, but sometimes I had to run errands with our housekeeper. We'd walk down a narrow passageway that dissected our block, and arrive at the Parián, a small market where they sold vegetables, fruit and groceries. Don Luis, Don Nacho, Don Pepe and Doña Josefina kept track of things they sold on credit, and wrote down everything on our list. Of course, Concha never let go of my hand, and I never knew if we were going to buy bread or to pick up clothes from the dry cleaner.

"My parents say that during the time when Fule was born, everything was going well. The store at La Lagunilla provided enough for many more children. Nevertheless, it seems that Papá neglected the business and didn't notice that the saleswoman was stealing money from him, until one day he couldn't pay the creditors, the landlord, or anybody else. My grandmother came to the rescue. She had bought the store originally and Mamá had worked there since she was twelve years old. They had given it to Papá as dowry. When Papá started looking for work elsewhere, Mamá went back to La Lagunilla. Although she never neglected us in the morning, she spent her afternoons at the store and we were left at home.

"Sometimes that was great because we'd organize all kinds of games and Concha couldn't stop us. Abram and Fule, running around and around the table, pillows flying through the air, Abram helping me do somersaults on the bed, Fule jumping on top of the tables, the baby screaming and crying, Jaime throwing rolled-up socks like guided missiles, Raquel wide-eyed watching every move. At nightfall when Mamá came home we all started shouting accusations.

"—Fule hit me in the eye and wanted to tear out my tongue so I couldn't say that he's a dope.

"—No, that's a lie, you fairy!

"—Those guys broke the flower pot, I saw them!

"—No, that happened when you fell against the table, because Fule pushed you.

"—Mamá, it's Saqui's fault, he took the legs off the table to play with the wheels and that's why everything fell down.

"—Bueno, that's enough already!—Mamá would finally shout. Concha, please give the boys their dinner and put them to bed. How's my darling, my sweetheart, my princess?

"It's strange that my memory is not precise in regard to the day of the week, the date, or the time of day. That's all a blur to me. But I know it must have happened between the time Musa was born and the twins arrived. Mamá was already pregnant and since the twins were born in August, then it probably happened in February, March or April of that year, which was 1962. I was about five years old and Raquel must have been about three. During my nights of insomnia, the accident happens over and over again. In my sleepless state, with my eyes wide open I walk down those desolate streets, toward that sudden avalanche of cars and that throng of people crowding around to see what happened.

"Mamá was working, as usual. Abram had a cold and had curled up on the bed in Mamá and Papá's room. An invisible hand had wound us up more than usual. We were so restless, we wanted to go out on the street, experience the city, jump up and down under the cloudless sky of Mexico. Fifty-nine times around the table in the dining room; two hundred and thirty bounces on the beds (who's got the record?); forty-six soldiers killed in the marbles game; nineteen paper airplanes that crash-landed on the floor; three books on painting skimmed over in a flash; zero soap operas on TV. The decision was made: --vámonos, let's get out of here.

"I always believed that I was responsible. In spite of my tender age, I was the instigator, I was leading the pack, and I was the only eyewitness. Perhaps right when we had first tried to escape from the apartment, the couple in the soap opera was surrendering to a kiss they had avoided for months on end, and our housekeeper was enjoying their long-anticipated embrace. At any rate, she ran to shut the door on us; I was so frantic that I bit her hand. Concha, enraged by the bite, shouted:

--You lousy, good-for-nothin' brats!

"We got past her and ran to the front entranceway, where the usual troublemakers were waiting for us: the Camhis, the Spaniard from number 15 and two of Señora Lucía's sons.

"—Where are we going?

"—To the swings.

"—To the Parián.

"—To the Ajusco Park to rent bicycles.

"—No, to the grass strip to play soccer.

"—Let's go get enchiladas!

"I don't know who suggested it. Now that I think about it, it sounds so absurd. What got into us? Why did we want to eat a dish that was so spicy we never could finish it? Maybe there was something strange or magical about the word; we were fascinated by the colorful image: rolled-up tortillas filled with chicken and smothered in green and red salsas, the red Mexican rice and black beans on the side, the cream that topped off the dish with a splash of white.

"Raquel took my hand. I was in front of the group, with Fule and Jaime in the rear. We set off through the streets of the neighborhood: Jalapa, Orizaba, Mérida and then with a right turn, Chihuahua, Guanajuato, Zacatecas, Querétaro. I know that we were heading south, but which one was the fatal corner?, which streets did I never dare to cross?, what model was the ill-fated car?, where did all the curious bystanders come from?

"Still holding hands, Raquel and I arrived at a major intersection. All the rest were far behind, some not even in sight. Maybe that's why I hesitated for a moment. Also, it was a long way across the street, and I was afraid of the speeding cars. Raquel, on the other hand, made up her mind quickly. She let go of my hand and ran to face her death. It was as if she knew that someone was waiting for her and she had been given an order. She had only taken a few steps when the car hurled her out of my sight. I don't know how far her body flew, but even now I still can't remember having seen her after the accident. I looked around for her and the only thing I saw in front of me was a red piece of clothing, a sweater or a blouse. I wanted to pick it up and take it with me, but I couldn't move, I was paralyzed. Did I let her go, or did she get away from me without my being able to stop her?

"Nearby, people were milling around. Some were looking at me curiously; others were arguing about what happened.

"—It was a Ford Falcon.

"—No, I'm sure it was a Chevrolet, this year's model, I saw it.

"—Some guy wrote down the license plate.

"—That damn bastard!, he just kept driving.

"—That miserable swine.

"—He has no shame, he didn't even slow down to see

if he had finished her off.

"—Son of a bitch, if he were still here I'd beat him to a pulp.

"—And who's that boy? He's not even crying.

"Our little gang had disappeared. Fule and Jaime came up to me, crying. The ambulance sirens were assaulting my ears and driving me crazy. I didn't know where Raquel was, or if some relative had gone in the Red Cross van. Jaime shook me by the shoulders. The onlookers had dispersed and the street was deserted again. Fule put his arm around me. I started to cry as I stumbled along in a daze, guided only by the pressure of my brother's arm. Back at the apartment, Abram had already heard the news; he was sobbing and his tears were mixing with snot from his nose. The baby was screaming incessantly.

"A while later we heard Mamá's voice in the corridor. I ran immediately to the apartment door, looked out, and saw her going toward the stairs to the third floor. She was carrying a bucket full of the one hundred eggs we received weekly from El Chaparrito at La Lagunilla. Her arms went limp when she heard the news, and the eggs spilled out of the bucket, rolled down through the gap between the stairs and the corridors and splattered at the bottom, near the lobby. In spite of the broken eggs, there was a long silence. Mamá had keeled over on the nearest landing, and she was lying on her back, disheveled, with torn stockings. Her fainting spell did not last long. Soon she was wailing at the top of her voice, hitting herself violently, shouting that she had to wake up from a nightmare, while the relatives who had rushed to the scene made cautious attempts to subdue her hands.

"Nobody noticed that I was hiding under the bed. They had brought chairs from the next apartment, where my grandmother lived. There were a lot of people. Somebody had to be in charge of making coffee and breakfasts for the men who came to pray. A family friend was looking for a button when she caught sight of me; she tried to get me out of there, but failed. My grandmother had to get down on her knees and hold her arms out to me: --Come on, roḥi, come here, honey.

"When we came out of the bedroom several people stroked my hair; some of them winked at me. Papá picked me up and pinched my cheeks. Mamá was prostrate on the floor, with her eyes glazed over.

"—My darling, my sweetheart, my princess. Oh Lord, why did I leave her?

"That was the last thing I saw. They took me to my cousins the Hanonos, a wealthy family with a huge house in Polanco. But that didn't make them any different from us, because the customs and food were identical. What did impress me was the way they fought. There they didn't just strike a shoulder to intimidate a younger brother; rather, with an open hand they slapped his back and the impact resonated throughout the high ceilings, which were illuminated by crystal chandaliers. From time to time I would listen in on my aunt's conversations:

"—Yes, he's better; he's not crying anymore. He always has his eyes wide open, looking around. Well, yes, they're finishing tomorrow. Simón? Ḥazito! He's had a hard time. First his papá, then his mamá, now his daughter. Can you imagine his suffering?

"Mamá says that she had to drag me back there. I don't remember that. I do recall biting and kicking, shouting in the middle of the street, crying desperately. My resistance tactics must have persuaded her, because we would make a long detour to get where we were going, or she'd simply postpone the errand and have one of my brothers do it. One day, she heard that I could be permanently traumatized, so she was convinced that she had to do something. She pulled me by the elbow along the street; then, as my resistance increased, she had to drag me. For the first time, she didn't care that I lost a shoe on the way and my socks were getting dirty, or that a group of people was gathering to watch the struggle. When we got to the ominous corner, she didn't know what to do, and I didn't either. I saw the cars rushing by again, through the wide intersection. The scuffle had ceased and a strange stillness possessed us.

"You see, nothing's going to happen. No one is going to run you over. Come on, hijo, let's cross, give me your hand.

"I held onto her as tightly as possible. As we advanced, Mamá looked bewildered, and a bit dazed. On the other side of the street, everything seemed strange, very different. We went back home, disheartened by the experience. We never spoke of it again; an exchange of looks was enough, at the right moment.

"Now that everybody is asleep, my sister appears before me as she always does, without saying a word. She hasn't changed a bit; our dialogue is the same. I gaze at the photo once more and watch Raquel as she gets off the swing and begins to fly high in the sky."

Mamá had been sobbing. *I do remember everything. Raquelita died on May 4, 1962; she was going to be three years old the next day; we had bought her a doll for her birthday but we never got to give it to her. According to what I was told, she wasn't killed by a speeding car, but rather by a parked car that suddenly backed up. The owner of the car gave the police a huge bribe so they would let him go free. I called him on the phone for a whole year to rant at him, but who was going to get my daughter back for me?* Saqui was astonished that Mamá had another version of the accident. He suspected that somebody lied to her so that it would seem less violent. Mamá felt like venting, *just imagine, right now she would be married, with children. You don't mention your papá, but he was deeply affected. I think that's why we became so poor back then (and even more, when the twins were born). He was numb for many years, not making any effort, not noticing that you boys really needed him. That's why I had to pull myself together: for you boys. If I hadn't had my sons, I don't think I could have overcome that pain. But your papá didn't talk to anybody, didn't cry, didn't want to get up in the morning. That's why when his brother León offered him work, I didn't want to interfere, because at least he had a routine and a reason for living. He always suffered alone. I never blamed him, but from then on we couldn't talk. And now he's dead. Do you know what it means to live forty-four years together? I feel all of his pain. He was a good man, but his sorrow for Raquel killed his ambition and his desire for success. Gambling was a distraction for him, to keep from thinking about things; he never made big bets because he wasn't interested in high stakes, and he didn't have the money anyway; he didn't even have the ambition to win at gambling. He preferred dominoes so he could pass the time just thinking about combinations of numbers. He loved you boys, but his soul was tortured by what happened to Raquel.*

Noting Mamá's willingness to talk about Papá, Saqui asked, *but he lost the store before Raquel died, he was ruined even before that, right?* Mamá explained, *actually, until then, gambling for him was just a passtime, something he had to do because all of his friends did it and he didn't like to be different. They all had their small businesses downtown and got together every afternoon in the apartment above Moi Kabli's store. When the others realized that their employees were stealing from them, they designed a daily inventory system that protected them very well. But your papá said that his saleswoman was not capable of stealing from him. I warned him a thousand times. One week out of sheer desperation I went to the store every night and counted the dresses myself, one by one. The clerk said that she hadn't sold anything those afternoons, but when I arrived at night, six or seven dresses had disappeared. Your papá refused to listen to me. Within a year he was ruined. My mamá loved the store because it had provided for us, her daughters. She couldn't stand for them to take it from us, so she decided to pay the debt and asked me to work there, but forbade me to give even one cent to your papá. When Raquelita died, your papá was trying to set up his own business. He had found a locale in the Roma district, to sell curtains; he didn't have to invest a lot of money like his brother did with the display furniture; he just had some fabrics and the models for the curtains on site. But he hadn't been there even three months when the tragedy happened. Of course he bombed out again, but this time he didn't owe money to anybody, just one month's rent for the locale. Six months later León took him to work at his store.* Saqui inquired, *so do you think he felt guilty? If you hadn't been working at the store that afternoon, we wouldn't have been allowed out on the street. Perhaps,* replied Mamá. *I felt so helpless that I wanted to drown myself. But I had five children and I was pregnant: I wasn't going to let everyone starve!* Just then Jaime and Fule interrupted the conversation as they entered the bedroom. Mamá said she was going to see who was downstairs. *You can rest a while, but then come downstairs. You can't lie in bed all day; it's haraam.*

Saqui tried to remember the times he had seen Papá happy. Almost automatically, he went to open the drawer of the chest where family photos had accumulated, all out of order. A photo from Mamá and Papá's honeymoon was under a picture from the birth of one of the grandchildren, and next there was a snapshot from a trip to Acapulco taken thirty years ago; the black and white photographs seemed more intense than those in color. Saqui wanted to prove to himself that Papá had been capable of being happy, even after having lost Raquel and his parents. He studied a photo in which Papá was smiling as he embraced Mamá, at the banquet of a nephew's wedding. Certainly he would find many pictures in which Papá was smiling or even laughing heartily, but how could he know what was going on behind the façade? Could Papá have learned to hide his bitterness? Saqui opened the bottom drawer, where

Mamá kept the professional albums, commissioned for each occasion. He found the album for his bar mitzvah: on the front there was a photo framed in a heart, in which Papá was showing him how to put on the tefillin. Musa was snooping around in the background, guessing he would be the next one, so he needed to start learning the religious ritual. Further back, caught unaware, was Jaime, sporting giant sideburns. Throughout the album, Papá was diligently giving instructions to Saqui. *That day,* thought Saqui, *we got behind schedule and Papá went through two red lights; he had to bribe a traffic cop.* But Papá didn't look agitated or nervous or irritated in the photos. Tío León wasn't in the pictures because he didn't wake up on time and, instead of going to the knis, he went directly to the breakfast at our house. Saqui couldn't recall seeing many of his cousins there: not the Hanonos, nor the Zonanas, nor the Mustris, nor the Benvenistes. *Caramba!,* thought Saqui, *nobody came to watch me put on the tefillin for the first time.* Only the Camhis were there, and they lived in the same building, in the apartment above ours, and the ḥakhamitos who always went to the knis every day anyhow. Maybe that's why his smile looked a bit forced. Saqui remembered the blue and white kippah they had given him, as well as the tefillin and the tallit, in a blue leather bag with the Star of David embroidered on it. *Where could that bag be now?* Even though he had studied with ḥakham Saal and he had memorized the berakhot, he allowed himself to be guided by Papá in the ceremony, repeating the words that Papá pronounced emphatically and clearly. In almost all the photos, Papá had a serious face, knowing he was faithfully fulfilling his duty. He was so attentive that even at the most delicate moment, when Saqui had to read the Torah, Papá appeared behind him, as if standing by to help in case he stumbled. Now Saqui looked at the pictures in which he was kissing Papá's hand and, on the upper level, Mamá's hand, too.

He could almost hear the *a'aris, papi, a'aris,* that they said to him, and he felt content. No, there was no way to tell if Papá had been happy. Not even by examining the snapshot in which he posed with everybody else, stretching his mouth in an obligatory smile. Was he lamenting then that his daughter Raquel wasn't in the photo? David and Beni had been born about three months after her death, almost like a palliative for the tragedy (that's why Papá and Mamá used to cry more vigorously every time they saw Pepe el Toro in the classic movie *"Nosotros los pobres").* Saqui remembered that a lot of people did show up for the breakfast at our house and he had to give a speech, accepting his religious responsibility. One week later, Elías and Salomón Hanono had declared they were going to take him to get laid. *Have you ever waxed your candle? Well then, it's about time,* Saqui recalled them saying, as he smiled to himself.

Saqui was the only one of us who worked at Papá's furniture store. He was studying history at the university and needed money for books. Papá told him to tend the store in the afternoons to make sure he wasn't robbed while he was playing dominoes. When Mamá found out that Saqui had agreed, she began to scold him in a very angry voice, *are you happy now?!, you're working for your Tío León!, he's going to exploit you just like he's exploiting your papá! So think it over carefully; if you wish, I'll help you buy what you need for your studies, but don't do this to me, hijo.* Saqui was determined not to be swayed by Mamá. *According to Papá, the store belongs to him; my uncle has nothing to do with it anymore; five years after opening it, Papá paid him off so he could have the business to himself.* Mamá had heard that argument many times, but she didn't believe it at all, *if that's true, why doesn't he contribute more to the household expenses?, why doesn't he show us the documents to prove it?* But Saqui didn't want to hear any complaints. The job with Papá was unbeatable: he could attend the university during the morning, then eat at home, arrive at the furniture store around three o'clock, and make use of the afternoon by studying for his classes there. He recalled the many times Papá would say to him, *come a little earlier, papi, we'll eat at Rafaello's, it will be my treat.* The waiters treated Papá very well. He would drink two or three martinis and become very animated; they served him Oysters Rockefeller and then a fried fish fillet. *Try the shrimp, hijo, you're going to love them.* He inhaled deeply on his cigar and stared into space. Saqui startled Papá out of his trance, *did you sell something today?, do I need to fill an order or send a last-minute shipment?* However, Papá never took the bait, *I don't like anything to be sent in the afternoon. Don't you worry about that.* As always, Papá tried to convince him to drop out of the university, *hijo, if you wish, I'll make you a partner, you can come work with me all day. Or, if you prefer, we can look for a locale for you and I'll help with the purchase. That will be a piece of cake because I have credit with the lenders; they can set you up with the display furniture at no cost, and you can get a good start. What's so great about studying history? Are you going to fix the past?* Saqui remembered savoring the gourmet food at Rafaello's, as he tried to stall his papá, *let me think it over, maybe, but for now I'm going to keep attending classes.*

Fule woke up from his siesta and told Saqui that it wasn't good to look at photographs during the week of mourning. But instead of putting away the pictures and closing the dresser drawers, Saqui asked him, *do you think Papá was happy?* Fule answered impatiently, *of course he was happy, don't be foolish, you're letting yourself be influenced by his last years, when he was so sick.* Saqui showed him a snapshot he had picked up haphazardly, *let's see, can you show me his happiness?* Fule reacted with some irritation, *I don't need to analyze any photos; just remember my wedding, there's no doubt about it.* Saqui contradicted him, *that was the period of time when Papá had to give up drinking because of his ulcer. He spent the whole wedding celebration complaining about not being able to toast with anybody!* Fule wasn't going to let Saqui change his memory of his own wedding, *that doesn't matter: he was happy! He was acting like a little boy, dancing with all of us!* Jaime, who had been listening, decided to contribute his two cents' worth, *how can you know that someone is happy? That question is irrelevant, you live and that's it. Papá enjoyed some luxuries, he ate in the best restaurants, he bought fine clothes, he managed to marry off almost all of his sons, who could ask for more than that? He enjoyed what he could. Did he suffer? Of course he did!, but that didn't keep him from having a good time at fiestas. Don't be an idiot! All this talk about happiness is a bunch of bull.*

David entered the bedroom to tell us that another ḥakham had arrived and we had to go downstairs to listen to him talk. It was twelve o'clock and the house had filled up with women again. We had never seen this rabbi; our cousin Tere Mustri introduced him to us. Tere's husband had become very religious and was one of the main sponsors of a group in one of the yeshivahs that was dedicated to studying the Torah. *He's the Rabbi Asher Zelig, from the Or group,* said Tere. The ḥakham asked us to sit down on the cushions. When we were all in our places, there was a silence that surprised even him. Although on other occasions the rabbis were constantly interrupted by cell phones and people chatting, this time everybody listened very attentively to his words.

As you know, these are the ten most sacred days of the year. These are the days in which we reaffirm our faith and we ask God to inscribe us in the book of life. But you are sitting on the floor, lamenting the death of your father. Hashem does everything for a reason, and you may be asking yourselves, why did our papá die a few minutes before the beginning of Rosh Hashanah?, what message is God sending us?, why are we sitting shiva during the first days of 5757? Although I am not the one to answer these questions for you, I can help you make some observations regarding our tradition. First of all, let's contemplate the word father. In Hebrew, you say ab (or aba, for papá) which is composed of two letters, aleph and bet. As you know, they are the first two letters of the alphabet; however, you should note that aleph-bet is also a way of referring to the alphabet, like "the ABCs." Therefore, the word father represents the complete alphabet, all the letters, and that signifies our tradition. The letters that comprise that word are, according to Zohar, the ones that give foundation to the origin. The Torah begins in Genesis with the words "Bereshit barah Elohim et hashamayim be'et ha'aretz," commonly translated as "In the beginning God created the heavens and the earth." The first two words, "bereshit" and "barah", begin with the letter bet; the second two words, "Elohim" and "et", with the letter aleph. In the Zohar it is told how all the letters ask God to let them be the first letters of the creation (and thus, of the Torah). For example, the first to speak is the last letter of the alphabet, the tav, which says it should begin because it is the last letter of the word "emet," meaning truth. Nonetheless, God responds that He cannot begin with tav because it is also the last letter of "mavet," which means death. Thus, each letter makes its case until they get to the bet, which says that it should come first because it begins the word "barukh," or blessed. Indeed, hashem utilizes the bet to begin everything. If you study the form of the letter, bet [ב] is the one that connects the upper world with the lower world (two horizontal bars, above and below, are united by a vertical bar); it also represents the form of a house with an open door, which, when rotated in any direction, will always remain open. The bet is our temple which always has open doors; it is the reception of God in the Olam haba. Furthermore, it is important to note that the letter bet, alone, means "in," which indicates that by itself it is an invitation to enter the world.

Next we have the word "reshit," the inception or begin-

ning. Within that word we have another, "rosh," which means head. Everything begins with the head; therefore, we call the new year Rosh Hashanah (head of the year). And the Zohar even explains that the anagram of "rosh" (resh, aleph, shin) is "asher" (aleph, shin, resh), which is the sacred temple, hidden and secret, so that before everything begins there is already a temple evoked by the letter bet and the word asher. Nevertheless, you may wonder why Genesis does not begin with the first letter of the alphabet, the aleph. In the Zohar, it is explained that the aleph did not go to make any request of the Lord; when God inquired why it had not asked to initiate creation as the other letters had done, the aleph replied that it was better to keep silent. Hashem considered the aleph to be a sacred letter and placed it at the beginning of our alphabet; moreover, he declared that unity can not be found anywhere but in the aleph. The aleph includes in its sign the name of God, which, as you know, consists of four letters: yod, hei, vav, hei. If you look carefully, the aleph [א] is composed of a transversal bar (which goes from left to right) and two vertical semi-bars; the yod [י] is represented by the semi-bar on the upper right part of the letter, the vav [ו]is the same bar (although it is tilted), and the letter "hei" [ה] is composed of the bar combined with the semi-bar of the lower part. The letter aleph does the same thing as the bet, which connects the upper world with the lower world: the bar functions as the element that connects one with the other: it points upward and downward. If the feminine principle can be attributed to the bet, the masculine appears in the aleph (although the aleph also has both poles: the masculine, represented by the vav, and the feminine, represented by the hei). The aleph is the initial letter of Elohim, the first word that designates God in the Torah. The aleph is the letter that summarizes all the other letters of the alphabet, the root of all beginnings and the maximum mystery of the creator. Therefore, when we say father, ab, we are alluding directly to the foundation of the world; we find in the ab the sum of all letters and the sum of all creation. Thus, for you, the loss of the ab is a very difficult blow to assimilate. However, you must always believe that the father has not disappeared completely; he remains in the heavens, protecting us.

We were all fascinated by the rabbi's explanations. Our prima Mustri asked without meeting his eyes, *well then, if the father is everything, what function does the mother have?* The rabbi kept quiet for a moment as he gathered his thoughts, then answered, *the word mother, "em", is written with two letters, aleph and mem. I have already spoken about the meaning of aleph. So, why the mem? Well, the letter mem is the letter that is exactly in the middle of the alphabet, which means the mother marks the road of life from the beginning to the middle. Now then, here is something curious, what happens if we add the last letter of the alphabet, the tav, to the word em? Well, we would have the word "emet," which means truth. Man needs to go through the entire alphabet, from the aleph to the tav, in order to know the truth. If the alphabet symbolizes life, then the mother takes us from the beginning to the midpoint of the journey. When we reach the midpoint, then she can allow us to walk on our own. The value of a woman is precisely that she has her children, raises them, educates them, and takes them halfway down the road, at which point they are capable of going on alone. Do you know what the children must do? They have to complete the journey.*

The father and the mother always go together, like a unit. We can see that in the fifth commandment, "kabed et avikha ve'et imekha," "honor thy father and thy mother." In the Talmud, it is said that the parents share with God the labor of producing life. That is to say, the parents are the partners of God in the creation of man. Notice that the fifth commandment comes immediately after the one that indicates the sanctity of the Shabbat. The Shabbat is totally connected to the act of creation. The sixth commandment, "Thou shalt not steal," is the one that establishes the laws that should reign among men. Between the fourth and the sixth stands the respect for your parents. The transition between the sphere of

God and that of men is made through the parents. To honor your parents is to honor God. The rabbi paused a moment and then concluded, *You may say: this is where it all ends; but that is not what it means to honor a father who gave everything to you. Honor is exactly the opposite; you must squeeze water out of the rock once more. Thus we discover what is "emet", the truth, the real concept of honoring our parents. We should not renounce anything; on the contrary, we should follow the example of the father. Think about how we light candles immediately after a person dies: the candle represents the person's soul; we make light even in the most fulminating moment of death. This is what we have to do; this is our function as yehudim. We do not believe that we end at death. The person is not here physically, but you carry his name. You should glorify that name. It is my wish that God will bless you, give you strength and consolation, but more than anything, you must rise up, take heart and honor your father and your mother; in two words, great energy and vitality: that is the real honor that you can give them.*

Our prima Tere said *amén*, blending in with the other voices. As he was walking out the door, the rabbi managed to answer, *may God give you strength.* We were all impressed by his speech. Mamá asked Tere if all the ḥakhamim of the Or group were like him. Tere looked around, making sure she could speak freely, *the truth is, tía, that they aren't. Most of them spend the whole day studying together in the yeshivah, and rarely speak to anyone else. They talk for hours among themselves, but I don't ever get to listen. Rubén, my husband, admires them a lot and gives them money, but they don't even speak with him. This rabbi is marvelous; he's the only one who has come to our house for dinner several times, with his family. He speaks divinely, which is why I invited him, tía.*

Before eating, Helfón taped on the wall an announcement of the memorial service:

THE DARUSH WILL TAKE PLACE

ON THURSDAY, AT 5:30 P.M.,
IN THE KNIS OF BET YOSEF.
PLEASE DON'T MISS IT,
IT'S A VERY IMPORTANT MITZVAH.

Four of Mamá's nieces (two of Tía Raquel's daughters and two of Tía Jasibe's daughters) had promised they would be in charge of the food that day. In the morning they had prepared ingredients for the meat pies and sent them to a bakery in the town for the final preparation. They also made two kinds of kibbe, as well as stuffed grape leaves and zucchinis. At about two thirty in the afternoon we sat down to eat. Helfón, feeling energized, spoke with Jaime in a loud voice. *The problem is that the ḥakhamim don't all agree on things: ḥakham Shueke shows up here and announces, as if you would go to hell if you didn't heed his warning, that you can't shake hands with the avelim; and ḥakham Mizrahi comes and declares that he can show you in the Shulkhan Arukh, the code of Jewish law, where it states you can say shalom. Then ḥakham Levi arrives and claims that it depends on the avel: if he greets you, you have to respond so you won't offend him, because the mitzvah of giving comfort to the avelim has priority over the ban on greetings. Who do you obey? They get you all confused, mano. This is driving me crazy.* Beni laughed at Helfón's complaint, and mockingly replied from the other side of the table, *and what do they say about hugging and kissing?* Helfón just ignored him and kept ranting, *why don't you ask Mizrahi when he comes: "ḥakham, why do we cover the mirrors?" and he'll tell you one version. Then ḥakham Shueke will tell you another story. If you ask Levi, he'll say that not all the mirrors of the house have to be covered, only the ones here in the prayer room, so we don't see our own image when we are saying the amidah, that's all, nothing more. Ḥakham Shueke says that it's an integral part of the mourning. Another says that it's because of the ghost of Benito...* We all laughed when he mentioned the ghost of Benito, but that didn't seem to bother Helfón, *I tremble every time Shueke opens his mouth because he starts talking about death. He doesn't talk about anything else. Before you know it, he's sent you to the cemetery! He talks about hell, death, the grave, oh how I wish he'd change his tune! You know what he says? That it's better to go to a house of mourning than to a fiesta, according to King Solomon. That's too much! You have to have some fun in life! The Torah celebrates life also, doesn't it? So you're going to have the darush tomorrow in the knis. But with all due respect, can I be honest with you? In the old days, we used to set out fruit in the house, invite someone to say a blessing, and that was it. Forty years ago there was no darush! The ḥakhamim invented it just to make a few bucks, mano.* We were all having a good laugh. *As for ḥakham Yedid... the truth is that many people know that he hasn't always been a saint, and may God forgive him, but now he's talking to everyone as if he were Moshé Rabenu, and that's not right! It's haraam, mano! The ḥakhamim must be humble, according to the Torah, but now they've become merchants. Forty years ago the ḥakhamim didn't make enough money to live; they had to work as tailors, butchers, cobblers, etc. When I was a boy, they all had a trade. Now they're only interested in how big your check is going to be.* One of Tía Jasibe's daughters interrupted angrily, *so, Isaac, are you such a saint? You receive money for praying, don't you? And do you think the ḥakham who came today, from the Or group, is only interested in making big bucks? No way! People who live in glass houses shouldn't throw stones!* Helfón answered our cousin calmly, *you're right. All I'm saying is that I accept my guilt and I'm not a hypocrite. I'm not going to preach as if I were God's gift to mankind. I observe the commandments as much as I can. I know how to recite all the prayers because as a boy I went to the Jewish school every day, and I learned many things about religion. And I can tell you that the ḥakhamim from the old days were a thousand times better than those we have now. That ḥakham from Or is the exception, but just so I won't shock you, I'm keeping to myself some stories I could tell on various members of that group.*

After eating we lay down for a while to take a siesta. Abram and Saqui recalled the time when they decided to set up a business together. Saqui was about to start taking classes at the university and Abram worked only at night. They decided to sell curtains and rugs, found a small locale on Chapultepec Avenue, and didn't have to invest much in the store to get set up. They named it "L'Art", thinking that the French name would make people believe that it was a European business with a branch in Mexico. A week after opening, with Mamá's help, they got their first big order: one of the Hanonos asked them to provide curtains and carpets for the house he had just bought. They had to poach the carpet layers from their competitors. Since they were inexperienced, they paid too much to the seamstress who made the curtains. After a couple weeks they had finished the job, but Hanono didn't want to pay because he wasn't satisfied with some decorations he had ordered for the living room. After much suffering, they managed to collect their money. They were very pleased to have done business and declared that they'd be able to devote themselves to their passions (music and history) because they were going to earn a lot of money in a short time. They hardly noticed that besides Hanono, they hadn't had a single customer since they set up the store. They opened at ten thirty, and all morning long they either read or chatted about the future; they'd go have lunch around two, have a siesta at home, and return around five o'clock. Abram would go to rehearse with his group and Saqui would stay at the store and read until seven, when it was time to close. That was their daily routine until one afternoon Saqui commented to Abram, *we've spent all our profits from Hanono's order; we don't have anything left to pay rent or electricity, even though we don't pay ourselves a salary.* When Jaime found out they were bankrupt, he scolded them, *that's what happens when you don't take my advice. The key to that business is a full-page ad in the Yellow Pages.* Anyway, by then Abram and Saqui had already realized that they weren't salesmen. From then on, they decided that business was not for them. Now Abram and Saqui laughed about that misadventure and revealed that they hadn't taken a siesta since then. Abram stopped talking when he noticed that Saqui had fallen asleep. Later, when Saqui woke up, he felt the need to tell his dream to Abram and Musa.

I'm in Madrid: I go walking down the street, everything's closed and everybody's asleep. I wonder if Spain has died and the people have disappeared, but suddenly I realize that it's just an illusion: there's such a crowd that I can hardly walk; more and more young people abruptly appear, with long manes, drinking from enormous bottles, lying down, sitting, standing in the streets, the plazas, everywhere. A loud burst of music makes them jump and shout, euphoric for having just been born. I feel depressed, my grey hairs have multiplied and a sharp pain in my knee makes me stop every so often. I can't go on: I have a terrible migraine and the sweat of the crowd begins to permeate my body. I've grown fat and now I begin to lose my hair so rapidly that I instantly become a furry bald man, with hair growing profusely on my back. I don't know why, but I want to get to the Puerta del Sol. I'm two streets away and I don't know how to gather the strength to make my way through the young folks, who are grabbing onto me so they can jump even higher. I wonder where the music is coming from, as it envelopes the city. Everybody's shouting but I can't make out their words; the closer I get to the Puerta del Sol, the more intense is the noise and less intelligible are the words they're spewing. I strain to hear what the closest ones are shouting, but my efforts are useless. A girl has grabbed my arm and doesn't let me go; during one of her jumps I hear, in the midst of the uproar, a cracking sound in my shoulder and then feel an abrupt, unbearable pain. I want to throw myself down on the ground and cry, but I can't because there are too many people. A grotesquely fat guy lifts me up in the air and throws me into the crowd: to my surprise, I don't fall to the ground, other hands are pushing me up and I bounce like an inflatable ball, rebounding with the music and the revelry. For the first time, I feel hope: I see the clock tower, it's 11:55. My bumpy ride through the air becomes more intense: I'm all battered up, my nose is bleeding, and my ribs are probably fractured. I am passed along from one set of hands to another, moving rapidly toward the plaza. Upon arriving, I understand for the first time why the young people are shouting. They're counting backwards: thirty, twenty-nine, twenty-eight, twenty-seven... My body seems as light as a feather, since I keep soaring higher and higher, as if bouncing on a trampoline. I'm terrified to think what might happen when we get to zero. My eardrums are about to burst; I have blood smeared on my lips, which have grown tired of howling in pain. Five, four, three, two, one, ZERO. *Just as we arrive at zero, everything stops: the music, the shouting, all the noise of the merrymaking. In my flight I have reached an illuminated clock that shows twelve o'clock on the dot: its hands don't move and I remain suspended in the air. I try to shift my eyes to see what's happening with the crowd in the plaza, but I can't: I can only look straight at the clock's face. I try to use logic to analyze what's happening, but I don't have a clue. Suddenly, on the front of the clock there appears a photo of Raquel, holding my hand, smiling, squeezing more and more. Stupefied, I watch what seems like a slide show on the clock's face: in the next picture I am with my friend Shulamit at the kibbutz. It's a snapshot that I took myself, stretching out my arm so we would both appear in the picture; we are pressed together and our faces barely fit in the frame. Shulamit is kissing me and I can smell the scent of cows that comes from the stable. Then there's a photo of Mamá, who turns my head violently to kiss me on one cheek and then the other and the other and the other; we're in the airport and her eyes are red from crying so much. Then, in Spain, amid the most absolute silence, some lips pronounce my name in Hebrew, Yitzḥak ben Rifka. A white cloud begins to move around the plaza, wiping out everything in its path, making circles around the central clock; when everything has disappeared, the cloud situates itself behind the clock, framing a photo that I can't decipher. The voice pronounces my name again and at that instant I realize that the picture, the clock, the cloud and I, suspended in the air, have all dissipated. The voice begins to pronounce other names that I recognize immediately: I can't see anything, just whiteness, but it is comforting to know that I am accompanied by the names.*

8

6/7 Tishrei 5757

19 September 1996 (Thursday)

DURING THESE DAYS THE AVEL MUST ABSTAIN FROM ALL KINDS OF PLEASURE, SUCH AS LISTENING TO MUSIC, WATCHING TELEVISION, LISTENING TO JOKES, OR PLAYING WITH A CHILD. THE AVEL WHO IS MOURNING HIS FATHER OR MOTHER SHOULD NOT ATTEND PARTIES FOR ONE YEAR, AND FOR OTHER CLOSE RELATIVES, FOR THIRTY DAYS. THIS MEANS THAT HE IS FORBIDDEN TO BE PRESENT AT PARTIES, EVEN IF HE DOES NOT PARTAKE OF THE FOOD; NEITHER SHALL HE GO TO ANY MEALS CELEBRATING A MITZVAH, OR FRIENDS' BANQUETS. FURTHERMORE, JOURNEYS AND EXCURSIONS SHOULD BE AVOIDED IF THEY ARE FOR PLEASURE OR RECREATION PURPOSES, EVEN IF THEY ARE NOT WITH A GROUP.

THE AVEL SHALL NOT GET MARRIED DURING THE FIRST MONTH. AFTER ONE MONTH, HE MAY MARRY, EVEN IF HE IS MOURNING A FATHER OR MOTHER; FOOD MAY BE PREPARED FOR THE WEDDING AND A JOYFUL CELEBRATION MAY TAKE PLACE.

THE DARUSH SHALL TAKE PLACE DURING THE WEEK OF MOURNING. IT IS PREFERABLE THAT IT TAKE

PLACE IN THE HOUSE WHERE THE PRAYERS ARE BEING RECITED. IN A FEW SPECIAL CASES, IT MAY BE CARRIED OUT IN THE SYNAGOGUE. THE AVEL MAY GO OUT, IF HE IS ACCOMPANIED AND WEARING A PIECE OF CLOTH ON HIS SHOULDER.

While we were having breakfast, Tía Jasibe cornered Musa at one end of the table, *your papá, ḥazito, didn't get to see you married, what a pity!, but it's never too late. You can do him that honor while he's in heaven, and you should give this pleasure to your mamá while she's still alive, before it's too late. I know that after a month you can go out with a muchacha and, if all goes well, you can even get married before the year is over.* Helfón, who was listening to the conversation, commented, *sí, your tía is right; you can get married, and you can even have a party and enjoy yourself.* Our tía continued, *my daughter told me that there's a muchacha named Atri (the daughter of Fortuna and Abud, my son-in-law's cousins) who hasn't been married. She's a good girl and I think you'll get along beautifully; as soon as Yom Kippur is over, go to the fiesta that they're having in the Deportivo and you can be introduced there. It's about time, Musa! What are you waiting for? You're never going to find the woman of your dreams, because she doesn't exist. You just have to get married, have children, treat each other well, and that's all!, because you're never going to find a soul mate and live your whole life with her.* Musa was used to these encounters and knew how to swim with the current, *sí, tía, you're right; I'll go to the fiesta and meet her, then I'll let you know what happens.* But later, sitting on the cushions, Musa whispered to Abram, *I've met that Atri girl; she's nice-enough, but a bit chubby, and you know, the snooty kind that wants you to take her to a good restaurant and spend loads of money.* We all knew that every time

Musa was given a girl's telephone number, he would call to test the water, *if you want, we can go to the Café New York, but they're like the gringos now and they don't let you smoke; do you smoke? Or, if you just want to go eat, I know a vegetarian restaurant in Anzures, because I'm a vegetarian, as you can probably guess...* And of course all the uppety girls would be turned off by the name Anzures because they had no idea where that neighborhood was. Venturing so far from the Jewish neighborhood seemed crazy to them, and they obviously preferred to be invited to VIPS on Palmas Avenue or a restaurant in Polanco. Before ever going out, they had already given him his walking papers. And Musa ended up staying at home, locked into a routine that allowed him to avoid social activities. We all wondered why Abram was so outgoing and Musa such a hermit.

Musa had done his high school studies at Preparatoria 3, the one on San Ildefonso Street that was famous for its Diego Rivera murals and the poets who had studied and taught there, although that didn't mean anything to Papá and Mamá. Musa would go to the store on Honduras Street in the morning, and in the afternoon he only had to walk a few blocks to school. During that time, encouraged by Abram, he began to learn how to play the trumpet. They used to talk about jazz and get excited listening to the casettes that were sent by his European friends. Musa was a dedicated student and his instructors were always so impressed that they wanted him to specialize in their field, which was very confusing to him because he didn't know whether to follow the advice of the teacher of mathematics, biology, literature, or philosophy.

Before choosing a career, Musa decided to go to a kibbutz but didn't want to attend the Shomer, so he consulted Abram on every detail. He secretly prepared for his trip, carefully planning everything, even what clothes to take, and saving every dime that Mamá paid him for working at the store. He calculated that after a year and a half he would have enough to pay for half his ticket, plus two hundred dollars for emergencies. He convinced the Jewish agency to pay for the rest of his ticket, declaring that he was going as an immigrant. The Soḥnut also found him a kibbutz that offered training in Hebrew at the Ulpan at the time he wanted to make the trip. All he had to do was convince Papá and Mamá to let him go before he was eighteen; the men of the Soḥnut had told him that their permission was absolutely necessary. So as not to prolong the battle, he let them know just three weeks before his trip; Papá and Mamá were probably expecting it because they didn't put up a big fuss like they did with Abram and Saqui. *Oh, Musa, we've suffered so much. Please reconsider, hijo, we don't want you to go.* Of course Mamá started to cry, but rather than an attempt to blackmail him, her tears were proof that she was just as sad to see him go as she was with her other sons; nevertheless, after a couple of days, Musa had the necessary signatures on his papers.

With intermediate stops, it took him two days to get as far as New York, where he suddenly felt lonely. It was mid-December and he trudged down the streets, freezing his butt off, not knowing where to go or what to do. When he made it to Israel he was taken aback by the customs officials' harsh treatment of him. They made him wait seven hours before allowing him to be taken to the kibbutz. As soon as he was assigned a room he fell into bed, exhausted by the journey, only to be disturbed two hours later by the shouts of an Australian who had lived in Brazil, who was furiously complaining about being given a Mexican roommate. In Musa's mind, Abram's wonderful stories about making friends with people from all over the world had created a marvelous house of cards, which came tumbling down around his dreams as the Aussie's temper tantrum shook him out of a deep sleep. After three weeks of protesting every day in the administrative office, Musa managed to get transferred to the room of a Guatemalan with whom nobody wanted to live. He was a corpulent fellow who spent his time smoking marijuana or hashish, and he sometimes became aggressive without warning. Even so, Musa liked him; they relaxed together, speaking Spanish and making fun of the others. Seeing them always together, people labeled them as a couple of troublemakers who had to be watched. Within a month, they called Musa to the office to tell him that he had to leave the kibbutz because of his drug use. No matter how much he insisted that he had never even tried any drugs, he couldn't convince the director of the Ulpan. Consequently, Musa was banished to a kibbutz without an Ulpan in the Negev Desert, where he was forced to work eight hours a day during his first month, instead of the usual six hours assigned to volunteers. Laboring in the debilitating heat of the desert, Musa's resentment grew as his backache became more severe from bending over to dig out weeds with a trowel that was totally inadequate for the job. All he could do in the evening was flop on his bed and try to sleep; he had no idea how long this situation was going to last, or how long he could bear it.

One day the Guatemalan came to visit and gave him some marijuana in a padded envelope plastered with stamps from Central America. *My friends sent me a lot of weed, but you can keep the whole wad; I've decided to go back home because I'm tired of them breaking my balls all the time.* A week later, Musa decided to smoke a little to see how it felt, but since he didn't want to experiment alone, he shared some with Harry Weiner, a friendly New Yorker who had offered him hashish when he had just arrived. Harry put on Pink Floyd music and explained how to inhale deeply and hold it in to get high. Musa was thrilled by the experience, and before he knew it, he had a small club that met in his room every Friday night to get stoned. The new friends, however, disappeared as soon as the pot had all gone up in smoke.

When summer arrived and the heat became unbearable, Musa decided to abandon the kibbutz and tour around Europe, following Abram's advice to travel from house to house, visiting friends he had met in Israel. But things didn't go well for him. He called on people who hardly remembered him; some made up excuses for not accommodating him (*we're painting the house* or *we've got other visitors this week*) and others claimed they were too busy to help. Even though he slept in train stations to avoid spending money on hotels, in a month and a half he was almost broke. He thought that the only way he could stay longer in Europe was to look for work. After a week of going door to door, he managed to get a job in a hotel in Basel, Switzerland, where the other workers were Turks, Yugoslavians, Italians and Spaniards. They let him sleep in a room in the basement and he never missed a meal for the employees. *This time,* he told himself, *at least I'm going to earn a salary.* He saved every cent he could; the only luxury he allowed himself was going every two weeks to a bar where jazz groups played. Sitting there alone, he despaired at not being able to share the moment with anybody.

One day in the early morning hours, he heard soft knocking on his door. It was Erika, the daughter of the hotel owners, who came to ask him to turn down the volume on his radio. Feeling confused, he offered an apology. In a rapid exchange of looks, Musa realized that Erika had come for something else. He hesitated, and before he could muster his courage, she was already kissing him. Musa didn't feel attracted to Erika because she was too strong and he was turned off by her hard muscles. Before leaving, she said with a laugh that she wanted to experiment with sex before getting married. He found out the next day that Erika had just become engaged to a bank executive. He was afraid their secret would be revealed, there would be a scandal, and he'd be deported or at least fired. Luckily, after three weeks the sex had become routine, no matter how creative Erika tried to be. Musa went back to being lonely and depressed. He figured that he had to work two more months to be able to travel through the rest of Europe.

When his departure date was near, he met Amy Burns, a girl from Chicago who lived in Switzerland as an exchange student. She was petite, with delicate features. They started chatting in the jazz bar, and stayed until closing time. It was the first time he had met somebody he really liked, so he was happy when Amy agreed to continue the conversation at the hotel where he worked. Erika saw them enter from her perch at the window, and before they could get comfortable, the watchman had intervened. The next day, the owners fired Musa, claiming that they had warned him from the beginning that having women in the room was forbidden. Musa asked to stay one more week so he could collect his salary for the whole month. Since Amy slept in a women's dorm, their only recourse was to spend the week kissing in the parks. Before leaving Basel, Musa invited her to spend the night in a different hotel. After anxiously awaiting the evening, they devoted the entire night to lovemaking, intensified by the imminent separation.

Upon returning to Mexico, Musa decided to continue with trumpet classes at the Conservatory. He took everything out of the storage room in the garage and turned it into a music studio, covering the walls with egg cartons to improve the acoustics, and thus created his own space where nobody bothered him and he didn't bother anybody else. He spent every night there, practicing until one in the morning or listening to jazz until he fell asleep on a mattress he had dragged in there. Papá tried to warn him, *hijo, you can play music as a hobby, but you need to find a real job. I know what I'm saying, believe me, you're going to starve to death; besides, the life of a musician is not right for you.* Papá's warning did not fall on deaf ears, but rather on the fine-tuned ear of a musician. Musa got it into his head that he wanted to form a free jazz group and with some effort he managed to incorporate people who played various instruments: bass, clarinet, sax, violin, piano, guitar, drums and Mexican percussion instruments. They took the name "Pasos en la azotea" (Footsteps on the Roof). He managed to find a rehearsal hall, but their practices were half-hearted because there was always somebody missing. After a while, the group fell apart.

Julio Vélez, the saxophone player, suggested to Musa that it would be cool to get together now and then to listen to jazz. Musa invited him to the storage room. With no forewarning, Julio showed up with several peyote buttons. He explained that you had to eat the entire button in order to have hallucinations. Impulsively, Musa took a bite and began to chew; he choked on the bitter taste and felt like he was going to vomit, but made a concerted effort and kept chewing until he had swallowed all the cloves of the button. In a short time, he began to have an intense hallucination, with astonishing clarity. It was like entering another reality, which he could perceive with all of his senses. They played their instruments and listened to music, enraptured by each note, in absolute delirium. The trip lasted all night. The next day, he woke up early and went running in Chapultepec Park. He didn't understand why he wasn't tired: after circling the park three times, he still had enough energy to keep going, but preferred to go home and play the trumpet. The saxophonist had left him a note in the storage room: "That was awesome. I left you a little gift. Hasta la vista." Musa was excited to see the nine peyote buttons spread out on a side table next to the mouthpieces for his trumpet.

He spent the following days in solitary rapture, eating one peyote button every twenty-four hours, going up to the house only to get more cassettes and returning immediately to the storage room to bask in the music of Ornette Coleman, Cecil Taylor, Miles Davis, Don Cherry or Anthony Braxton.

One afternoon Papá insisted, *come have dinner with me, hijo; Concha is going to make pita bread with cheese and avocado.* Musa didn't understand where we had all gone and why Papá was left alone. Even though he preferred not to eat so that the hallucination would be more intense, that night he stayed in Papá's room, gazing out the window at the sky. Musa could hear the neighbors' dog barking, and was infuriated by the piercing sound. *That damn dog, why doesn't he shut up?* Papá kept talking and talking, but Musa was in a daze and didn't even try to follow the conversation. Instead, he baffled Papá with his comments, *have you noticed the sky?, it's red; no, not red, maybe maroon; or violet? The clouds are stretching out and a ring of stars is shining through them.* Papá saw Musa grasping at the air as if he wanted to catch a fly. *Grab the newspaper and swat it...* But Musa turned to look at Papá and declared, *the moon is ripe for the picking, like a shiny honeydew melon, but it slips through my hands,* and then he burst into uncontrollable laughter. In spite of Musa's strange behavior, Papá was happy to hang out with one of us, especially because he often felt excluded from the intimate relationship we shared with Mamá.

Musa signed up to study modern dance at the Casa del Lago. At first he went one hour a day, but soon he was staying all afternoon, trying to learn new moves and exercise better control over his body. After a month, seeing that he took dance very seriously, the teacher suggested that he join the Independent Ballet of Mexico. Even though most of the members of the company had been dancing for years, Musa wasn't one to be intimidated, and he began practicing with tremendous discipline. He became so obsessed with the idea of being a professional dancer that he started to wonder if he should quit the trumpet and the Conservatory. He decided to stick with both for a while, until he could make up his mind. His day was very structured: he'd go running in Chapultepec at six in the morning; around nine he'd go to the Conservatory; later he'd return home to eat and at four he'd go practice with the ballet company. At night he would practice the trumpet a bit and listen to free jazz. He'd eat a peyote button, wait exactly twenty minutes and then take a toke on a joint to intensify the hallucinogen. Needless to say, he couldn't keep up that routine for very long. Mamá got tired of giving him money, and told him to find a job. He had no choice but to go work at Jaime and Fule's factory, where his job was to fill the orders; he worked out a very efficient system that allowed him to finish everything by about one o'clock. Since he didn't have anything else to do, he'd abandon the factory without saying a word, and go to the dance company practices. Jaime and Fule would scold him vehemently, *you're an employee here and you can't leave until we give you permission. You have to be on the ball all the time, that's why we hired you. Don't blow it! You've got to give up all that music-and-dance nonsense and settle down to work, like decent people do.* Musa defended himself, *you hired me to fill the orders and I always finish my work, without fail. I'm not going to be stuck here like an idiot all day, with nothing to do. Dance and music are my lifeline and you can't change that.*

As could be expected, after three months Musa decided to look for work on his own. His trumpet teacher suggested that he join a symphonic band, for starters; he got hired as the third trumpet in the Naucalpan Symphonic Band. He was surprised not to see anybody from the Conservatory playing wind instruments. It was depressing to think that even in music there were political games and cronyism. Not much time had passed when the director called him to his office and said their budget had been cut and he had to fire him. Thus, Musa bounced between different bands and orchestras every six months or so; from the Naucalpan band he went on to the Poli and then to the Cuauhtémoc delegation.

One day, Julio Vélez, the saxophonist, invited him to take a trip to San Luis Potosí. *It will be a wild trip, mano; we're going to a town called La Maroma, south of Real de Catorce; it's right on the Tropic of Cancer, and June 21 is the perfect day to see more stars than you've ever seen before. I know where to find peyote and we can play music in the desert every day: there's absolute silence, it's incredible!* Musa took the bait, as did another friend that Julio invited, Lázaro Vives. They brought provisions in a backpack: dried fruit, nuts, canned goods and several bottles of water. A señora from the town knew Julio and they had arranged to make a trade: Julio would give her some of the canned goods and fruit in exchange for tortillas, beans, and nopalitos made from the local cactus. They spent four carefree days eating peyote and playing music in the middle of the desert, with no interruptions. Musa felt that he had reached a hypnotic state in which only the world of sound existed. The notes he played resonated in the desert air, soaring off on their own, returning now and then to intertwine with the melody lines his friends were creating. They had brought two boom boxes to play John Coltrane's album *Interstellar Space*, which they listened to endlessly, sometimes playing their instruments and imbedding their improvisations into Coltrane's music. Sometimes they felt like playing each of the planets according to the moment: Mars at midday, Jupiter in the afternoon, Saturn at dusk, and Venus at the spellbinding hour of midnight. With the other tape player they recorded themselves jamming with Coltrane, then listened to their recording when they were tired. One day at dawn, while they were listening to the previous evening's jam session, a bird approached and sang during the pauses of the trumpet solo, establishing a dialogue so fresh and intriguing that it gave them goose bumps. They grabbed their instruments and began to play again. They played for hours and hours, tirelessly, until their instruments morphed into appendages of their bodies. Any dissonance between them melted into harmony, and soon they had the sensation that the whole world was vibrating with one spirit. The realm of the unconscious was revealed in all its truth, without masks or deceptive appearances. They contemplated each other with fascination as their bodies evaporated and only their souls existed as they sang in unison and in tune with the magical atmosphere of the desert. When they were totally exhausted, they lay down on the sand. After a long silence, Julio whispered, *we've tapped into the mystical power of music.*

Two days later, they had to pack up and go home early because Lázaro had decided to take a drink from a bottle that the señora from town had given them, even though Julio had warned him, *don't drink that water, it's full of amoebas.* They had to rush him to a hospital in Mexico City. Lázaro survived the adventure, but he was so alarmed by what happened to him that he swore off peyote and marijuana for good.

Three years after coming back from Europe, Musa received a letter from Amy, the girl from Chicago he had met in Switzerland; she was desperate to escape the winter storms and had decided to spend a week in Mexico. When she learned of the impending visit, Mamá asked him if she was Jewish. He fudged a bit as he answered, *I think she's ashkenazi.* Papá had his reservations, too, *where's she going to sleep? The storage room is really cold and she could get sick.* Even though Musa had been forced to change the carpet remnants in the storage space several times because of rot from the humidity, he answered confidently, *that's not a problem; I bought an electric heater and now it's more comfortable.* Amy had trouble recognizing Musa at the airport. *I'm sorry. I only saw you for a week, and I didn't have any pictures of you.* He didn't remember that she had moles on her neck, but that didn't diminish his joy. Tired from her journey, Amy tried to evade Musa's advances when she arrived at the house. She was irritated because she didn't understand why it was cold in Mexico, and had never imagined that the house in Tecamachalco would be freezing. They spent the rest of the afternoon listening to the new cassettes that Musa had bought the previous week. She was surprised that Musa was still so obsessed with free jazz. That night Musa introduced her to us. Amy was astonished that there were so many of us, *oh, my God, you all look alike.* Even though Mamá didn't know English, she managed to ferret out the important information with Saqui's help, *she says her mother is Jewish, from New York, but her father's family was Irish Catholic. She grew up without knowing anything about religion, but she's becoming more and more interested.* Amy thought it was strange that Papá and Mamá spoke Arabic to each other, even though we were Jewish. *It's Hanukkah. Aren't you guys going to celebrate? No,* replied Jaime, *that's something you gringos made up. Hanukkah is a minor fiesta; only the most religious families light candles for it. Here it's no big deal.*

At ten p.m., Mamá asked Saqui to translate for her, *we're going to eat quesadillas at a stand next to the supermarket. Tell her they can make them with mushrooms, cheese, pepper slices, potatoes, huitlacoche and squash flowers. They're kosher because they don't use meat at that stand.* We all went except Papá, who thought that eating while standing was a vulgarity that should be avoided at all cost. Finally one of Amy's expectations for her trip was met, *this is delicious! Please, order two more mushroom and cheese tostadas!* Later, she blew up when she found out she was supposed to sleep in the storage room. *Forget it! Take me to a hotel; I'm not going to sleep in that shithole! It's fucking freezing in there!* No matter how much Musa insisted that the electric heater was very efficient, he wasn't able to soften her resolve; she finally agreed to stay at the house, but in the living room, not the storage area. The next day, he followed Amy around like a deer in rut, but her bad mood thwarted any intimacy. Musa was confused; he thought she had come to sleep with him and have a good time. Irritated by his persistence, she finally explained so he would leave her alone, *I'm having my period, okay, so just wait three more days.* Two days later, Musa received a call from a Frenchman who was at the airport and said they had met at the kibbutz in the Negev desert. Although Musa didn't remember him, he was happy to put up the foreigner in the storage room. When he arrived, Musa recognized him immediately: he had long, stiff hair that looked like hay, his beard was dirty and tangled, and he had the same lost look of the guy who came to his room in search of marijuana. Mamá was shocked when she laid eyes on him, and said to Musa, thinking the Frenchman wouldn't understand anything, *what's wrong with you?! You can't bring home drug addicts or bums; this isn't a hotel!, understand?!* The foreigner interjected with rudimentary Spanish that he only wished for permission to spend one night at the house.

The next day, before going to the Conservatory, Musa told Amy he would be back in the afternoon; on his way out he stopped at the storage room to say good-bye to the Frenchman. When he arrived at the Conservatory, he wondered why nobody was there; but then he saw that the room where he usually practiced was locked, and he remembered that it was December 12th, the day of the Virgin of Guadalupe. He went home, excited that he was going to see Amy earlier than expected. From the street he could hear loud music coming from the storage area. By that time, the Frenchman should have left already, so he thought, with relief, that Amy had finally rediscovered jazz. He opened the door, hoping to resume the joyous relationship that had been interrupted in Switzerland. But the first thing he saw was the Frenchman's body heaving up and down; then, from underneath, Amy's face peered out at him. Frozen in his tracks, Musa barely managed to shout, *get out!, out!, out!* The Frenchman wasn't even bothered, but Amy, on the other hand, reacted violently, *you've been hassling me every day!, fucking asshole!* When they left, Musa noticed they had eaten a peyote button. He recalled the definitions that Julio Vélez, the saxophonist, had offered him: *peyote is the root of the devil; mushrooms are the blood of the gods.*

Instead of practicing the trumpet that day, Musa ate a couple of peyote buttons, choosing the two largest ones. In contrast to the pleasant hallucinations he usually enjoyed, this trip went bad, as he sunk deeper and deeper into his anger. Music seemed to stoke his fury; he whirled around, striking the wall with his fists until they began to bleed. Feeling disoriented, he went running aimlessly through Tecamachalco. That week the Symphonic Orchestra in which he played had planned a tour in the state of Sinaloa. Musa got on the bus for the musicians and organizers, and found a seat in back, next to a percussionist that he had chatted with a few times. The drummer took out a bottle of tequila and passed it around the back rows. When they arrived in Sinaloa, the first trumpet, a young man from Guerrero nicknamed El Niño, got feisty with Musa, *hey, dude, let's get something straight: when the tour is over, you take your sorry ass and go play for another orchestra. I gotta clear the deck for my pal Ignacio.* Later one of the flutists consoled him, *don't sweat it, buddy, he's drunk; El Niño's like that: he gets riled up sometimes, but he'll be over it tomorrow; he's okay when he's sober.* Musa was so wasted that he couldn't see straight. He stumbled to the bathroom and vomited his insides out. Then it occurred to him that perhaps a peyote button would smooth out the bad vibes. He invited the trombonist and the clarinet player, with whom he was sharing a room, to go play music with him in the outdoors, to commune with the earth and sky. They just laughed at him, *You're crazy! We're staying here, but if you go, watch out for stray dogs!* Musa wolfed down two peyote buttons, hoping that the hallucinogen would calm his nerves.

When he returned to the room two hours later, he noticed that one of his roommates was in the bathroom. He lay down with his eyes wide open, unable to sleep. Ten minutes later, he was startled to see El Niño himself coming out of the bathroom. Gripped with fear, Musa rushed out of the room, thinking he was going to be killed. It occurred to him that his life was in danger as long as he was near Guasave, the town where the orchestra was staying. He ran all night as if his life depended on it, sticking to the shoulder of the highway, but not knowing where he was headed. At dawn, he stopped at a stand to buy water; his legs were shaking with fatigue and he couldn't hold them still. He saw a sign with the name Guamúchil; he couldn't remember the route the orchestra was taking, so he was afraid that this town would be their next stop. It didn't surprise him that he was still tripping, even though many hours had passed. He decided to keep walking until he found a smaller town where he could sleep a while, but no matter how long he walked, he could not feel comfortable in any of the places he saw. When his legs refused to take another step, he lay down to sleep under a tree at the side of the highway. Upon awakening, he was alarmed once more by the thought that they might be coming after him with intent to kill, and he began to run again. With the few pesos he had in his pocket he ate at the roadside stands, but immediately continued walking or running. He arrived at Culiacán on December 24, after eight days of not knowing where he was. With no money left, all he could do was call Mamá and ask her to send him a plane ticket so he could come home. Since the police had told her that Musa might have been kidnapped, she had been beside herself with worry. Musa could hardly understand her harsh words, punctuated by wails and sobs, *where the hell have you been?!, why didn't you call us?!*

When he arrived at the airport, Musa had trouble recognizing Saqui and Mamá. He thought El Niño might have disguised himself as Saqui, so he could kill him. At home he seemed to be following the conversation, but then he would suddenly cut us off and disappear to the storage room, where he would sit down to cry, *God, if you exist and have given me life, I promise that I will never touch peyote again.* Then he would imagine that we were all hit men masquerading as his brothers; he would only eat after someone tasted his food, for fear of being poisoned. He had delusions of having to die so he could accompany Raquel in Heaven. Then it occurred to him that our names were creating rhymes that sentenced him to death: *Jaime: he'll tie me; Fule: he'll fool me; Beni: can he?; Daveed: I'll plead; Saqui: he's cocky; Abram: wham, bam!* He was being persecuted by sounds; the names of the towns in Sinaloa became twisted in his mind: *Guasave: what say he?; Guamúchil: watch you chill!; Culiacán: Who's a con?* He recalled that in our religion, when someone is threatened by death, it is customary to change his name to save his life; he decided that we should call him Samuel. Mamá replied with a nervous laugh, *you've got to be kidding!* In his delirium, Musa believed he was Jesus Christ, destined to be crucified.

On his birthday, January 25, Musa woke up in the storage room, covered in sweat. His fever had broken and he realized immediately that the hallucinations had passed. His friends Julio and Lázaro called him to ask if he wanted to get together with them to play music. He told them everything and resolved to stop taking drugs, cold turkey. The next day, Lázaro encouraged him to go to the Hare Krishna temple, *thanks to them, my life is on track; I've finally found true meaning and spirituality.* Upon entering the temple, Musa hesitated, wondering if he should bow to the two deities represented there; *well,* he thought, *it couldn't hurt anything.* He remembered the karate classes he had as a teenager and the meditations they did before starting to work out. Kneeling down, he lowered his head to the floor; he closed his eyes for a few minutes and tried to relax. Afterwards, he entered a room where everyone was singing joyfully. Within ten minutes he had identified the words. Lázaro tried to explain, *this is a mantra that you have to repeat in order to liberate the kundalini.* Noticing that Musa didn't understand, he added, *the kundalini is the coiled serpent: the vital energy that must be awoken.* Later, Musa sang with the others, *"Hare-Krishna, Hare-Krishna, Krishna-Krishna, Hare-Hare, Hare-Rama, Hare-Rama, Rama-Rama, Hare-Hare". If you repeat this all day long, you'll liberate yourself from the material world and access the spiritual world and God. Every day you should say the mantra, completing 108 cycles of 16 repetitions each, for a total of 1728 times. With the mantra you create a sonorous vibration which allows you to feel closer to God. Moreover, since the last word you utter before you die decides the path of your future life, if you have the habit of saying the mantra, it's likely that word will be Krishna, so Krishna is where you will go.*

Later, the guru gave a lecture, which Musa thought was enlightening. Afterwards he was so fired up about the idea of a more spiritual life that he decided to learn yoga in order to assimilate more completely into that world; thus he gave up dancing, believing he had started too late in life anyway, and would never become a first-rate performer. Accustomed as he was to discipline, it wasn't difficult for him to adjust to the new regimen. He resolved to follow the religion's rules: don't eat meat, seafood, or eggs; don't gamble; don't become intoxicated by alcohol, drugs, tobacco or coffee; don't have illicit sexual affairs; recite as much as possible the mantra of the Hare-Krishna. Mamá had a hard time accepting the fact that Musa had become a vegetarian. *You have to eat well: meat, eggs, chicken; you're crazy, you're going to become malnourished. Hijo, you're so skinny; you look anemic.* Musa was very stubborn, and he wouldn't even let them put chicken broth on his rice. *You're acting like a health inspector, following us around the kitchen; you're worse than a rabbi, making sure everything's kosher.* On Fridays, for him, they had to stuff the grape leaves and squash with just rice. Mamá wouldn't let him be, *come on, hijo, eat the bacha kibbe: I made it especially for you; remember how you loved this when you were a boy?* Musa was learning to cook for himself; he bought semola and various spices from India and he served himself heaping helpings of food that looked very unappetizing to the rest of us. Exasperated, Papá would say, *you're just like a horse, eating a bunch of alfalfa; all you need is a feedbag!*

Musa had begun to run long distances, and Chapultepec seemed too small for him now; he preferred to go to the forest at the Desierto de los Leones. After six months, he managed to get a break from the trainer of the Olympic marathon team that trained there. Musa told us enthusiastically, *I'm training with the second string of the Mexican team; I might get to go to the Olympic Games in Korea!* By then, Jaime and Fule had gotten married, Abram was living with Alicia, and Saqui had just gone to Austin to work on a doctorate in Mexican history. Musa finally had his own room in our house. Encouraged by his teachers at the Conservatory and by his newfound privacy, he bought a piano, which he kept covered with a blanket. He would lock himself in his room and play free jazz, trying to sound like Cecil Taylor. One day he confided to Abram that sometimes after running twelve miles in the Desierto de los Leones, he would climb to the top of the mountain, assume a yoga pose, meditate a while, and then without changing position, begin to play the trumpet, trying to vibrate with the music and believing that with each note he was drawing closer to the name and representation of Krishna.

Ten years after the Sinaloa fiasco, the house was almost empty; Papá had been diagnosed with advanced emphysema and Mamá had moved into the room that used to belong to David and Beni. Gradually, Musa and Papá had learned to get along better. Musa was the only one who pampered Papá and did favors for him, even when the rest of us objected. Musa no longer ate dinner with the family on Sunday, the only day of the week that he varied his routine: yoga occupied him for most of the morning, then he went with Lázaro to a vegetarian restaurant and from there to the temple of the Hare-Krishnas. One Sunday he met Margarita Rosas, a young woman from Guadalajara who had just moved to the city with her parents. Impressed by her delicate manners, he asked her parents' permission to take her out to eat. They had been devoted to the Hare Krishnas for twenty years and were pleased that someone of the same faith wanted to date their daughter. Since the university was on strike, she began to visit him in the storage room almost every day. At first Musa controlled his emotion and they just listened to music; but eventually, moved by her tenderness, he began to kiss and then to caress her. He was surprised by the affectionate way in which she responded, which was a new experience for him. Within six months, just as Papá suffered his worst crisis, Musa discovered that he was in love. Dreading the prospect of fighting with his family, he decided not to propose marriage until Papá came home from the hospital and his condition had stabilized. The Sunday of August 11, 1996, two days before Papá's birthday, Musa and Margarita got together in the storage room to listen to music. Soon, feeling the urgent magnetism of their bodies, they went beyond their usual caresses and made love, whispering the mantra in each other's ears and feeling as if they were levitating, being transported by a sublime force. Nevertheless, a few days later Margarita coldly announced, *either you marry me or you'll never see me again.* Musa didn't have time to react because that Sunday Papá had another serious complication, from which he would not recover.

Now, sitting on his cushion, Musa was tortured not only by Papá's death, but also by his separation from Margarita. He wondered if he should follow his heart and marry her, or respect his family's mourning period and renounce his love. Ḥakham Rayek had been talking in the living room for more than half an hour, but Musa hadn't paid attention to anything he said. Afterwards, Musa approached him and asked to speak with him alone. In spite of his surprise at the request, the rabbi agreed. Pinning his hopes on the ḥakham's reputation as a modern leader, Musa dared to reveal his secrets and ask for advice. As he poured out his whole life's story, not sparing any details, the rabbi's eyes opened wide with obvious consternation. *However, ḥakham,* Musa hastened to clarify, *the Hare-Krishnas don't mind if someone follows his own religion, as long as he shows devotion to Krishna...* When Musa faltered, the rabbi began to speak slowly and emphatically, *in the first place, you are Jewish and your obligation is to your people. You have disobeyed the first commandment which, as you should know, is the foundation of our religion. As if that weren't enough, now you want to trample the honor and respect that your parents deserve. But, barukh hashem, barukh hashem, you have come to me right before Yom Kippur. And I'm telling you that there's still time to do teshuvah and repent of all your sins. These are the most sacred days and God put me in your path so you would remember him. You have to abandon that temple with idols immediately, for that is a great sin, and forget about that young woman. I am going to lead you down the road to goodness. You must promise to obey my orders, and I will promise to help you get out of this mess.* Musa decided to defend himself for once, instead of just going with the flow. *Ḥakham, I would like to comment on various things that you just said; yes, I am a Jew, but I am also a human being. Some Jews follow tradition and others may find God through love, music, or yoga. Now then, just as you claim that hashem put you in my path, I could say that hashem also put this young woman in my path, and I have fallen in love with her. "Death and love, both come from above," as the saying goes, so why didn't God rule out this relationship, if that is his will? I love God and believe I am a good human being and a good Jew. I don't see anything wrong with climbing a mountain, assuming a yoga pose, playing music and communing with the divine.* The ḥakham was not used to anybody questioning his words, and he began to get angry even though he continued to speak calmly, *the only way to be a good Jew is by following the principles of the Torah and its mitzvot. Hashem did not put anywhere in the Torah that you should do yoga or chant mantras in order to reach him. The only way to be sure he is listening to us is to obey his commandments, and you are not doing that. Think it over carefully: if you marry a goy, you're going to provoke a great tragedy in your family; your children will not be yehudim, you'll abandon your tradition, and you'll be ostracized from the community forever. Hashem has given us free will so we can make the right choices; perhaps hashem put this girl in front of you as a test. You must carefully consider your actions and their consequences: your papá has just died, may he rest in peace, and this is the time of year to do teshuvah. The circumstances that hashem has chosen are very clear. There are many yehudim who justify their disrespect of the commandments by alluding to secular ideas, which offer false shelter for impious acts. Such yehudim live comfortable lives, not bothering to make any effort. They will never cease to be Jews, but we must always remind them that we are only here briefly, our true life is in the*

Olam haba: there we will have comforts, but first we have to answer to hashem, who is the supreme judge, as it is written. The ḥakham was getting ready to leave when he realized that Musa had not yet surrendered to his wisdom, *ḥakham, I appreciate your answering me so calmly, but I still have something to say. First of all, I don't live a comfortable life. I get up at six in the morning, run for almost two hours, then go practice with the orchestra; I don't stop all day: after rehearsal I come home to practice the trumpet and piano until eleven at night, read for half an hour, and go to sleep. If, as you say, only hashem has the right to judge, then why are you criticizing my secularism? Besides, I think that in the daily prayer book it says we should praise God; well I do that in my own way, with love, happiness, and music. And finally, I might add that I have known Jews who never married and seem unhappy, or they're divorced from Jewish women and never re-married and they seem unhappy, too. There are also Jews who think they are observing religion to the letter, but they're not happy, or they beat their wives or con innocent people out of their money. It's not my place to judge them, but I'm just saying that we're all being tested, not just those of us who are secular. I'm not a thief or an assassin or a rapist or any other kind of criminal. My transgression is not observing Shabbat, although I try to rest on that day, in my own way. If I decide to marry her, maybe that will make Mamá sad and disturb Papá's soul, but that's why I'm uncertain. I love this woman and I also love my parents and God. Why should I have to choose?* The ḥakham was completely exasperated and unwilling to listen any more, *all I can say before I leave is that you should not marry that girl. It would be a serious mistake. Don't let yourself be influenced by your fleeting desires of the moment; think of the eternal life that will be yours before you know it. Don't be childish and follow your whim; grow up and recognize the reward that awaits you. I wish with all my heart that hashem will illuminate for you the righteous path, so you will make the right decision. You must not defile your father's memory.*

Struggling to suppress the rage that was distorting his face, the rabbi quickly left the room. He refused a cup of coffee that was offered to him, and strode out without bidding farewell to anybody. We all wondered what Musa had said to provoke such anger. During lunch, Mamá besieged him with questions, but Musa clammed up and didn't reveal a thing. Afterwards, at about four o'clock in the afternoon, Musa was pleased to greet Natán Zarfati, a yoga guru that he had met at the Hare-Krishna temple. When Zarfati and Musa went up to his room, Fule revealed to Jaime and Mamá, *I know that guy; he goes to the Deportivo in the mornings and does yoga exercises in front of the pool. He never talks to anybody. He puts on some sheets, hindu style, and begins to breathe deeply as if he were crazy. They say he went to India and came back a lunatic.*

Natán sat on the rug with his legs crossed; Musa decided to ask his advice, *for a year now I've been going out with Margarita, the daughter of Mr. and Mrs. Flores. A month ago we had sex and from that day on she's refused to go out with me, and just before my papá died she told me she hadn't had her period. I'm afraid she might be pregnant. But you know how the ḥakhamim are, and the rest of our community; if I marry her, there will be a big scandal, and I feel really confused because my papá has just passed away.* Natán listened to him with his eyes closed, concentrating on each and every word. Afterwards, he started talking about the most important concepts regarding the process of enlightenment. He talked endlessly, but didn't seem to get to the point of responding to Musa's concerns. Here and there, Musa managed to grasp the essence of his answer, *...we are all influenced from conception by the planets and stars; in the womb we are gradually formed according to their forces. Jupiter gives heat and humidity, the sun gives energy so the heart may be born, Venus reigns while we acquire our sex organs. Your dilemma might be caused by the karma you got from a star. You have to assimilate your* *fate and learn to accept that the galaxies are influencing your destiny. You must practice certain exercises so you can pay attention to the chakra produced by the emanation from a particular planet. You have to learn to vibrate in unison with the stars, creating cosmic unity, but in order to do that you must liberate your body from the corresponding chakra. Once you accomplish this, you will be surrounded by light and you will radiate like a star.* Musa tried several times to pin him down, *for sure, mano, but what does this all mean?, should I get married?, should I go against my parents' wishes?* But rather than give him a direct answer, Natán continued to speak elliptically, *have you noticed that the star of David is made of two triangles?, one points upward and represents the macro cosmos, and one points downward and signifies the micro cosmos. It is the perfect equilibrium of everything, including the dimensions of space and time, the spiritualization of matter and the materialization of the spirit. If we analyze it according to the Vedic perspective, we would have Shiva pointing upward, representing the transformation, the body that becomes spirit, and Shakti pointing downward, signifying the opposite, the spirit that comes down and materializes. Examine, also, the tree of the Sephirot of the Kabbalah, and you will see there are three upper emanations and seven lower ones. The ten emanations combine with the 22 letters to form the 32 ways of wisdom. Likewise, the 33 consonants and the 16 vowels of the Sanskrit alphabet are situated on the 50 petals of the 7 chakras (one letter is repeated to complete the number); each chakra carries out the multiplication of 7 times 7, in order to interconnect one with the other, just like what occurs with the cabalistic tree. We don't limit ourselves to one alphabet, we use two; everything serves us in our spiritual search. As we free ourselves of the material world and try to purify our bodies, we also try to dress ourselves with the tunics of humility and grace that represent the wisdom of different religions.* As Natán rattled on and on, Musa didn't dare interrupt him. Finally, Mamá knocked on the door and came in, *excuse me...Musa, we have to go to the knis for the darush... maybe your friend would like to go with us...* When Natán left, Mamá warned Musa, *watch out for that guy, they say he's nuts; more than twenty years ago he left his wife and children. His family was loaded with money, but he just threw it all away and went on a trip. They didn't hear anything from him until he finally returned with his crazy notions, dressed in sheets and huarache sandals. Don't let him put ideas in your head, understand?!*

When we arrived at the knis, Jaime instructed the rest of us, *keep an eye out for the ratero, but try to stay calm.* We sat down in the third row. Saqui was ready to punch Azra in the face; his hand was gnarled up in a fist so tight that it hurt; he could just imagine smashing that guy's face, right in the knis. Just then Tío León walked in, with his three sons parading behind him as if they were bodyguards. He also was accompanied by Tía Rosa, Tía Pola and Terri, but at the entrance they had separated from him to go sit with the women. Jaime stood up and greeted him enthusiastically. The rest of us popped up as if we were on springs; Abram even gave him a kiss on the cheek. Surprised at our show of affection, Tío León turned to look at his sons with disbelief. As we embraced him, we were watching the entrance to see if the ratero appeared. Saqui muttered mockingly, *he's a coward; he's not going to come.*

We stared at the golden lions and the large Hebrew letters of the Ten Commandments. When the shammash opened the doors to let in some air, we felt a gust of wind and smelled the scent of rain that had been threatening to fall since morning. The señoras were sitting up front on the left, as they did for weddings; Mamá didn't have the strength to climb the stairs. David had said, *stay down here, the shammash won't say anything. If it's okay for weddings, why not now?* We hadn't worried about it until we heard the shammash arguing vehemently with Salomón Amiga, and saw the shammash's face turn red as he struggled to be polite, *señoras, we beg of you with all due respect, please go upstairs; the ḥakhamim cannot recite the prayers.* Salomón intervened to clarify for some of the older ladies, *if any of you have difficulty climbing stairs, please sit in the back.* Mamá's sisters said angrily, *don't pay any attention to him, Rebeca, we'll stay down here with you; he can have a fit, but we're not moving.*

After a while, Rabbi Aarón Levi took the microphone; his voice echoed against the high ceiling so much that sometimes we could hardly understand what he was saying, but after a while we adjusted, and could follow his words:

The custom of saying the ereye, a speech which is given in memory of the deceased, is established by the ḥakhamim as a way of advocating for the dead and emphasizing his virtues so that his soul will be elevated, and the words said in his favor will be heard in heaven. There is not the slightest doubt that Señor Simón must be on high, because he never harmed anyone and always demonstrated his good and noble sentiments. Although his body suffered, it does not suffer anymore and his soul is rejoicing. He no longer has to endure the maladies and limitations that plagued his body, which is only the soul's temporary shelter; when the soul leaves the body, it is liberated from all limitations. Now his soul is truly free, and is experiencing pure joy. Besides having a noble spirit, Señor Simón displayed such integrity, such dignity, that he was an example for us all. In the ereye, besides advocating for a person, we should learn from his virtues and assimilate them.

I would like to refer today to a fragment of the perashah Vayigash (Genesis, 47: 7-9). The perashah describes the encounter between our patriarch Yaakov Havinu and Paroh, the pharaoh of Egypt. Yaakov was a recognized spiritual personage and Paroh a very powerful man; the dialogue that occurred between them is noteworthy. Paroh asks Yaakov: "Kama yemeh sheneh hayekha?" "How many are the years of the days of your life?", that is to say, how old are you?, a fairly simple question. But Yaakov gives him a strange answer. I am going to quote what the Torah says: "The days of the years of my pilgrimage are 130 years: few and of poor quality were the years of my life; and they didn't reach the days of the years of my parents' life on the day of their pilgrimages." What does he mean by such an unwonted answer, to such a simple question? Although this seems to have no transcendence, there is a very revealing message for us all, in which Yaakov's philosophy of life is reflected. The question, how many years are the years of your life? gives the message that this life is over; did you really enjoy it? it ends here. That is the focus of the materialistic and limited existence of life in this world, and it ends here. That was the pharaoh's focus. Indirectly, Yaakov is challenging it. In the Torah, life does not mean what we call life. What we call life is something fleeting. The body lives momentarily and then it ends. In contrast, the soul –in the abstract, or as manifested by good works-- cannot end, that remains for eternity. Has anyone seen a soul die?, has anyone seen a thought die? It cannot die. Yaakov speaks again and tells the pharaoh that this life is a pilgrimage, one passes through and then disappears. He was very humble and did not consider his merits to be great. They did not reach the level of his parents' virtues. If the body suffers somewhat, that is not important. What matters is what one takes from here for all eternity. Now let's return to Señor Simón, may he rest in peace. If we focus on the quality of his physical life, his pilgrimage, then yes, he may use the same expression as Yaakov, "meat veraim," few years and of poor quality. His body suffered, but that doesn't tell the whole story. That explains the anxiety that Paroh felt, for he was focusing on the enjoyment of life. Obviously, we take care of our bodies and try to enjoy good health; this is appropriate, accepted by the Torah, and totally valid, but it's not everything because it is a limited approach. The concept of life with which we must concern ourselves is eternal, unlimited life, which we do want to be plentiful and of good quality, "arveh ve tov".

When I spoke with Don Simón's sons to prepare the ereye, I asked them about their father. They responded that their father had not left them an inheritance: that is, he had not left material assets. And then they mentioned the virtues of Don Simón, may he rest in peace: dignity, humility, modesty, courtesy, gallantry, kindness, respect, and the ability to express affection and love for his fellow man. The truth is very clear: Don Simón's heritage is, precisely, his moral legacy, having taught his sons these values that are so essential to our faith. Don Simón could have signed a famous letter written to his son by Ramban, the Rabbi Moshe ben Nahman, also known as Nahmanides, a Sephardic wise man of the thirteen century. I would like to quote some excerpts from this letter to illustrate the ideas of this great ḥakham. It begins with some words that come from Proverbs: "Listen, my son, to the discipline of thy father and forget not the teachings of thy mother." Contemplate for a moment the exhortation of the fifth commandment: honoring your parents is one of the essential principles of our faith. Parents have the obligation to lead their children down the path of goodness. The abovementioned "discipline" of the father certainly alludes to obedience of our Jewish laws; and the "teachings" of the mother refer to the ways in which she has molded her child and educated him according to our customs. Now then, I believe that the following sentence is very appropriate, given Don Simón's personality, "Make it your custom to speak in a friendly manner to all people, on all occasions." That friendliness or kindness does not depend on the other person; it should be an attribute of your personality. Furthermore, notice that this friendliness should be directed "lekhol adam," "to all people," which means that nobody should be excluded, even those who may have behaved in an inappropriate way. Immediately after this, Nahmanides says in his letter, "and this shall protect thee from ire, which provokes people to sin." He insists that ire will be severely punished. It does not help human beings; on the contrary, it makes them lose their head and forget their love for their fellow man. If ire takes control of us, then we lose all sense of ethics and thus we are only one step away from "doing evil" and committing sins.

Therefore, Nahmanides says to his son: "Expel ire from thy heart and eliminate evil from thy flesh." And further on he adds: "And when thou hast expelled ire, then into thy heart will come the virtue of humility, which is the most blessed of all virtues." May hashem help us to assimilate these words of great wisdom. What is Nahamnides trying to say to us?, why so much emphasis on humility? Upon reading the entire letter, it is obvious that this virtue is directly related to the fear of God. Only God may give us wealth and wisdom; only He may take it from us. The humble person knows that man is nothing compared to the magnitude of hashem. The virtue of humility is what allows us to draw near to the Torah. The most important message of the letter is that we must act with kindness and humility, and thus God will compensate us on judgement day. We may achieve wealth, honor and wisdom due to divine favor, as a loan, but we should not boast about our fortune, or succumb to the temptation of arrogance. Señor Simón might not have been wealthy, but he knew how to be an example to his sons so they could follow the path of goodness and obey the commandments of our Torah.

Before concluding, permit me to refer to the perashah of the week, Haazinu. As you know, Moshe is about to die. The perashah is a final song that he dedicates to his people, like a swan song; the lyrics trace the history of our people, from creation to the days in which Messiah was to arrive. Basically, this musical legacy is an admonition as well as an invitation to observe the precepts of our Torah. Here we have the same idea expressed in Nahmanides' letter, but this time in a collective manner, addressing all the people of Israel. There is a verse that is particularly relevant these days, which says, "Remember times that have passed; understand the years of all generations; ask thy father and he shall tell thee, thy ancestors and they shall tell thee." This episode clearly tells us that we must understand the history of all our people: we are an unbreakable chain that must be extended indefinitely, passed on from fathers to sons. A yehudi must be aware of who his forefathers were, of what has happened throughout all the years of history; we all have the obligation to remember and understand our heritage. The transmission of this tradition, the weight of our faith, is on our parents' shoulders. They have the duty to teach their children the obligations we have to hashem and the study of the Torah, so that from generation to generation we assure the survival of our people.

If we consider this passage of the perashah of the week, along with the message of Nahmanides and the encounter between Yaakov and Paroh, we can see that there is a lesson to learn, and with this we will conclude. Don Simón was here in passing, as we all are. Perhaps toward the end of his days, his body suffered here, but now certainly he is enjoying eternity. There in the Olam haba he has his true residence; there he will have good spiritual health. He fulfilled his role as father with love, humility, tenderness, and dignity, teaching his children with his example. It's not necessary to be a great rabbi, like Nahmanides, or a great prophet, like Moshe; each one of us should follow his own conscience. For this reason, these days are sacred, and everyone is asked to do teshuvah. Don Simón has the benefit of having been quite worthy and righteous, and thus certainly he will be with God. It is my fervent hope that he will intercede on our behalf, and for his family in particular, and God will send his blessings.

The rabbi paused and the prayers of Minḥah and Arvit began. Afterwards, we went down to eat. Fule commented to Jaime, *the ḥakham spoke well, but why so much emphasis on humility? It was obvious to everybody how kind Papá was, and of course he wasn't going to flaunt what he didn't have; he was very dignified and proud. For many years, he enjoyed good health, so why focus so much on his suffering?* We couldn't discuss it because the room was packed with people. There were three rows of tables placed end to end, like long banquet tables that stretched from wall to wall; two rows were reserved for men, while the third was for women. The tables were laden with platters of fresh fruit (canteloupe, papaya, watermelon, pineapple), nuts, dried fruit, olive oil and spices, cheese, olives, tahini, yogurt, pastries, hardboiled eggs and boiled potatoes. Small bottles of Coke, Sidral, and other soft drinks were spread out along the tables. The shammash circulated around the room, making sure that everybody had enough food and drink. Saqui wondered if it was more of a mitzvah to come to a darush than to go to a house of mourning, since the knis was so crowded that day. There we could finally see the whole family, as well as friends of Papá and Mamá. Jaime remarked, *if we have any friends or relatives who didn't come today to offer their condolences, then they won't ever come.*

9

6/7 Tishrei 5757

20 September 1996 (Friday)

A FEW MINUTES BEFORE LIGHTING THE CANDLES FOR SHABBAT, THE AVELIM SHALL RISE FROM THE FLOOR, PUT ON LEATHER SHOES AND CHANGE OUT OF THEIR TORN CLOTHING. THE LAWS OF AVELUT ARE NOT IN FORCE ON THE SHABBAT FOR VISIBLE THINGS SUCH AS CLOTHING AND SHOES. FOR THINGS THAT ARE NOT VISIBLE, SUCH AS BATHING AND HAVING CONJUGAL RELATIONS, THE LAWS OF AVELUT CONTINUE TO BE IN FORCE EVEN ON THE SHABBAT. IF THE SEVENTH DAY WERE TO FALL ON SHABBAT, THE VISIT TO BET HAḤAIM SHALL OCCUR ON THE FOLLOWING DAY.

Although there were enough people for minyan, we were all surprised by the small number who had come to breakfast. None of the ḥakhamim had appeared that morning and Helfón told us that he could only stay until noon. *We have to prepare for Shabbat. You get up from the shiva today and you don't have to sit down again. Since the shiva began on Sunday, the day of the funeral, today is the sixth day and tomorrow the last. When Shabbat is over you can bathe, but remember that on Sunday you have to go to the knis for Seliḥot: it's the eve of Yom Kippur. And from there you go to the bet haḥaim like everybody else.* Jaime asked Helfón for a precise calendar for mourning throughout the year. Sounding like a typical bureaucrat, Helfón answered, *that's not my job; you should ask ḥakham Tawil in the bet haḥaim. He's the one who can calculate the exact days when the kaddish can be interrupted, and the exact day of next year's anniversary memorial. For the years after that it's very simple: the memorial will always fall on the Shabbat before Rosh Hashanah.* After breakfast, we expected to see all the women who had been crowding into the house on previous days –cousins, friends, some we scarcely knew— but they didn't show up.

We sat on the floor, staring at the empty chairs all around us, feeling abandoned. Without the constant hustle and bustle, we had nothing to distract us from our grief. Jaime took a deep breath and let it out in a prolonged sigh that felt like it came from all of us. After a pause that probably seemed longer than it was, a delivery boy arrived with an enormous bouquet of flowers sent by Miguel Caso, a friend of Abram's from a new orchestra that was being formed. In spite of the white carnations' agreeable aroma, Jaime said we had to throw them in the garbage. Abram wanted to put the bouquet in one of the upstairs rooms so as not to insult Miguel, but Jaime didn't waver, *when he comes, if he asks where they are, just explain to him that it's not our custom to display flowers at this time, he'll understand.* Half an hour later, Miguel arrived. He was surprised by our torn shirts, foul-smelling bodies, stubby beards and greasy hair. Miguel had met Papá seven years ago in a nightclub where they danced salsa. On that occasion, Papá was dancing with Tía Rosa and a circle of people had formed to watch their swaying hips and smooth moves. Miguel was playing the conga, which gave Papá a pretext for mentioning Abram and his musical group, so they owed their friendship to Papá. Now with guitar in hand, Miguel announced, *with your permission, I'd like to pay tribute to Don Simón by playing some of his favorite songs.* Alarmed, Jaime said brusquely, *I'm sorry, but that's out of the question; we're not allowed to listen to music for a whole year, out of respect for our father's memory.* Miguel politely kept quiet, but before leaving he commented to Abram, *if your papá loved music so much, why is it a lack of respect to remember him by listening to the songs he enjoyed? You have to follow your heart and not just your faith. So, does this mean you can't work for a year?* Abram explained, *since music is my profession, I am allowed to play; besides, you know I'm not very religious. I've done my duty for the week of mourning, and to top it off, I'll follow the rules for the Day of Pardon, but that's as far as I'll go. My brothers are the ones who have suddenly become orthodox; they want to follow the mourning rituals to the letter, although I doubt that they'll become kosher or completely observe Shabbat.*

Around two in the afternoon, the waiter began to stack the folding chairs and drag the regular furniture back in place. The Friday smells were in the air: rice with peas, small kibbes, radishes with lemon, green peppers, and other spices. We ate in silence, not really tasting the food. The atmosphere had changed, and we each felt our loss in a more solitary, and introspective way.

Toward evening, the sisters-in-law arrived with all the children, who looked at us with intense curiosity. Beni's son Simón was fascinated by his papá's scrubby beard, while Rebe, David's daughter, latched onto his leg, making him drag her as he walked, and laughing at her father's clumsy dance as he played at trying to shake her off. Jaime's little Simón asked us why we couldn't take off our torn shirts, and he also wanted to know if he could go to the Deportivo to play soccer. When Beni looked at his son he remembered his circumcision, and shuddered. Papá was already showing the symptoms of emphysema, although he still managed to go to the Deportivo to play dominoes. They had brought the enormous chair from Monte Sinai and placed it against the same wall where we had recently been sitting on cushions. That Sunday we had taken turns to see how it felt to sit on a chair that was so tall and so wide. Even though it was Papá's duty to hold the baby, Beni's in-laws had insinuated that perhaps Papá, with his trembling hands, wasn't up for the role of godfather. Beni didn't see anything wrong with his father-in-law's request to hold the baby during the ceremony, but the smoke coming out of Mamá's ears only hinted at the intensity of her fury, *that's an insult!, don't be an idiot! The honor of holding the child belongs to us, understand?! The next thing you know, they'll be saying they want Fortuna's mother to be the godmother!* Papá listened to the argument, but gave no sign of taking offense. Back then he was drinking heavily every day and didn't care about anything, except for going to restaurants at lunchtime and playing dominoes in the afternoon. Mamá reminded Beni about all the trouble his in-laws had caused.

Seven years earlier, Beni broke up with his girlfriend from the university and soon began to date Fortuna, the cousin of Jaime's wife. They had only been going out for a few months when her parents, Yusef and Yemile Yedid, asked Beni what his intentions were. Beni believed that at 23 he was still too young to get married, *let me finish my degree and find work.* In spite of the father's objections, the mother allowed them to date for three more months. Fortuna had just turned 17, and was very excited about the idea of a wedding. By the end of the year, her father was so exasperated that he gave her an ultimatum: she would have to break up with Beni, unless they came to speak with him to formalize the engagement. Mamá was glad they were pressuring Beni; she had suffered a lot from the suspicion that Beni had a girlfriend at the university who was goy. *If they give you a good dowry, you don't even have to finish your degree; you can start working right away.* However, Beni wasn't sure he wanted to get married, so he stopped going out with Fortuna and called Debbie Shapiro, a woman he had met at the Deportivo. She was studying art history at the Anáhuac University, and her mother was pleased that her daughter was going out with *a boy from the Arabic quarter.* Debbie was more liberal, and not put off by Beni's sexual advances. One Saturday night when he was dropping her off at home, he was invited in to chat with her mamá; after a while, the mother said good-night and went to bed. If it hadn't been for the maid making noise in the kitchen, Debbie and Beni would have made love right there on the sofa.

The next day, he ran into Fortuna at the Deportivo; she had heard the gossip about Debbie, so without a moment's hesitation she threw her arms around him and gave him a prolonged kiss. They were standing in the middle of the patio of the Deportivo, and before Beni could react, Debbie walked out of the gymnasium and saw them. *You bastard! Don't you ever call me again!* she shouted with indignation. Later, a friend of hers commented bitterly, *you can't trust those Syrians!, they're backwards, not a cultured bone in them. Don't worry yourself about that stupid macho; you're better off without him. You deserve someone who will respect you.*

Beni liked the way Fortuna's hair fell to her shoulders in shiny waves, and how her long lashes framed her lively, dark eyes. Although her body was fully developed, her gestures sometimes revealed glimpses of her recent childhood. Beni confessed to David that he preferred Fortuna's seduction to the not-so-subtle ways in which Debbie dominated the contact between their bodies. After much pleading, Fortuna's mother allowed her to go out with Beni again. When her papá found out, he shouted furiously at his wife, *What's wrong with you?, are you crazy?, Fortuna is an attractive girl, and she's at the best age for marriage. Right now she could find herself a rich boy who isn't going to want a dowry, it wouldn't cost us a penny! What does she see in Beni?! She shouldn't be wasting her time with that imbecile!* The mother tried to defend her, alluding to Bella's marriage to Jaime, *his brother turned out to be a fine husband, just ask my brother Beto.* But Yusef Yedid was stuck on the idea that his daughter should marry a millionaire. *Listen to me, now that Fortuna is a precious flower we have to find a good match for her. You should go visit Tía Latife to see if she can recommend somebody.* With her back against the wall, Fortuna's mamá had no choice but to forbid her daughter to go out with Beni. Señora Latife knew all the families of the community, and every time she went to cure the evil eye or bless a new house, she would spread the word. *By the way, roḥi, I have a beautiful girl from a good family for your son; give him this telephone number and have him ask her out, no strings attached. If, gracias a Dios, they get along well, then we take the next step.* They always replied, *God willing.* Fortuna missed Beni's sense of humor, and soon became bored with the rich boys who took her on dates, *they don't say a word, and the silence drags on and on; so I always want to listen to music because at least the time goes faster that way.*

During that year, Beni had started going out with Debbie again. Every Saturday they went to a hotel on the highway to Toluca, and stayed there from ten at night to three in the morning. Beni was learning how to arouse her, and she rewarded his desire to please her with fiery passion. One day, Fortuna called Beni and said, *I want to be with you, I don't care if my parents give me permission or not; I'm willing to run away from home, if necessary.* Beni didn't know what to say; he vacillated because he didn't want to hurt Debbie. He asked for a week to think it over, and during that time, conveniently enough, Debbie called to break up, *I've met someone who turns me on intellectually; he's working on his Ph.D. in anthropology at Princeton; I have to be honest with you: I don't want to hurt you, but I think it's best if we stop seeing each other.* Beni had finished his degree in business administration and just found work in the Coca Cola company in Mexico City. He thought that might make Fortuna's papá change his mind. Yusef Yedid was impressed by the name of the company where Beni worked, and agreed to allow Fortuna to go out with him again. After his experience with Debbie, holding hands wasn't enough for Beni anymore, so he and Fortuna resorted to steaming up the windows of his car parked outside the building where the Yedids lived, until one night a couple of police officers knocked on the windshield and Beni had to give them a bribe. After four months they were desperate to be alone together in comfort, so Beni suggested going to the hotel on the highway to Toluca, with the promise they would not have sex. Fortuna hesitated, but only for an instant, since she felt that her love for Beni had intensified during their time together. During their first few visits to the hotel, they struggled through a game of start and stop that only served to increase the temptation, until one night Fortuna couldn't take it any longer and she told Beni she was ready to lose her virginity. Thinking they would remember that night for the rest of their lives, they planned everything very carefully. They went to a ritzy hotel in the Zona Rosa, ordered room service, and got into the jacuzzi to relax. Even though Beni was very patient --employing all the foreplay techniques he had learned from Debbie-- for Fortuna the pain surpassed the pleasure.

Afterwards, Fortuna was plagued with anxiety, fearing that if Beni abandoned her now that she'd sacrificed her virginity, nobody from the community would marry her. She didn't dare tell her parents, but hinted to her mamá, *Beni's job is going really well; it's about time he asks for my hand, don't you think?* Without consulting Beni, Señora Yedid called Mamá, *I've got to tell you, Rebeca, my daughter is almost 19; we need to know if her relationship with Beni is serious; we can't lose any more time, you know.* Beni agreed to have Tío Jacobo Zonana, the husband of Tía Raquel, negotiate the engagement. Our uncle called Yusef Yedid and set up a meeting at the VIPS in Palmas. Yusef arrived at the restaurant, accompanied by his brother Nissim. After an hour of conversation, Tío Zonana formally announced that he was there to represent the Galante family in their request for Fortuna's hand in marriage. *They want to know what you have planned for the couple's wellbeing.* Yusef Yedid was ready with the answer, *Jacobo, I'm going to be honest with you. As you know, I have a women's clothing store downtown; that's my only asset. With the economic crises we have suffered, I can scarcely pay all my expenses and I haven't been able to save any money. Time has slipped through my fingers like water. I have two daughters, barukh hashem, who are my pride and joy. Since my brother-in-law Beto is very pleased with his son-in-law Jaime, I would agree to give my daughter's hand in marriage, but I don't have a cent to contribute, even for a small party.* Tío Zonana had been around this block before, so he was able to stay cool, commenting very politely, *Yusef, I'm sure you want the best for your daughter; that's precisely why you have to make the greatest effort to assure that her marriage goes well. You think it over, I'll try to soften up my brother-in-law and, if you wish, we can get together again next week.*

When Tío Zonana reported to Papá and Mamá that Yedid didn't want to pay any dowry, Mamá couldn't believe it, *caramba, how is it possible that he didn't save anything for the dowry? Everybody knows a father has to start saving as soon as they announce in the hospital, "it's a girl!" What planet is he from? We're not going to ask him for the pearls of the Virgin, but at least he could help make the down payment on a condo. Where's his daughter going to live? Is he going to let them go live in the Roma neighborhood, or the Condesa? With what he earns, Beni will scarcely be able to pay the bills, and they won't be able to make ends meet once the babies start arriving.* Papá barely participated in the conversation, only nodding his head as Mamá spoke. Tío Zonana found out through a friend that Yusef Yedid had indeed saved some money, but was very tight-fisted and would require some cajoling before he'd relax his grip. So Tío Zonana met with Señor Yedid several more times, but no matter how hard he tried to persuade him, Yusef Yedid did not budge an inch. After six meetings, Tío Zonana sputtered, *okay, so why don't you just say it outright, "I'm not going to give any dowry; you guys figure it out, because I'm not interested in my daughter's wellbeing."* And of course, Señor Yedid's reaction was categorical, *Well, now I'm more opposed than ever to this marriage! I'm going to forbid my daughter to see that worthless boy, and I'm sure a better suitor will turn up.*

Soon after, Fortuna got a call from Abdo Hop, whose father owned the largest textile factory in Mexico. Yusef Yedid couldn't imagine a better solution to his problem; he pressured Fortuna so relentlessly that she felt obligated to go out with the young man at least once. Señor Yedid was so pleased that he gave his daughter money for a new dress. Her mamá helped her with her hair and make-up, trying to make Fortuna look as attractive as possible for the date. Abdo Hop picked her up in a new Ferrari; he was wearing a heavy gold bracelet with his named engraved on it. He was used to getting his way, so when Fortuna refused to give him a kiss, he started showing off his bad manners, farting and burping in the restaurant. She was so disgusted that she told him she never wanted to see him again. Yusef Yedid couldn't understand why his daughter would pass up such a great opportunity. *The Hops have so much money that even their great-great-great grandchildren will receive a huge inheritance. Don't be a fool, hija, I'm telling you this for your own good. That Beni is just an employee and he's going to be just-an-employee all his life. You should give Abdo some time. Who said you have to be in love to get mar-*

ried? Fortuna was tempted by the thought of so much money, but she was afraid to imagine Abdo's reaction when he found out she wasn't a virgin. She went out with him a couple more times, only to confirm that he made her nauseous and she could never be happy by his side. Beni felt the hairs on his neck stand up like the quills of a porcupine when he heard that Fortuna had gone out with somebody else, but he calmed down when she called and suggested they return to the hotel on the highway to Toluca. And thus they began a clandestine affair; they had trysts during lunch hour, or whenever a friend of Fortuna's would cover for her.

One day Fortuna's brother Moisés was coming out of the same hotel with his mistress when he spotted Beni's car. He parked at the exit to see who was with Beni, and his stomach turned when he saw his sister. She saw her older brother out of the corner of her eye and wondered who was with him. Moisés had been married for two years; he had a fifteen-month-old son and his wife was about to give birth a second time. That Friday night, Moisés and Fortuna went into her room, closed the door, and told each other off, but neither one dared to rat on the other. When she turned twenty, her mamá began to fret. During the Shabbat dinner, Fortuna announced defiantly, *I'm not going to date anybody else; the only man I'll ever love is Benjamín Galante.* Made suspicious by his daughter's outburst, Yusef Yedid decided to send an employee to spy on Fortuna. A week later, he was horrified to hear that his daughter had gone with Beni to a hotel. Feeling extremely offended, he called Tío Zonana to complain, but rather than bemoaning the scandal, our uncle pointed out, *now there's even more reason to marry them; calm down, they're going to be husband and wife, after all. You should consult your brothers to see if they'll help you with a little money for the sake of the newlyweds.* Mamá heard the gossip from her sister Raquel. Yedid agreed to share the expense of a small banquet in a restaurant.

The bride and groom would look for an apartment in Polanco that Beni could afford. Mamá complained, *with seven sons, I hoped that at least ONE of you would receive a good dowry!* and Saqui replied sarcastically, *well, don't lose hope, there's still David and Musa.*

Three weeks later the Yedid family invited us to celebrate the engagement. When we arrived at their home, we weren't surprised that the living-room armchairs were covered with plastic, because we had seen such upholstery-protectors in many homes when we were children. Mamá had a fit because at the last minute Fortuna's mother had invited her brothers and sisters and all their kids, as well as her mother and mother-in-law, without giving us the opportunity to notify our own relatives. Yemile Yedid tried to apologize, *you'll have to forgive me, Rebeca, but one of my sisters found out today and then I felt obliged to invite the others; I didn't tell you because we have such a large family and with your relatives, too, there wouldn't be enough room for everybody. I've got five brothers and a sister, and they all have families, too.* Mamá launched a furious counterattack, *Oh yeah?, that's strange; I've got seven children: five older boys, plus twins. But don't you worry, your apartment is small and we understand,* and then she turned to say to us, *ḥamseh! five times over, ḥamseh!*, opening her hand wide to ward off the evil eye. According to Papá, the shrab il'los, the white almond drink usually served to celebrate weddings, had not turned out well, *it's too thick, I can hardly swallow it*, but nevertheless, he politely complimented his son's future father-in-law, *the shrab il'los is delicious, may you have health and prosperity; you know, may you see them as bride and groom. May they live long and prosperous lives, may you live to be 120.* Yusef was the brother of the mother of Bella, who was Jaime's wife; and Yemile was the sister of Bella's father; moreover, the four of them were first cousins. Fortuna and Bella had the same last names: Yedid Yedid. Saqui commented drolly that when

Fortuna and Beni had a son, he would have exactly the same name as Jaime's son: Simón Galante Yedid.

After Mamá and Yemile broke a plate, as is the custom, the ḥakham carried out a brief ceremony in which he asked the engaged couple to hold a handkerchief between them while he gave the corresponding blessing. Before bidding farewell, Mamá took out the engagement ring and gave it to Fortuna. Since he hadn't seen it yet, Beni came over to satisfy his curiosity. He carefully inspected the shiny diamond ring, and we all wished them the best of luck. When we got back home, Mamá told Fule, *I gave your wife a ring with a larger stone because they offered a better dowry, but I don't see why I should give these Yedids such a diamond after they were so stingy with us.*

Mamá didn't have a dinner in response to the engagement party because she was furious with the bouquet of yellow flowers that the Yedids had sent. *They're turning their noses up at us; by this time, they should know perfectly well that I hate the color yellow, since I've told Bella that several times.* Beni and Fortuna were so excited about the wedding that the family feuding paled in comparison to their bliss. Fortuna started coming to the dinners on Shabbat; one of those nights, as we were discussing the details of the religious ceremony, Fortuna told Mamá that she didn't want to have flower girls. Mamá had already made arrangements with several relatives: *I already asked my niece Judith Hanono to allow her two-year-old daughter to accompany you, as well as the two Zonana girls and one of the Mustris.* Fortuna was furious that Mamá had made plans without consulting her, *this is my wedding and I'll decide who walks down the aisle or not!* Mamá retorted, *Oh, yeah? And are you going to pay for the wedding, too?, because it seems that you've forgotten that your papá refused to give a dowry.* Fortuna, feeling a wave of rebellion rise from the pit of her stomach and rush to her head, took off the engagement ring and flung it on the table, *here's your wedding and your piece-of-junk ring, you can stuff it you-know-where...* and she stomped out of the house. Outside it was pouring rain; when her mind cleared enough to realize that she had no transportation, she came back inside, *Beni, Beni, damn it, take me home!* As they went out, she slipped and fell on the sidewalk. We all watched from the doorway as she got into the car, covered with mud and with runs in her stockings. Afterwards we had trouble finding the ring; Musa finally discovered it in the plate of guacamole. Yusef Yedid was very nervous about the wedding being cancelled. He came to the house to talk to Papá, *Fortuna is very young, Simón, she doesn't know what she's doing. Barukh hashem, the kids love each other. Let's not let a minor upset like this ruin their future.* Papá nodded, then told Musa to ask for the Turkish coffee and pastries for Beni's future father-in-law. A few minutes later Mamá came home from the store; she was surprised to see Yedid there, and she mumbled to herself that he probably was desperate to have his daughter get married. *Fortuna offended the whole family; she has to come apologize to us all. And I assure you, there will be flower girls in the ceremony because I've already made promises to my relatives.* Fortuna resisted for two weeks, complaining to Beni that Mamá wanted to humiliate her in front of the whole family. Finally, exhausted by having to mediate between Mamá and his future wife, Beni managed to negotiate that the apology would be addressed exclusively to Mamá and Papá.

There were only two months left before the wedding. Mamá chose to send the bateh to Fortuna on the day of Pesaḥ. She explained to us, *in the bateh you are obliged to send 101 coins in a gold, silver or glass coffer; the coins can be pesos, silver dollars, or any other pieces. They stay in the newlyweds' home, so they will always have money. The bateh must include a box of chocolate and almond candy, as well as something made of gold (it could be a coin, neck-*

lace, earrings, whatever you want), and the rest is optional: perfume, purses, shoes, swimsuits, hats, handkerchiefs, according to the families' situation. A wealthy family would give many earrings, necklaces, bracelets, different kinds of rings, perfumes, lotions, and a fur coat, but I can only afford a few things: I bought her a beautiful leather purse, a hat, some silk handkerchiefs, earrings, and a gold necklace with her name engraved on it. I'm saving a bracelet to give her when we go to the purification, before the wedding. Everything must be wrapped as a gift. I'm going to ask Judith Hanono to do me the favor of delivering everything to the bride's home. But if the Yedids want to host a gathering to show off the presents, that's another story. Relieved that the wedding plans were progressing, Fortuna and her parents were happy to receive the bateh.

About that time, Fortuna's younger sister, Bella, got engaged to Abdo Hop. Yusef Yedid was overjoyed. The Hops were going to pay all the expenses of the wedding and he was sure that in the long run, his son-in-law was going to help the rest of the family. We planned Beni's bachelor party according to custom, on a Thursday night, and somebody suggested that we invite Abdo Hop. Then Abdo told Jaime he would organize the party. He invited us all to a suite in a ritzy hotel in the Zona Rosa. We usually went to a striptease bar for bachelor parties, so we were excited that this time would be different. Abdo had ordered all kinds of booze: cognac, whisky, rum, tequila, vodka, and more. Two hours into the party, when we were all bombed, two heavily-made-up girls arrived at the suite. One of them greeted Abdo very affectionately, revealing the intimate nature of their relationship. We all started yelling at once. Shouting over the uproar, Abdo announced there would be a raffle to decide who would get to take the hookers into the bedrooms. David drew the winning number from a bag full of slips of paper prepared for the occasion, but David told Musa he was in love with his girlfriend Ceci and didn't want to cheat on her. He offered him the ticket, but Musa replied that he was going through a period of sexual abstinence and it would be better to give it to Abram. Several guys began to razz David and Musa. Abram yanked the slip of paper away from David, grabbed the hand of the prostitute with enormous breasts, and led her into one of the bedrooms as the rest of us cheered him on. We all doubted Abdo's integrity when he pulled out the next winning ticket. Somebody accused him of hiding it between his fingers. Someone else hollered *cheater!*, and the rest of us mocked him in unison, *cheat-er!, cheat-er!, cheat-er!* Abdo became so enfuriated by our taunts that he pounded on the door where Abram and the hooker were secluded, exclaiming, *Verónica, come out of there! We're leaving right this minute!* The woman opened the door, with her clothes half on. Beni tried to detain Abdo, but was shaken off, *this is bullshit!, I set you guys up with some first-rate call girls, a suite, all you can drink, and this is how you thank me?* From the doorway of the bedroom, with his dick still erect, Abram shouted scornfully, *you can take your filthy money and shove it up your ass, you miserable bastard!* After Abdo left, Jaime called the lobby and found out that the suite and drinks were all paid for in advance, whereupon we all rejoiced and continued the fiesta until five in the morning.

Only Musa and Jaime had stayed sober. Jaime told Beni that we had to go serenade his fiancée, so we drove to Garibaldi Plaza to pick up some mariachis, and from there to Fortuna's place, where we proceeded to wake up the neighbors. Fortuna had been waiting there with her sister Bella and four friends ever since the bachelorette party had ended. Bella was very curious about what had happened to Abdo. Saqui answered that they had to take him home because he drank too much tequila. Yemile Yedid had prepared some very spicey chilaquiles, knowing that we would need them to cure our hangovers. After an hour of what seemed like extremely loud music, the mariachis left and we all sat down to eat breakfast. Upon taking his first bite, Fule, who was totally blitzed, ran to the bathroom to puke. The stench of his vomit ended the visit prematurely. Yemile Yedid declared that the bride and groom could not see each other again until the wedding ceremony.

It was time to get ready for the tebilah. Several women were invited to accompany Fortuna for the ceremony. After intense pressure, Mamá finally agreed to tell us about the ritual, *on Thursday the family of the groom sends the bride a tray with a rosca in the shape of a star of David and 51 other pastries (so bread will never be lacking in the new home); candles to be lit during the tebilah; soft and hard sugar and candy (so sweetness will reign in the home). They also send slippers, a silk robe, some fine towels, exquisite soaps, everything the girl uses for the bath: shampoos, conditioners, creams. Before noon on Friday, the mother of the groom, the tías, the hermanas, and primas all go to the tebilah. There is a woman in the tebilah who has the responsibility of examining the bride: her nails must be short and unpolished, her hair combed smooth, her face free of make-up, and her body scrubbed clean before entering the tebilah. After she arrives, she is submerged in water three times, berakhot are said, and then she is submerged seven more times without speaking, while only the señora prays; all the other women must be there with their candles lit. Some powder should have been sent, to use on the bride (Jafif will sell you the whole tray, complete with a star, pastries, sugar candy, the candles, and the powder). Also, each guest brings something: pastries, candy, gelatin, and so forth. After getting out of the water, she breaks the star on her head, sprinkles sugar on herself, and spreads the powder on her back and legs. Finally, they all sing. Thus, she is purified, ready to get married, and can't leave the house or she'll lose her purity. From the tebilah, we go to someone's home for breakfast.*

On the Friday afternoon before the wedding,

Mamá threw her own version of a bachelorette party, without the bride or the bride's mother (so there wouldn't be unnecessary contact between the families). Her guests included her sisters, their daughters and daughters-in-law, our sisters-in-law, and other friends. Saqui was content to listen from upstairs. A musical group from Veracruz was playing raunchy songs full of double meanings. Mamá did impressions of the women in her future daughter-in-law's family. There was a lot of boisterous laughter and clinking of glasses, and the party became increasingly rowdy as the afternoon progressed. After drinking so much, Mamá couldn't stay awake for Shabbat dinner.

That Saturday morning at the knis, Yusef Yedid fawned upon Abdo Hop's father more than on our family. He was so intent on buttering him up that he invited Señor Hop to go up to read the Torah in his place. Papá was irate, *that's not right, no matter who he is, the custom is that only the groom and the fathers of the bride and groom go up.* From the balcony, Mamá and the sisters-in-law threw chocolate-and-almond candy when Beni finished reading the passage; one of the candies hit Señor Hop on his baldspot and Yusef Yedid thought that someone from our family had done it on purpose.

One month before the wedding, Mamá had decided to throw a big party after all, and take the opportunity to get even with the Yedids. Besides telling them at the last minute, she warned them that it was going to be a small banquet and there would only be forty places for their family members. She reasoned that since the Yedids were going to contribute very little money, she had the right to invite more guests, so she told the caterers to prepare for 120 people. Since there wasn't any mention of the banquet on the wedding invitations, the word spread during the ceremony that the party would be in the hall of the Turkish knis, on Monterrey street. Papá's cheek began to twitch, betraying his nerves, when he saw Tío León and his family come in, and he realized there were no more tables available. We calculated that we needed seven more tables; we were astonished when the caterer told Mamá and Yusef Yedid, *don't worry, we'll set up all the tables you need right now, and settle accounts later.* Mamá was furious that there were so many party-crashers, but Señor Yedid calmed her down by offering to pay for the extra tables. We all wondered why he had changed his tune so dramatically: he had been so stubborn about not offering any dowry and now he was cheerfully insisting that it would be his pleasure to cover the additional expenses.

Beni's thoughts returned to his son's t'hur. Papá's hands had trembled so much that the mohel asked Jaime to help him hold the baby. Two days later the baby had a fever and they had to admit him to the hospital. Of course the Yedids blamed Papá, alleging that his shaking had caused the mohel to make the incision improperly. The mohel assured us that, on his part, there had not been any slip of the scalpel. We never knew what caused the fever, but the boy left the hospital after three days.

Beni was brought back to the present when Jaime said we should change our shirts and put on clean underwear, pants, and socks to go to the knis. We still couldn't bathe, but at least changing clothes reduced our week-long discomfort. We decided to go to the knis of Bet Yosef because it was closest to the house. Since it was almost Yom Kippur, there were a lot of people in the knis. We sat in the middle, all in the same row. We no longer felt the pressure of people staring at us like the previous week, so we were able to relax a bit and chat with several friends who came over to give us a hug.

When it came time to say the kiddush that evening, we felt the sting of Papá's absence once more. Fule took the cup and said it as quickly as any ḥakham. The children were making noise and David shouted impatiently at them to go play upstairs. Sitting at the table after dinner, as we swirled the last sips of Turkish coffee around in our cups, Musa reminded us of the time Mamá called Señora Latife to see if a cure for the evil eye could help Papá. He had just been released from the hospital, which seemed miraculous to us. Although Papá had always been slender, now he was reduced to just skin and bones, and it wrenched Musa's heart to see him like that. He thought of the photographs of people with AIDS, and it occurred to him that emphysema had the same emaciating effect, which hindered any improvement. He recalled Dr. Charabati's words, *with so little oxygen in the blood, the whole body suffers and the organs lose their ability to function.*

When Señora Latife arrived, Mamá had gone to the store. Papá had a bandage on his hand because Beni's son Simón had stepped on him, and the fragile skin had fallen away to expose his flesh, like saran wrap being torn off a piece of raw meat. Señora Latife spoke to Musa, *roḥi, your papá is going to get through this; we have to give him a very good cure and then, God willing, he'll get better.* Musa had helped him put on a robe, and walked him to the kitchen, carrying most of his weight. He felt Papá's ribs rub against his side and he shivered with the sensation that Papá was almost a skeleton. Señora Latife had taken out all her supplies and organized them. She greeted Papá with a big smile, revealing her rotten teeth. Accustomed as she was to seeing the sick, Señora Latife was not shocked by Papá's morbid appearance. She began to smack her lips and mumble under her breath, *ḥazito, ḥazito, I think several people have given you the evil eye; ḥamseh, ḥamseh, don't worry, Simón, you're going to get better.* Musa watched as she placed buckshot and alum in a pan with a lid, and then covered Papá with a white sheet, reciting in Arabic, "*Ehn shafet ta'et mate*". Musa couldn't resist asking her to translate, and Señora Latife, upset by the request, protested: *por favor, roḥi, let me do my work, I need to concentrate on finding the eye.* Then she repeated the phrase, but this time she followed each word with its translation: *"Ehn (eye) – shafet (it looked) – ta'et (it was broken) – mate (it died)".* As he surrendered to the treatment, Papá was submerged in a silence that conveyed his total lack of energy or desire to live. Señora Latife carefully proceeded with the healing, following the steps of a ritual that very few people in the community knew. Musa wondered what it signified when she poked holes in blue paper with needles; then he watched curiously as she poured the water with lead into a dish next to Papá's body, taking precautions so as not to burn him and making sure she poured seven separate times. Sounding like she was talking to herself, she murmured: *Dios mío, Dios mío, please help Simón to get better; he's done no evil, he wishes no harm on anybody; we wish no harm on anybody, so that no harm comes to us; help me to free him from the evil eye; may the eye disintegrate. Out, out, evil eye!* Immediately, Señora Latife took out the shebbe and put it on the fire. Musa noticed how the white stone was melting and acquiring unusual contours, with bubbles or air pockets. Señora Latife paid close attention, scrutinizing each droplet, until she exclaimed, *aquí está!, here it is!, I knew it!* And she uncovered Papá so he could look at the stone. Pointing at it, she shouted, *look, here's the eye!* Papá mumbled a word of approval. She put the shebbe in a white linen napkin and asked Papá to step on it hard enough to break it, *roḥi, por favor, step on it so the eye will disappear.* But Papá didn't have enough strength in his legs to comply so as a last resort, Señora Latife asked Musa to step on it for his father, and to hold onto him when he did so. Musa put his hand on Papá's shoulder and stomped on the napkin as if he were trying to kill a scorpion that was threatening Papá's life. Afterwards Señora Latife told them she had cut locks of hair from seven people close to Papá (although she didn't specify which ones); she found a pot and put in the hairs, the shebbe, and the perforated paper. After breaking the needles and throwing them into the pot, she cracked a fresh egg and added that, too. She stirred it all up and then dabbed some of it behind Papá's ears, under his arms, on the back of his knees, and on the soles of his feet. She looked upward as if she were praying intensely, then went to the street to throw everything out. *May the evil eye disintegrate. Out, out, evil eye!*

Now, as he pondered that last-ditch effort to save Papá, Musa muttered, *It didn't do any good.*

10

9/10 Tishrei 5757 (the eve and day of Yom Kippur)

22/23 September 1996 (Sunday and Monday)

ON YOM KIPPUR WE ALL APPEAR BEFORE THE SUPREME JUDGE, THE KING OF KINGS, THE LORD OUR GOD, TO RECEIVE THE FINAL SENTENCE FOR OUR ACTIONS DURING THE YEAR. THE RABBIS ADVISE US TO DEVOTE OURSELVES TO THE PRACTICE OF THREE PRECEPTS: FASTING, PRAYER AND CHARITY. FASTING WEAKENS THE CORPORAL STRENGTH, ENTHUSIASM, AND VIGOR WITH WHICH THE ACT OF SIN WAS COMMITTED. PRAYER RECOVERS THE FAITH THAT WAS LACKING IN THE MOMENT OF COMMITTING IT, AND CHARITY ELIMINATES EGOTISM, REQUIRING THAT ONE DO GOOD DEEDS FOR HIS FELLOW MAN BEFORE BEING CONCERNED WITH HIS OWN WELLBEING.

A horn was blasting away as if sounding the alarm for some unseen disaster. It was Jaime, pounding on his car's horn like a maniac. From the window, Musa spotted one of the neighbors peering through his curtains to see who was making such a racket. Abram woke up with a headache and in a bad mood, but he was relieved to be able to put on clean underwear and feel that his body was no longer grimey. Saqui, Musa and Abram hustled down the stairs and got into Jaime's car, *I've been waiting for fifteen minutes! We said four-thirty, right? Musa, didn't I tell you to wake them up at four?!* Saqui and Abram were so drowsy they couldn't even protest. Jaime changed his tone to explain what was going to happen, *my father-in-law changed some money for me: today is when we have to give the most donations to charity. I've got a wad of small bills for each of you; each time someone passes by with a collection box, you put in twenty or thirty pesos.*

When we entered the knis, we were amazed by the large number of people who had made it there so early in the morning. Fule commented to Saqui, *Papá never missed the prayers of Seliḥot; he always honored his commitment, even when he was sick. Last year he insisted so much that we were forced to bring him, oxygen tank and all.* For most of us, attending the prayers of Seliḥot was a new experience. Only Jaime and Fule had come with Papá in recent years, because of his delicate health. We were seated in the fourth row, from eldest to youngest, although the order was slightly askew because Abram sat next to Saqui. Abram was fed up with all the praying, and even more so now that we had woken up so early. We stood up each time we had to say the kaddish, and we could immediately identify all the people in mourning. Since Fule went to the knis every Saturday, he knew the personal circumstances of the families. *The Zagas have almost completed the year; their mamá died of a heart attack eleven months ago. Those two Betechs lost an older brother eight weeks ago in an accident on the highway to Acapulco; over there is the only son of Señor Jacobo Masri, who's in the grave next to Papá. Those guys are the Abadis, but I don't know who died in their family: it probably happened during the last few days.* Since Fule hadn't identified all those who were reciting the kaddish, Jaime remarked, *either they're saying it because it's the anniversary of the death of some relative, or they're not very religious and only come today because it's the eve of Yom Kippur.*

We stopped whispering when we saw a man circulating through the rows with a medium-sized money box; when he approached us, he implored, *for the Keren Hayesod, a most worthy cause, gentlemen.* We all took out the bundles of bills that Jaime had given us and, following his example, put twenty pesos into the box. A few minutes later, a large number of men stood up all at once, as if their springs had all been released by the same lever; they picked up collection boxes that had been deposited in the lower compartments of the tevah, where the Torah was placed, and began to circulate through the entire knis. Rather than following the prayers, Jaime and Fule were busy trying to identify each of the volunteers. We all immediately recognized Moni, who had been in charge of Papá's grave. Since we were standing at the time, Abram took the opportunity to leave the row and approach him, *what's up, mano?; we didn't even get to thank you for your work. How long have you been with the Ḥevra?* Moni poured out the story, *my mamá died from a blood clot four years ago. I had treated her very poorly and didn't have a chance to ask for forgiveness before she died. I had a bad-luck streak: I was mugged by armed robbers in the middle of the day, right downtown, when I had just come from the bank with the payroll for all the workers in my papá's factory, and nobody made a move to help me. They beat me up pretty bad and left me unconscious in the street. After that, my brother suffered such a severe depression that we had to take him to the hospital. Then, to top it off, I had an accident on the freeway and was almost killed. It occurred to me that those were signs from God and so I decided to do teshuvah and, barukh hashem, nothing has happened to me since. A couple of years ago I became close friends with Buzali and he invited me to work in the Ḥevra. And here I am; right now I'm helping out the elderly. This collection box is for the Eishel, the nursing home in Cuernavaca. I've only heard news about you from Simón Jasqui; he told me you've left your wife and you're living with your parents. I know what I'm talking about, Abram; now that it's Yom Kippur, you should do teshuvah, too. I know a lot of women from the community who want to get married. You could make a new life for yourself.* Abram smiled, took fifty pesos from his wad, and put them in Moni's box, *don't worry about me, Moni; I went to live with my parents out of necessity, not by choice. As soon as I get back on my feet, with this new musical group I'm forming, I'll move. After Yom Kippur is over, I'm done with this religious nonsense. You know, in the music world we have to stay up really late and it would be impossible to get up early to come to the knis. I've respected the customs this week in memory of my papá and I'll stick it out for Yom Kippur, but then I'm out of here.* Moni knew his efforts were futile, so he chose to go back to collecting contributions, *we'll talk later, I've got to convince you, you don't know what you're missing...*

By that time, collection boxes from all kinds of altruistic organizations were circulating: the Mexican Red Cross; a group providing funds for the poor families of the community; the Bikur Cholim, which pays hospital bills for indigent people; and various charitable associations for victims of cancer, cerebral palsy, or polio. There were also collections for various community organizations, as well as the representatives of religious schools, including some of the most famous from Israel and New York; religious committees; and funds to help marry girls whose families couldn't provide a dowry for their wedding. We usually followed Jaime's lead in regard to the amount donated to each cause, which was about the same for all the boxes, but from time to time some of us felt particularly motivated by a cause, *we should give more for cerebral palsy; remember the fellow with that problem who sold stockings in the street in the Roma neighborhood?; he was always being attacked and could scarcely walk...*

By the end of Seliḥot, Abram and Saqui had handed out all their money. Jaime scolded them, *I told you to hold onto a third of the bills because in the bet haḥaim they're going to ask us for more donations!* Rather than respond to his brother, Abram rushed over to the entrance, where Turkish coffee and roscas were being served. We had to wait half an hour to continue with morning prayers. Pepe Smeke came over to chat with Jaime, *how much do you think they collect in each box in just a short while? Let's say that each one of us here put in an average of thirty pesos. Do the math: thirty times two hundred people is six thousand. And that can be multiplied by the number of knises, let's say thirty. Now we're talking about almost 200,000 pesos, in just a little while, and that's not counting what they can collect in the bet haḥaims. Plus, there are people who like to be generous and donate large amounts on this day. Now, how many organizations do you think take a collection today? I'm guessing there were at least thirty.* Jaime was paying careful attention to Pepe Smeke's calculations; Pepe concluded somewhat cynically, *adding it up, we're paying all together more than six million pesos so God will pardon us. That's pretty cheap, wouldn't you say?* Suddenly he realized that his comments could hurt Jaime's feelings, *perdón, mano, I wasn't talking about you and your brothers; I know it's really important for you to give donations right now, since you've just gotten up from mourning your papá.* Jaime replied calmly, *don't worry about it, we've followed all the rules to the letter and, barukh hashem, my papá's soul is resting in Heaven.*

The shammash came to call us back because they were going to begin Shaḥarit; we all took out our tefillin and prepared for the prayers. The coffee had revived us and we were conversing with greater enthusiasm. After a few minutes, David looked up to the balcony and noticed Mamá was arriving. Since we were chattering nonstop, a group of men in the front rows looked back at us and scowled, but didn't dare hush us; then the shammash passed by, thumping the prayer book with his hand, *silence, señores, silence!* The noise had intensified; there were more of us chatting than reciting prayers. Several of us remembered Papá in the knis, singing in a proud voice from his seat next to the main aisle, where Jaime was sitting now. It turned our stomachs to think that we would never hear him again. Abram confided to Saqui, *I don't know if I'll ever come back to the knis; for me, Papá was the knis. I came to kiss his hand and see the happiness on his face; I came to watch him kiss the sefer, say the shema, greet his friends and make jokes; I came to be with him, even if we didn't say a word to each other, to convince myself that this world belongs to me. But I think it won't make sense any more: I'm here with his soul, accompanying him for the last time, before he goes up to heaven.* Jaime heard part of what Abram was saying, and immediately tried to console him, *and what about your brothers?, don't we count for something?, and Mamá? You have to remember what the ḥakham said: Papá didn't die; his soul will live for eternity. You have to keep respecting him, even though his body is no longer with us.* Abram looked at him with disbelief, but then said, *you're right, Papá will still be alive as long as we have memories of him. Do you know when he will truly die? When nobody remembers him; that's the ultimate death.* Jaime didn't know how to react to Abram's comment, but Fule's response was that Abram was deviating from what the ḥakhamim had said, *you're wrong, mano, you're wrong. On Rosh Hashanah, God inscribed Papá in the book of life and he's going to remain forever in the Olam haba and from there he's going to watch over us and our children, and our children's children, and the children of our children's children, and so on to infinity.* Since Fule had raised his voice over the hubbub of the crowd, the shammash strode directly over to our row, *silence, gentlemen, silence, por favor; we're reciting the amidah, and you must be quiet!* Nevertheless, Abram kept talking to Saqui until shaḥarit had ended.

We went in several cars to the Deportivo, where we got on one of the six school buses chartered to take people to the bet haḥaim. Jaime explained to us, *since six buses won't be enough for everybody, they'll be coming and going all morning.* On the way to the cemetery we were struck by the desolation of the street, *caramba!, on a normal day, you'd spend an hour getting through the traffic on one of these streets, but now all the cars are circulating like water.* Fule informed David, *Papá went to the bet haḥaim five times a year: on the eve of Yom Kippur, like today; on the day of the anniversary of his papá's death and that of his mamá, on father's day and on mother's day. The ḥakhamim forbid you to go on father's day and mother's day, but he didn't pay any attention to them. For religious reasons, you should only go three times a year. They say if you go often to the cemetery (as Mamá did after her mother died), the person's soul cannot rest; you're supposed to leave the soul in peace and not cry or become bitter.*

It seemed like a holiday in the bet haḥaim, in spite of the expressions of pain on people's faces as they remembered their loved ones. Just inside the entrance they had set up some long tables with food, as if it were a meal at the knis, although there were few chairs to sit on and most people were standing with plates balanced in their hands. Helfón circulated around the crowd saying, *the food is so you can say the four blessings, por favor.* Since we didn't know what to do, we paid attention to what everybody else was doing. Jaime thought we should wait for Tío León so we could go together to visit Papá's grave. Our cousins on Mamá's side would not be accompanying us because they had to go to the bet haḥaim of the Ḥalabis. Mamá complained to Jaime, *why should we bend over backwards for León?, it's bad enough that he snubbed us by not coming to the house since the quarrel; besides, what if he comes with the ratero?, are you going to ask for his pardon, too?* Several of us sided with Mamá, *sí, por favor, let's go alone, without waiting for anybody.* Musa managed to say, almost in a whisper, *what about our tías?,* but Mamá cut him off, *they live far away; they're always showing up late. Your Papá always got very impatient with the delay.* As we were talking, three more buses pulled up and began to unload; in the boisterous pack of people that crowded into the cemetery, we spotted Salomón Behar and his friend, Elías Cababie. Salomón greeted each of us with an exuberant hug. *Primos, I'll accompany you to my Tío Simón's grave. And then I hope you'll do me the great favor of going to my papá's grave and that of my older brother, to say the kaddish with me.* Beni asked him if his brother Jaime was coming. *I don't know, maybe he will, maybe he won't; he's unpredictable. My mamá won't be coming because her health is delicate.* Cababie, in turn, asked us to accompany him to say kaddish at his mamá's grave. Saqui went around whispering to each one of us, *listen, if the ratero shows up, there's going to be a blowup because I'm going to punch his lights out, so we'd better tend to our business pretty soon. With the seven of us, Salomón, his friend, and a ḥakham we have minyan for the kaddish.*

The central path through the bet haḥaim was so crowded that we had to walk very slowly and stop now and then. On both sides of the path we could hear the kaddish being repeated. All the ḥakhamim of the community were going from one small family group to another, receiving a donation after reciting several psalms. Jaime commented, *now they're really making a killing; it's like selling toys on Christmas. Everybody wants them to pray for their dead, and of course they have to loosen the pursestrings afterwards.* When we reached the point where the cemetery fanned outward, we noticed there were two piles of white stones. Fule instructed us, *pick up some rocks, we're going to have to place them on the graves.*

We had to wait for ḥakham Rayek to be available. Jaime didn't have to explain anything to him. The ḥakham joined our group, even though he was interrupted at every step by people wanting him to pray at the other tombs; he answered them emphatically, *as soon as I finish with the Galante family, I'll be happy to accompany you; just give me five minutes.*

Papá's grave was in the last row. We noticed there wasn't much available space left in the cemetery. David made some calculations and said in a worried voice, *I think that in about seven years the bet haḥaim will be full to capacity, and then what will we do?* To our surprise, Jaime had an answer for him, *don't worry about it; they already bought the piece of land in back as well as two lots on the side.* Salomón Behar commented, *did you know that the "official" foundation of the Jewish community in Mexico happened because of a death?* Mamá glanced over at him with curiosity. *Sí, tía, the community was very small and they prayed in different houses, kept kosher homes, with shoḥet to slaughter animals, and rabbis and all that, but there wasn't an organization to bring everybody together. Then an elderly woman died and they found themselves in the predicament of not having a cemetery in which to perform the burial according to our customs. That's how Monte Sinai was founded in 1912, in order to raise funds to buy this piece of land, where we are standing now, tía.*

Papá's tomb was the third one from the corner. We noticed there was one grave that had been dug even more recently. That row was the only one in the entire bet haḥaim that didn't have the three-foot marble headstones engraved with the star of David, name of the deceased, dates of birth and death (according to the lay calendar and the Jewish one), and an appropriate thought expressed in both Spanish and Hebrew. On the ground where Papá was buried there was a plaque. Seeing his name spelled out there was like being slapped in the face; suddenly overwhelmed with grief, we began to sob and wail. The ḥakham kept respectfully silent, waiting for us to calm down. Mamá didn't thrash around like she had at first, but just stared at the ground, mumbling something to herself as the tears rolled freely down her cheeks. When we were quiet, the ḥakham took out a briefcase with four prayer books and distributed them among us so we could share. Before beginning the prayers, he confirmed Papá's name: *Shimon ben Raḥel, right?* When we nodded, he specified a page number and began to read. Saqui wept as he gazed at the title of that section of the psalms, "To free oneself from fear of an enemy," and wondered why the rabbi had chosen to start with that one. Upon completing each page, the ḥakham paused and then indicated a new number. Saqui followed along, reading the titles in Spanish: "To heal the right hand," "To heal the left hand," "To free oneself from a lawsuit," "To be recited by someone leaving on a trip," "To cure oneself of forgetfulness," "To be recited by someone leaving on a trip" (*he already said this one, could it be a mistake?*), "To heal the right ear," "To heal the upper abdomen," and "For someone going to trial." Then, almost without interruption, the ḥakham said a series of prayers that ended with the mention of Papá's name. When we heard this, we all raised our heels, standing on tiptoes to indicate that his soul was rising to heaven. As the ḥakham was about to bid farewell, Saqui asked him why he had chosen those sections of the psalms, and was told: *according to custom, we followed the order of the letters of your papá's name: SHIMON in Hebrew is spelled shin, mem, ayin, vav and nun; then* BEN is spelled bet and nun; and finally, RAḤEL, resh, ḥet and lamed. Before leaving, the ḥakham gave each of us a piece of paper on which he had written the dates we should observe throughout the year:

Mourning for Papá

THE DATE OF THE DECEASED, MAY HE REST IN PEACE, WAS:

Friday (afternoon), September 13, 1996

WHICH CORRESPONDS TO THE DATE: Elul 29, 575 6

THESE DATES ARE ACCORDING TO THE DATE OF BURIAL:

YOU MAY SHAVE ON: October 15, 1996

SUSPEND THE KADDISH AS OF "ARVIT" ON: August 4, 1997

UNTIL "MINḤAH" ON: August 11, 199 7

YOU FINISH THE YEAR ON: September 13, 1997

MAY YOUR SADNESS BE ALLEVIATED.

Upon consulting the calendar we had been given when we arrived, Jaime noticed that September 13 of 1997 did not fall on Elul 29, but on Elul 11. The ḥakham explained, *that's because next year is a leap year; the month of Adar is repeated in order to compensate for falling behind the solar calendar. But it is forbidden to be in mourning for longer than a solar year. In subsequent years, you will commemorate the anniversary of your father's death on the Saturday before Rosh Hashanah.*

We were preparing ourselves to visit the other graves when we noticed that Fule was kneeling on the ground, kissing the earth where Papá was buried. After a couple minutes, Abram forced him to get up. Before our primo Salomón Behar could speak, Saqui announced that he wanted to go to Raquel's tomb. Mamá agreed immediately, *she's in the children's section, on the far side of the cemetery.* As we walked over there, we noticed that four men had occupied one of the benches, and were passing around a bottle of tequila. One of them called to Jaime, *what's happening? come over here; how 'bout a little tequila to dull the pain?...* We thought it odd that they would want to drink so early in the day; one of them was obviously tipsy. Jaime refused the offer with a wave of his hand to thank them for the gesture. Abram interjected, *I'll take a drink.* They handed him a shot in a plastic cup and he tossed it down with one flip of the wrist. *That's got to be forbidden,* David thought, but the rabbis passed by without saying anything or even scowling at us. Raquel had a tiny grave, with a marble headstone that Mamá had bought about four years ago. Saqui fell to the ground and hugged the stone as if it were our sister in the flesh. Then he asked us to say the kaddish, but Fule objected, *no, we can't; children don't need help getting up to heaven; they go directly there, without intervention. Do you think such a sweet, innocent child could commit a sin? She was an angel.* Saqui nodded sadly, and didn't insist. We each left a white stone on her tomb.

Our primo Salomón Behar was anxious to go to his papá's grave. *We'll be right there, Salo,* Jaime assured him. *Where is he buried?* Salomón gestured toward the middle of the cemetery. Since the children's section was located beyond that of the women, in the far left corner of the bet haḥaim, we had to walk against the flow of the most of the people. David ran into an old friend from Monte Sinai who was obviously in distress. *Por favor, David, there's a bunch of you guys and we could complete the minyan; have a heart and help me say the kaddish for my mamá; she's right here, in this row.* Without hesitating, Musa turned to walk down the row, with the rest of us following him. Thus we advanced very slowly and with frequent stops, because we were besieged with such requests. Abram kept an eye out for bottles of booze, and went from one group to another for shots of tequila, whisky or cognac. In addition to those impediments, there were all the volunteers asking us for donations to their cause. Jaime had managed to save some bills so he could distribute some at the cemetery, but most of us had given all of our money away at the knis. We decided to visit the tombs of the women first, starting with Elías Cababie's mamá, then Mamá's mamá, and even Mamá's grandma. Then Musa wanted to see our paternal grandmother's grave. We wondered why we had waited so long to see the sites where our ancestors' remains were buried. When it was finally time to go to the tomb of our cousin's papá, we spotted Tío León in the distance, accompanied by his sons. Musa tried to determine if the ratero had arrived, but couldn't see him. *He's a coward! He'll never show his face around here,* Beni remarked sarcastically. David, on the other hand, had already seen him standing alone, in a row we had passed without turning to look; fearing trouble, he decided not to sound the alert. Our heads ached from having said the kaddish so many times, and our progress was hindered further when Mamá's legs got tired and she had to sit a while on almost every bench. In one of the rows for women, we discovered the names of some men; Fule clarified for us, *when a family dies in an accident, they can make an exception and bury them all together; these people passed away when their van turned over on the highway to Toluca.* Then we saw the Palombos.

When we were children, the news that their papá had thrown himself off a third-floor balcony had upset the whole community. Whenever we saw them, we could tell they were still suffering from that death, by their tragic expression, knitted brows, and eagerness to fight at the slightest provocation. We never found out what could have pushed their father over the edge.

At the entrance, people were still milling around, eating and drinking; now and then more busloads would arrive. Jaime quipped, *here come the lazy bums who get up really late and just wander in whenever they feel like it.* It was almost noon by the time we left. At the parking lot of the Deportivo, we made plans to have breakfast at the VIPS in Palmas. Even though it wasn't lunchtime, the restaurant was full of friends and relatives. We recognized a lot of people we had just seen in the cemetery, as well as fourteen of our Hanono cousins who were occupying two large tables. They had gone to the bet haḥaim of the Ḥalabis; their shirts were unbuttoned, revealing their hairy chests. The eldest Hanono, Jaime, was wearing a heavy gold pendant. Abram asked him, *Jaime, did you wear that gold to the cemetery?, that's dangerous!* Jaime answered with bravado, *it's all a question of luck: you could get mugged or hit by a car, you could have a heart attack... there are no guarantees. You never know when something might happen. So why waste your time worrying about it?* While his mamá, Tía Zequíe, was scolding him for talking like that, we were summoned to our table for eight.

Afterwards we all went to Mamá's house because we had an appointment with a shoḥet who was going to perform the ritual slaughter of the chickens. While we waited for him, we stretched out on the sofas to rest. Mamá had asked Concha to start cooking the small kibbes for the ḥamut, as well as the bacha and the rice kibbes. She was also preparing what Mamá called "food for kings," which was a stew with small kibbe, red mushrooms and potatoes. With all that cooking, the house smelled like Friday.

The shoḥet Abud Chacruka bounded up the

stairs two by two, followed by a fat boy who was carrying two live chickens in each hand. He set them down in the patio and ran to get the other four. *Well then, Señora Rebeca, here are the seven roosters and one hen you ordered. Call your sons because I don't have time to mess around.* We went to wake up Abram, but we couldn't get him out of bed. Beni observed, *he's not just tired, he's bombed.* As if to prove Beni's diagnosis, Abram pulled himself up and stumbled to the bathroom to vomit. Out on the patio, the shoḥet was ready to perform the first sacrifice. Before killing the chicken, he held it up and made it make three circles over Jaime's head. Then he recited some words that our brother repeated after him, *ze halifati, ze temurati, ze kaparati; ze hatarnegol yelekh lemita, veani, Ḥaim ben Rifka, elekh leḥayim tovim ulshalom.* He translated for us, *this is my substitute, this is in my stead, a symbol for my pardon; this rooster will die and I, Ḥaim ben Rifka, will be destined for life and peace.* Next he took out a knife and slit the bird's throat, spilling blood on the cement floor. He repeated the ritual for each of us and for Mamá. Upon finishing, he said, *Víctor will stay behind to pluck the chickens; I'll be back for him in an hour. If you wish to donate the animals, I'll deliver them to the poor myself.* Mamá was exhausted and didn't want to deal with the chickens, so she quickly agreed.

The sisters-in-law and the children arrived around two-thirty in the afternoon. Saqui accompanied Mamá to the knis of Bet Yosef to light candles. The children started bouncing around and using the railing of the suspended stairs as a slide. Seated on the sofas, we passed the time discussing the people we had seen at the bet haḥaim. *I hadn't seen Moi Penhos since high school,* said David, alluding to one of his closest friends during adolescence. *We used to hang out together every Sunday afternoon, but then he went to work at his brother Jacobo's store and, since they were always busy on Sundays, I never saw him again. He was a wiz on the guitar; the music teacher would play a tune on the piano, and Moi could pick up the tune and play it on the guitar immediately.* Saqui commented, *it's incredible that he didn't become a musician, with his tal-*

ent! But Jaime, looking sideways at Abram, countered, *he was smart; you can't make a good living with music; it's okay to play the guitar at fiestas, but first you have to support your wife and kids.* Abram was in no mood to argue with Jaime. Ignoring him completely, he went up to Papá's room and instinctively turned on the television. Fule, who heard the noise from the bathroom, yelled, *that's forbidden, turn off the TV!* When he came out and saw it was Abram who had turned it on, he tried to explain, *we're not allowed to watch television. The mourning period is one full year; you can deal with it as you wish, but at least don't break the rules while we're here. As for music, you can decide that for yourself; you can set your own limits: for example, you could play music at rehearsals or fiestas where you've got a gig, but maybe not listen to music at home... Ah, and you should go to the knis every day to say the kaddish.* Abram answered, trying to avoid talking any more about the subject, *don't worry, mano, I'll figure it out.*

Jaime had arranged to spend the night of Yom Kippur in a hotel in the Roma neighborhood, along with Musa, Fule, and David. Mamá told us we had to eat early so we could leave our things at the hotel before it got dark. With the usual nervousness on the eve of fasting, we ate voraciously, dreading the inevitable migraines of the next day. Fule mentioned that eating on the eve of Yom Kippur was as important as fasting; Abram and Saqui laughed at his observation, *hey, no problem! Let's do our duty and stuff ourselves!* Musa told Mamá that the more salt she put on her food, the thirstier she would be later on. *Don't you worry about me; I know how to control myself, so just leave me alone,* she snapped back impatiently. Papá had taught us that Yom Kippur was the most sacred day of the year. *I might be a real haramero most of the year, but I always follow the rules for Yom Kippur. You know I can't live without smoking; well, that's the only day I don't smoke. If I leave the knis for a moment, it's only to get some fresh air.*

We had fond memories of the knis on Querétaro Street. Inaugurated in 1953, it was certainly the most splendid of all the sinagogues of its time. Mamá used to buy us new clothes: underwear, socks, shirts, ties (which were kept in a drawer that we all shared) and suits made to order at a store in La Lagunilla that gave us a special discount for buying in bulk. We recalled the blisters we got from the hard, shiney shoes. The community had grown and, even though the knis was very large, on holy days they provided an additional service in the Dorado hall, where the meals and banquets were normally held. Since Papá had lost the store of La Lagunilla, we spent Rosh Hashanah and Yom Kippur downstairs, with those who couldn't afford the seats in the main hall. The atmosphere in the Dorado hall was more relaxed; there were about twenty serious ḥakhamitos, but most of us chatted during the prayers and caught up with old friends. With the passing years, the community moved away and new synagogues were opened, first in Polanco and then in Tecamachalco. The knis of Querétaro, in all its glory, became a thing of the past, only revisited on holy days. Fule had been an ardent defender of that knis, demanding that it be remodeled, including re-upholstering the chairs, replacing the carpets, painting the walls, and cleaning the enormous candelabra that hung from the high ceiling. After lengthy negotiations, the board of directors finally agreed to make some minor improvements, with the promise to set aside as much money as possible in the future to preserve the knis. Now, as people entered the knis, Fule greeted them as if he were the host in his own house.

The prayer on the night of Yom Kippur, Papá had told us, *is the longest one of the year. It's the only night when you have to put on the tallit.* We had been amazed at Papá's transformation, seeing him suddenly immersed in another world, praying in a language he scarcely knew, with pride and confidence in his identity. Now we were seated, repeating the *Adonai, Adonai, el rachun bechanun...,* with the echo of Papá's voice in our ears. We looked around, convinced that someone with a similar voice was there, but after a while we realized that it was just an acoustic illusion. Then Saqui decided that the sound was coming from Musa's mouth; laughing, he declared to the rest of us, *it's Musa!, it's Musa!, exactly like Papá; caramba!* But we thought Saqui was hallucinating. Jaime commented, *Fule is the one who is really a carbon copy of Papá; he has the same gestures, the same manners, the same temperament; he's just as reckless with his money, and he loves gambling and smoking.* Abram added, *the difference is that he's had better luck, plus he doesn't dance as well.* Beni thought Abram was comparing Fule to himself with his last comment, since Abram was the only one who could compete with Papá on the dance floor. Then Beni pointed out, *Saqui and David may be very different from Papá physically, but they are just as good-natured.* Musa had been observing a man who was sitting two rows ahead, watching how he pursed his lips, covered his face with the tallit upon saying the shema, and stared at the tevah. He turned to Saqui, *look , that guy has the same gestures as Papá. Do you think it's generational?* Saqui had been so absorbed that he didn't listen to Musa and had to ask him to repeat the question. But by then the man had turned around and any similarity to Papá had vanished.

After the prayers ended, we walked together down the street, nervous about getting mugged, especially since a heavy cloud cover made the night darker than usual. At the Ajusco plaza we remembered the sunny days when we rented bicycles and rode around and around in the park. We also passed by the Orizaba ice cream shop and the long island of grass that divided Alvaro Obregón Avenue. As we observed some young men drinking beer in the street, we recalled a time when some teenagers grabbed the kippahs off our heads; nobody dared protest because we knew they belonged to a gang, and we wanted to avoid more serious problems. Papá said calmly, *don't worry, there are a lot of kippahs in the knis; they're just fishing for trouble, so don't take the bait.* We saw the building where we lived as children and remembered Papá parking the pick-up truck out front, and how we used to all pile into the back of the truck and sit on the floor, since it was set up for delivering furniture for Tío León's business. We thought of the countless Sundays when we'd go to the Deportivo in the pick-up, and Papá would stay for hours and hours, lying on a towel, and then at about three in the afternoon, he'd jump into the pool to cool off and we would climb on his back and shoulders, and he'd show us how strong he was by throwing us into the water. We all waited for that time of day when we could play with Papá. Back at the house, we'd listen to his favorite Arabic music and watch him prepare a whisky with mineral water.

The next day Abram woke up craving a cup of coffee, but immediately remembered the fast, *even though we finished the shiva, it seems like it's not over, since we have almost the same prohibitions: we can't bathe or wear leather shoes, and what's worse, we can't eat or even drink water.* Saqui replied, *Yom Kippur seems like a cross between mourning and getting a taste of death. Fasting makes you realize that our life consists of physical wellbeing (since the body enjoys everything that produces pleasure) and to a certain point it dulls the sensation of life in order to stimulate spiritual reflection; think about the last hours of fasting, when you have the sensation of being a survivor.* As Abram entered the bathroom, he said to Saqui, *may God forgive me, but I'm going to brush my teeth.* Saqui had to wait a long time for Abram, so they didn't go to the knis until about nine-thirty in the morning. They arrived when the auction of the sefer was almost over. Abram remembered how Papá used to leave the knis at that time; he went out to the street on Rosh Hashanah to smoke a cigarette, and on Yom Kippur just to get some fresh air. In recent years, Jaime had been very generous and had paid for the chance for Papá to read the Torah, thinking that perhaps such closeness to God would help him fight his illness. Papá was smiling, proud to have the opportunity, and he went up nervously, with a trembling lip. Solemnly, he kissed the Torah and then we saw him focus on the words and assume a dignified pose, in spite of being weak and out of breath after climbing the four or five steps up to the tevah. Everybody was watching us, and when he had finished, they yelled to Papá, *you are blessed!* After greeting about twenty people, we kissed his hand and Papá greeted us all, and to Musa he repeated, *a'aris, a'aris.*

Now Jaime was irritated by Abram and Saqui's delay, *You missed several kaddishes!*, but without paying attention to him, they put on the tallit and approached the tevah because the sefer was going to be taken out soon. The knis was so full that they could scarcely make their way down the aisle. When it came time to sing the *Leolam Adonai,* to get the Torah out, all chatting ceased and the united voices resonated on the high ceiling of the knis with such power that it seemed they would escape through the roof and rise up to heaven. Inspired by the chant, we felt our voices vibrating in unison with the rest of the community; then the cantor responded by singing his part, prolonging the vowels in different tones, imitating the Arabic melody of medieval time. As children we had never appreciated this music, but now Papá pulsated in each note, in each syllable that escaped the cantor's lips. We discovered a newborn nostalgia for a music that all of us, except for Abram, had ignored. When they placed the sefer on the tevah and we sat down, Jaime informed us that he had paid for the sixth reading, which is the one used to say the kaddish in front of the sefer.

The shammash came to ask us who was going up: Jaime gestured toward Saqui, *he lives in the United States and is leaving tomorrow, Allah ma'ak.* Saqui wanted someone else to have the honor, but the shammash was already asking for his Hebrew name. Later, as he climbed up to the tevah, he felt like an angel. He had never before gone for a reading on Yom Kippur, and thought that Papá's soul would be right there with him. *If you had the chance to talk to Papá again, what would you say?*, but he couldn't even imagine an answer. He grabbed onto the knots of the tallit in order to kiss the letters of the Torah that initiated the passage and, after reciting the blessing, concentrated on each word in the corresponding section.

As the reading progressed, memories were swirling around in Saqui's head; there, standing before the sacred book, he thought of the time Papá's car broke down on the way up a mountain as we were returning from Acapulco on the old highway. He heard Mamá's voice saying a prayer, and saw Papá's anguished face as he tried to comfort us, *calm down, kids, calm down.* Next came the moment when the surgeon in a Houston clinic came out to tell us that the operation on Mamá's back had been successful, and Papá urged Saqui to translate for him, *tell him may God bless, may God grant every happiness to him and all of his loved ones,* and Saqui noticed the doctor's confusion as he turned to answer with his back to us, *yes, thank you for your blessing.* Then there was the memory of Papá wearing Saqui's jacket, which was too short for him, in the middle of a New York winter, trembling with cold and limping from the bunions on his feet, *there's no place like Mexico;* and on the same trip, Papá seated at an oak table from the twenties, holding Simoncito for his t'hur and watching with intense emotion as the mohel from Brooklyn, who was more orthodox than the one in Mexico, sucked the baby's member after the circumcision. At the same time, Saqui was a child again, smelling the fragrance of Papá's cologne right after shaving; Papá took his hand and made him caress his smooth cheek, which would be stubbly within a few hours; then he could see the pock marks on Papá's neck, and remembered how they had ironically nicknamed him "Camay" for having such "smooth skin". He could see Papá in the nightclub Adonis at five a.m. on New Year's Day, listening to Arabic music with an ecstatic expression on his face, oblivious to anything else. Finally, he relived the scene in the bet haḥaim, gazing with horror at the inanimate face that had been prepared for burial. Saqui had to return to Yom Kippur and react when the rabbi pointed to the blessing that he had to say to conclude the reading. As Saqui said it he was thinking that he had been so distracted that he hadn't paid attention to the words of the Torah, and hadn't even asked for pardon during such a solemn act. As he greeted all those who came forward to shake his hand, he looked up at Mamá and managed to read her lips as she said, *congratulations, hijo, may you live to be 120 years old.*

While Beni was reading the perashah in Spanish, he realized that with this passage all Jewish people were asking for forgiveness for having venerated a golden calf; Aaron had to arrange for the sacrificial slaughter of several animals in order to obtain collective redemption. Even though we had been very young, Beni still remembered the inauguration of the Hanonos' house in Polanco. Tío Rafael had just won the lottery, so he decided to follow the ancient customs of the community and sacrifice a sheep as an offering. There were so many people that we couldn't see the actual slitting of the animal's throat, but we did see the pool of blood on the sidewalk that led to the parking garage. For many nights we dreamed of the bloody flesh and matted wool of the sheep, until the impact of the scene diminished with time. Beni relived the moment when Tío Rafael, while yelling at his wife Zequíe, used a blasphemous expression that implicated her mother in a very unflattering way, and our grandma, who was standing right in front of him, didn't dare respond. Papá, however, rushed to her defense, and Tío Rafael shouted at him, *fuck you AND your mother-in-law! you can both go to hell!*, and suddenly everyone at the fiesta fell silent, including the mariachis, and Papá held his head high as he said to us, *vulgar people do not deserve a response,* and Mamá was happy as she walked out to the street because someone had finally dared to stand up to her brother-in-law and defend her mother. And grandma, for the first time, forgave Papá for bankrupting the store in La Lagunilla. However, the next day we were all shocked to see Tía Zequíe's bruised face, and all the Hanonos trembling with fear.

What will we be today, the sacrificial sheep or the savage who beats his wife?, Beni asked Abram. *What do you suppose is the crime that we have inadvertently commited?*

Must we feel guilty for having kicked out Tío León's daughter? How many times have we shown a lack of respect for Papá? How can we cleanse ourselves of evil?, how can we live without hurting our neighbor?, to what extent can we rid ourselves of sin? Abram replied that there were no answers, *a ḥakham would say that today is when you should decide to do teshuvah and become kosher and observe the shabbat and all the holy days. I say that we are human beings and we all make mistakes, even the ḥakhamim. If there is a God who's going to judge us when we die and if that God is omniscient, then he'll take pity on us and forgive our sins.*

David's headache was intensifying. He was irritated by the squabbles of the children, who were accusing each other of breaking the fast, *you ate something, you ate something, let's see your tongue!, look, it's red!, it's red!* And a while later the same boy was bragging to his uncles, *I'm going to fast until four o'clock and next year, before my bar mitzvah, I'm going to fast the whole day.* The prayers had stopped for a half-hour break and David's throbbing headache kept him from concentrating on anything. Abram held out two aspirins, *swallow them without water, it's not haraam to take medicine if you need it,* but David rejected his suggestion immediately, *that allowance is only for the people who are really sick; I'm not sick, I just have to put up with the pain.*

Saqui and Beni were stretched out on some chairs in the back of the knis. Señor Carlos Meta, a childhood friend of Papá's, sat down next to Jaime. *Your papá was very kind, and so gentle that people took advantage of him. But I know a lot of stories about his life that nobody else knows.* Jaime turned to look at him with curiosity, sensing that Señor Meta wanted to share some intimate details that we didn't know. *When we were young, Moi Atri, Salomón Amiga, your papá, and I would go to the tea dances at the social club of Coahuila. I think we were almost twenty years old when there was a contest to choose the Queen of Damascus, in which the most beautiful girls of the community competed. That year the winner was Adela Palombo, a young lady we all thought was a knockout. They had decided to have a raffle to raise funds for the club; the prize was a dance with the queen and a movie date with her the next day (with a chaperone, of course). Since your papá didn't have any money, I gave him one of the ten tickets I bought and --who could have guessed-- by crazy luck he was holding the winning number. Our friends and I got all excited and pushed him out on the floor to go claim his dance with the queen. Your papá was very elegant, and carried himself well. They danced a danzón cheek-to-cheek and we all noticed how Adela Palombo was blushing. Afterwards, just for fun, we all chanted, "encore, encore, encore." And the orchestra, without skipping a beat, started playing a mambo. We all started dancing frantically and the party was in full swing. Adela and your papá couldn't stop dancing all night long. The next day they went to see the movie "To Have and Have Not," accompanied by her younger brother. We had just found out that Lauren Bacall and Humphrey Bogart had started seeing each other while making the movie, and were going to get married. It occurred to Moi Atri that Adela looked like Lauren Bacall, so by deduction your papá had to be Bogart, even though his acne was acting up that day, which of course, totally mortified him. We went to the movie theater to spy on them, stationing ourselves in the balcony so we could look down and watch your papá make his move, but all he did was put his arm around her; when they were saying goodnight we could see your papá revving up to kiss her, but she turned away from him and he was left standing there with a silly pucker on his lips. After that we teased him mercilessly, "You know how to whistle, don't you? Just put your lips together and blow..." Poor Simón, it was pitiful to see his pimply puppy-dog face, hopelessly in love with Lauren Bacall, personified by Adela Palombo.* Jaime had been listening attentively. He asked if Elvira Palombo was related to the Palombo girl in the story and Señor Meta replied, *sí, Elvira's her niece, the daughter of her youngest brother. Adela ended up marrying Isaac Romano.*

Come on, I'll point her out to you; look upstairs, she's sitting in the fourth row, on the end. Jaime scrutinized the woman carefully, but couldn't find the slightest resemblance to the Hollywood actress.

It was six in the afternoon when they passed around lemon peels and poured lotion on our hands. We knew the fast was almost over and suddenly recuperated our energy and good humor. We could almost taste the chamomile tea, consomé, hardboiled eggs, boiled potatoes and shredded chicken that was waiting for us at home. All the children and sisters-in-law had arrived. We prayed with renewed fervor, knowing that relief was imminent. Fule remembered how fragile Papá looked as a child, in a family photograph from the late twenties: Papá, wearing shorts and a buttoned-up sweater, with a cap in his hand, was gazing directly at the eye of the camera; his sister Rosa was standing next to him with her arm around his shoulders; there was Papá, so small and fragile, captured in his innocence.

Finally, we heard the long blow of the shofar. While the rest of us smiled and relaxed, Fule's mind was occupied by one more image: this time it was Papá, seriously ill, struggling to carry the Sefer Torah that the Hanonos had purchased and brought to the house –before turning it over to the knis— in hopes of being blessed with a miracle.

After we left the knis, hand in hand with our children, we noticed that a heavy rain had fallen because the potholes on the street were filled with water, but now the sky was clear. As our eyes adjusted to the relative darkness, we spotted three stars shining on the horizon.

* * *

GLOSSARY

Pronounce letters **ḥ** or **kh** like the Spanish **j** , as in Juan. Abbreviations: Ar. = Arabic; Heb. = Hebrew; Sp. = Spanish.

A'aris. Ar. Groom. [May I see you a groom.]

Aliyah. Heb. Going up. Part of the religious ritual that consists of "going up" to read the Torah.

Allah Ma'ak. Ar. May God go with you.

Amidah. Heb. Prayer in silence while standing, or repeated in unison (responsively) as a congregation.

Arvit. Heb. Prayers after sunset.

Avel [Plural: **Avelim**]. Heb. Mourner after the burial (during a year).

Avelut. Heb. Mourning.

Barukh hashem. Heb. God Bless.

Berakha [Plural: **Berakhot**]: Heb. Blessing.

Bet Haḥaim. Heb. Cemetery; literally "house of life".

Carajo. Sp. Hell, or damn.

Darush. Heb. Speech. Act to commemorate the deceased.

Deportivo. Refers to Centro Deportivo Israelita [Jewish

Sports Club in Mexico City].

Derbekeh. Ar. Drum. In Hebrew, tov.

Ereye. Ar. Speech to commemorate the deceased.

Goy. Heb. Non-Jewish person.

Gracias a Dios. Sp. Thank God.

Ḥakham. [Plural: **Hakhamim**] Heb and Ar. Literally, wise man; it's used at times as synonym of rabbi.

Ḥakhamito. Neologism combining Hebrew/Arabic and Spanish, to indicate that someone became religious or adheres strictly to the religious commandments.

Ḥalabi. Ar. Person from Aleppo, Syria.

Ḥamseh. Heb. Five. Expression to deter the evil eye.

Haraam. Ar. Sin. Prohibited by religious law.

Haramero. Neologism combining Arabic (haraam) and Spanish. Sinner.

Hashem: Heb. Literally, "the name". Way of referring to God, without pronouncing the word.

Ḥazito. Neologism combining Arabic and Spanish. Poor guy.

Ḥevra [Kaddisha]. Heb. "Holy society". Jewish organization in charge of the Jewish burial.

Hijo. Sp. Son.

Kaddish: Heb. Sanctification. Prayer in sanctification and glorification of God. Mourners' prayer.

Keriah. Heb. Ritual that consists of tearing a garment, as a sign of grief for mourners.

Kibbe. Ar. Typical dish in Lebanon and Syria. With different sizes and forms, it is basically a stuffed meat croquette.

Kiddush. Heb. Same root in Hebrew as **kaddish.** Prayer to receive the Shabbat and other holy days.

Kippah. Heb. Skullcap worn by observant Jews.

Knis. Ar. Synagogue.

Mano. Sp. Man, bro. From "hermano" (brother).

Mehila. Heb. Forgiveness.

Minḥah. Heb. Afternoon prayer.

Minyan: Heb. Minimum of 10 men to recite prayers in congregation .

Mitzvah [Plural: **Mitzvot**]. Heb. Obligation of all Jews to do "good deeds" and fulfill the 613 commandments given in the Torah.

Mohel. Heb. Person in charge of the circumcision.

Monte Sinai. Mount Sinai. First public association of Jews in Mexico, also refers to a K -- 12 day school.

Olam haba. Heb. World to come ; world after death.

Onen. Heb. Mourner before the burial.

Oye. Sp. Listen, hey.

Perashah. Heb. Fragment of the Torah, read on Shabbat at the synagogue.

Pesaḥ. Heb. Holiday that commemorates the exodus of Jews from Egypt and their freedom from slavery.

Prima/o(s). Sp. Cousin(s).

Ratero. Sp. Thief.

Roḥi. Ar. Term of endearment. My soul.

Rosca(s). Sp. Middle Eastern ring-shaped bread, with sesame seeds.

Rosh Hashanah. Heb. Jewish New Year, celebrated for two days. Literally, it means "head of the year".

Sefer [Torah]. Heb. The Pentateuch. First 5 books of the Bible.

Seliḥot. Heb. Prayers before sunrise.

Shabbat. Heb. Religious day of rest and observance. It starts Friday at sunset, and it ends Saturday at sunset.

Shafalkon. Ar. I commiserate with you.

Shaḥarit. Heb. Morning prayers.

Shami. Ar. Person from Damascus, Syria.

Shammash. Heb. Assistant in the synagogue.

Sharmuta. Ar. Prostitute.

Shebbe. Ar. White stone that protects against the evil eye.

Shema. Heb. Main prayer of the Jewish liturgy.

Shiva. Heb. From number seven. Period of first seven days of mourning.

Shofar. Heb. Ram's horn that produces a deep sound. It is used in Rosh Hashanah, and at the end of Yom Kippur.

Shoḥet. Heb. Person in charge of slaughtering the animals according to rabbinical laws.

Shomer [Hatzair]. Zionist organization with socialist ideals.

Soḥnut. Heb. Jewish agency.

T'hur. Ar. Circumcision.

Tallit. Heb. Prayer shawl used in the morning services.

Tebilah. Heb. Ritual bath of purification that women perform after menstruation or before a wedding.

Tefilah. Heb. Prayer book.

Tefillin. Heb. Phylacteries worn on the hand and on the head, during the morning prayers. Also, among Sephardic Jews, a reference to the Bar Mitzvah.

Teshuvah. Heb. Regret over sins, and the return to

religion.

Tevah. Heb. Place where the Torah is set to be read.

Tía. Sp. Aunt.

Tío. Sp. Uncle.

Torta(s). Sp. Mexican sandwich with French bread.

Ulpan. Heb. Program to study Hebrew.

Vámonos. Sp. Let's go.

Yehudi. [Plural: **Yehudim**]. Heb. Jew.

Yeshivah. Heb. Place to study Torah. Religious school.

Breinigsville, PA USA
18 May 2010
238229BV00001B/4/P
9 781888 205312